THE
TEMPUS
IMPERIUM

The Tempus Imperium

© Juliet A. Paine, 2024

Cover Illustrated by Carmen Dougherty.
Layout by Rhiza Press

978-1-76111-164-8

Published by Rhiza Edge, 2024
PO Box 302,
Chinchilla QLD 4413
Australia
www.wombatrhiza.com.au

A catalogue record for this
book is available from the
National Library of Australia

THE TEMPUS IMPERIUM

JULIET A. PAINE

Like as the waves make towards the pebbl'd shore,
So do our minutes hasten to their end.
William Shakespeare

'I could tell you my adventures — beginning from this morning,'
said Alice a little timidly: 'but it's no use going back to yesterday,
because I was a different person then.'
Lewis Carroll

For grandparents everywhere,
and the bond they have with
their grandchildren.

PROLOGUE

Adelaide, August 2011

My grandmother always said to be careful of shadows. However, by the time I turned fourteen, fear had taken on a different form. It could be that strange man, who followed you home until they suddenly turned left and entered a block of units. Or it was a car that passed by driving slowly, before doing a U-turn and coming back. *Should I run?* The driver pulling up alongside you, beginning to roll down the window. The breath clenched tight inside your lungs. *Waiting. Holding.* Only letting go when the driver asked for directions.

When I went for a run after school, I stuck to the main roads and only kept one headphone in, so that I could always hear behind me. If I walked to the shops after dinner, I went in a pair with another boarder. Both of us held our room keys in our fists, with the metal tip jutting out, like we'd been told in self-defence classes. These were the rules as a teenage girl that I understood. My grandmother's warnings about the shadows seemed as though they belonged in a fairy-tale, along with the bogey-man, and monsters lurking under the bed.

1

Growing up, my Grandma Penny had been my best friend. I'd often stay at her house on weekends, where we'd cook together in the kitchen, and drive to Semaphore and take long walks on the beach. My favourite moments were when she told me about her life: being a secretary during the London Blitz or travelling to China during the Cultural Revolution. I loved the little details she shared: about the heroics of the Fire Watch at St Cuthbert's, the damaged gas lines, and the mystery novels she read in the Anderson shelter during German bombing raids.

Yet, as I grew older, sport and parties had begun to fill my weekends. It was often easier to stay with a day-girl, then Grandma Penny on an Exeat, as they were already going to the same hockey match or some party two suburbs over that evening. Sure, we still talked regularly on the phone, but I missed the smell of my grandmother's baking, the sound of her cat purring, and our laughter.

Yet, one weekend, I found myself at my grandmother's place. My parents were interstate for a funeral, and they had cancelled hockey. The thought of sleeping-in on Saturday morning, and then spending the afternoon in front of the fire, cuddling her cat, Telemachus, seemed for once more appealing than a party up in the hills.

Penny picked me up on Friday afternoon from the boarding school in her mustard Volkswagen beetle, the exhaust backfiring like a series of gunshots that made Mr Mortimer, the teacher on duty, flinch.

'Darling, I've missed you,' she said, squeezing my arm.

I grinned. 'Me too.'

The next morning, Penny made us Anzac biscuits while playing Bach cello concertos on her record player. We set up the chessboard on the kitchen table and played several rounds before lunch. Afterwards, we replaced a washer on the laundry tap and patched some cracks in the living room ceiling with plaster and then painted over them. However, the highlight was always our matinee movie sessions at 3 pm. My grandmother, never bothered much about whether a film was rated M or PG. To her, watching movies with me was a formal part of my education that she took seriously, even if I still have flashbacks from watching Alfred Hitchcock's *The Birds* at age eleven. Together, we had viewed *The Bridge on the River Kwai*, *Dr Zhivago*, *The Great Escape*, *To Kill A Mockingbird*, *Psycho* and *Lawrence of Arabia*. Movies that I told my friends 'sucked,' even though I secretly liked them. Today Penny's choice was *Schindler's List*. According to the summary I found online, the film told the story of how Oskar Schindler tried to save the Polish Jews from the Nazi concentration camps.

Afterwards we went for a twilight walk, or a pre-dinner 'constitutional', as Penny liked to call it, beside the river. Between the gum trees that lined the riverbank, the light was the colour of cold water. Our breaths rose in clouds of steam as I questioned my grandmother about Hitler. The image of that girl from *Schindler's List* lying dead amongst the black-and-white bodies had seared itself into my fourteen-year-old brain.

'Why didn't someone just assassinate Hitler?' I asked.

'Oh, they tried. Von Stauffenberg even placed a bomb under a table in 1944, but Hitler survived,' said Penny.

The shadows were lengthening, their branches strangling our silhouettes.

'But think, Grandma, how many lives would have been saved if they had assassinated Hitler before the start of World War Two? There would have been no Holocaust. No ghettos or gas chambers.'

A branch snapped in the bushes nearby.

'True, that's one way of thinking about it. But also consider this—World War Two and the Holocaust might never have occurred if they had accepted Hitler into art school. Think about it. He was a lonely child beaten by his father, then a failed artist, and last, an angry war veteran. Imagine if someone had intervened and showed him some kindness.'

'Well, it's a pity then that no one has invented a time machine yet,' I snorted. 'Imagine all the suffering that might have been avoided if we could just go back in history and offer young Adolf a pack of tissues and a comforting shoulder.'

For a second, my words sat there between us. Penny glanced at me as she adjusted the crown on the oversized watch called a Tempus Imperium that she liked to wear.

'Unfortunately, time doesn't work like that. It's a stream built on cause and consequence. One small change can have a billion unintended effects. In meteorological science, they describe it as the Butterfly Effect. That's why physicists don't build time machines; they fear the havoc they could create.' Yet Penny had glanced down at her watch again when she said that final sentence. Usually, when my grandmother made a point, her gaze didn't move. She believed in eye contact and directness.

'Gosh, its got dark quickly tonight,' I paused, sensing the silence surrounding us. We hadn't seen another person since Penny and I had begun our walk. *Where were the dog-walkers and cyclists? The children on their scooters? The joggers with their heart rate monitors?*

'Let's get moving, it's cold.' Penny hooked her arm through mine and started to hurry.

I kept my eyes on the black tangle of scrub and fallen branches that ran along the edge of the pathway. The last thing I needed was a sprained ankle with hockey finals in two weeks. *Crack!* Another branch splintered in the scrub. Two yellow eyes flashed ahead.

'Huh? What was that?'

Penny snapped around, her eyes darting between the trees and bushes.

'Two eyes over there!'

'Where?'

I pointed down the pathway to the right. *Hu-huff… Hu-huff… Hu-huff.* Something was panting nearby.

Penny pushed in front of me, her hand hovering over her Tempus Imperium.

'Stay behind me, and be prepared to—'

'What? I don't understand!'

Woof! Woof!

A black Labrador bolted out of the scrub and ran past us.

'Rufus! Rufus, come here!'

A man in running shorts and a headlamp came running down the path at full speed.

'Sorry! I'm trying to catch my dog,' he panted, whizzing past.

'Phew!' I said, letting my shoulders slump. 'That was a false alarm, wasn't it?'

Penny turned to me and grabbed my wrist. 'Charlie, promise me. You'll always be careful of the shadows. Promise me!'

'Ouch! That's too tight!'

'Promise me!'

'Okay, okay. I promise.' I said, as she let me go.

It was only four years later that I finally learnt what that promise meant.

PART 1

1

Adelaide, January 2015

I spent the summer between the end of high school and the start of university working at Happy Jack's Pizza Shack on Portrush Road in Adelaide. Five nights a week, 2 pm to midnight, trying to save enough money for university. My parents had been able to afford to put me through boarding school, but the drought had badly affected our family agricultural supplies business. Now that I was almost eighteen, I needed to fend for myself. Luckily, I could stay with my grandmother in the city.

These months between the end of Year 12 and the start of university felt like a form of purgatory. Even the weather obliged, with a series of heatwaves that melted the asphalt; the government warned of 'catastrophic' fire conditions and the air tasted of ash. After each shift I tried to sleep under the arthritic ceiling fan in Grandma Penny's spare room, but still woke bathed in sweat at least twice a night. Every night I counted down the days to university: *thirty-three, thirty-two, thirty-one, thirty,* a countdown meant to convince me that a double degree in Law and Arts was what I really wanted to do with my life.

My friends all seemed to be so clear about their futures. Lynn, by the age of ten, had already known she wanted to be a doctor like her parents. Annabel planned to be a dentist, while Jacinta aspired to be a concert pianist. At the end of Year 10, the Careers Counsellor had met with each student and helped us select subjects and a career pathway. Despite my indifference, I somehow ended up with a plan to study Law.

Twenty-three, twenty-two, twenty-one … Those numbers were my daily mantra now. I had achieved the required results and my parents appeared happy to brag that there would soon be a lawyer in the family, but something felt wrong about my course choice. A hint of unease hid like a reef or rocky outcrop under the surface of the ocean, waiting to snag unsuspecting ships.

Each morning I woke up, ticked off another day and scrolled through my phone to see what my friends were doing. Even Dan, my boyfriend, seemed to be having fun in his R. M. Williams boots, moleskin trousers and Akubra hat, standing outside a shed where a wool sale was about to start. Unlike me, Dan had taken a proper gap year to work on his parents' farm while playing halfback for the Currency Creek Cougars. Part of me envied the ease of Dan's choices, an ugly barnacle of a feeling that felt abrasive, until I put my phone away. At least when I worked at Happy Jack's Pizza Shack, time passed quickly, between pizza preparation and fielding customer complaints as an assistant manager.

Tonight was quiet for a Tuesday night, despite the heat. Only fifteen days to go and I could reduce the number of shifts I worked. A cricket match played on the radio and the delivery drivers took bets on the highest-scoring batter.

It was 9 pm when my phone buzzed in my pocket. One missed call, then another—8:01, then 8:20, 9:15 and so on, each from my grandmother. Eventually she rang Pizza Shack's landline and I picked up.

'Charlotte … Charlie, be careful. The syneghasts, they've come,' she wheezed.

'The what?'

'Syneghasts.'

'Grandma, I don't have time for this. I'm at work.'

'*Be careful of shadows.* They hide there.'

I loved Grandma Penny, but this last month had been exhausting. I had agreed to stay with her—firstly to reduce my accommodation costs, but also to help care for my grandmother until Mum found her a bed in a nursing home. Her faculties, once sharpened on crosswords, sudoku and reading a book a week, had dulled. When Penny squeezed my hand at night while we watched television, her grip felt brittle like tissue paper. *And, what if she fell and I wasn't there?* Last November, Penny had fallen and spent a week in the hospital recovering. These worries had a way of narrowing my vision and making it hard to breathe.

Two nights ago, I'd even dreamt she had died. Me holding my grandmother's hand as she lay on the ground. Her last breath escaping, despite my best attempts at CPR. A mahogany coffin positioned in front of an altar. Mum's face streaked with tears, while my own shoulders heaved with sobs. I'd been too late, but too late for what? I always hated how these dreams forced me to speculate. When I told Grandma Penny the next morning, she had said with a sigh, 'Not to worry, dear. I'm old. I know I'll die one day.'

'Charlie, tell me you'll watch for those syneghasts?' she implored now.

'I'll be home just after midnight, Gran,' I sighed. 'Make sure you take your tablets before bed. Bye.'

Yet *Be careful of shadows* hung like a bat in my mind. *Why was she returning to this now? Why–after so many years?* The logical part of me dismissed it, but I couldn't forget the way her voice trembled.

«·✕·»

At 12:30 am I checked my phone, but only Dan had texted. He had sent me three hearts and a reminder about booking a weekend off to go to his cousin's wedding with him. I counted the change and closed the cash register. I could hear Mario, the owner, humming Led Zeppelin in the kitchen, so I locked the front door and went out back to see him.

'Finished, Charlie?'

'Yes, I just need you to lock the takings in the safe.'

'No worries, just give me a second to finish here.'

Mario took another huge swipe over the kitchen bench with his sponge. His forearms bulged from lifting sacks of flour and carrying twenty pizza pans at a time. When he cleaned, the bench got punished for being dirty, smacked with sweeping strokes that left it shiny and clean.

'Charlie, would you be able to pick up an extra shift this Saturday? My Nona's been struggling, and I promised I'd make her dinner this weekend and also do her gardening?'

'All right, will do.' I sighed, but still nodded. The best part of working late on a Saturday evening was the penalty rates, and I did want to buy a new laptop before university started. My parents had bought my current one when I was in Year 7, and it ran so slowly that video watching and web browsing were close to impossible.

'What would I do without you, Charlie? You're always willing to pick up an extra shift.'

'Um, just a reminder, Mario, but the following weekend I've got to go home for a wedding?'

'Yeah, no problem. Hitansh will take your shifts.'

I left the bag containing the night's cash takings on the kitchen bench and grabbed my backpack.

'Bye Mario! See you on Thursday!'

Penny still owned an old manual VW Beetle that hadn't been driven since 2013. I preferred to bus it to Happy Jack's Pizza Shack and get a delivery driver like Sayad to drop me home afterwards.

Sayad, as he often explained to me, had come from a wealthy New Delhi family to study commerce and law at UniSA. In India, he always wore starched shirts and long pants, with his hair trimmed and parted in the middle. However, in Adelaide, he liked to dye his hair green on the right side, pop in a nose ring, and wear skinny jeans and a white t-shirt. All night, he fielded messages on his phone and asked my opinion about the boys that he talked to.

'A lift, Charlie? Girlfriend, I'd love to,' he said.

Sayad's car was a Subaru WRX that shone even at night because of his daily polishing. Other drivers flooded their back seats and footwells with burger wrappers, parking tickets and empty water bottles, but Sayad's smelt of pine freshener rather than stale McDonalds.

'Bollywood okay?' he grinned before flicking on the car stereo. A thumping rhythm in Hindi rocked the car as we drove towards Grandma Penny's place. She lived in a tree-lined inner suburb of endless cul-de-sacs and roundabouts. Fifteen years ago, she'd moved to a smaller place in a housing estate where the builders had placed streetlights on every corner. Yet as we approached, darkness massed at the edge of the estate.

'That's weird,' I yelled over the music at Sayad. 'It must be a power blackout.'

Each house seemed braced against the night with blinds and security shutters drawn, the residents tucked up inside under their blankets of sleep and dreams. Only our two headlights fought back against the thick fog.

'Where is it again?' Sayad asked. 'My phone's cut out and there's no GPS.'

That's strange, I thought. Grandma Penny lived so close to the city that you always had at least four bars.

Slowly, we negotiated the turns and roundabouts of Grandma Penny's estate. Usually the solar-powered security lights above each driveway would flick on and off as a car passed by, but tonight, nothing.

Sayad turned off his Bollywood playlist, plunging us into silence. A shroud of nothingness came down abruptly and startled me, like the first and only time I'd taken a sleeping pill. One moment the world was outlined sharply in shadows and muted colours, and then naught.

When Sayad spoke again, I was surprised at how relieved I felt.

'Charlie, you'll have to guide me. I can barely see the road signs.'

'A left then a right,' I answered, but was it two lefts then a right? The fog made the street signs difficult to read. 'Go straight ahead and through the roundabout.'

These estate houses appeared so similar, arranged in rows like desks in a classroom, their residents' foibles hard to see in the dark: the prize-winning roses, the *ADVENTURE BEFORE DEMENTIA* bumper sticker on the caravan in the driveway, and a garden gnome in boxer shorts sitting on a toilet reading.

'I think it's the next right and then two houses from the corner on the left.'

Sayad parked the car alongside Penny's driveway. He took in a deep breath and looked around. 'You okay, girl? I'll wait until you're inside.'

I stepped out of the car. Even the dots of the solar-powered garden lights were out. Odd. I flicked on the torch app on my phone. Above me, a creature scuttled across the power lines. *A possum?* Something hissed in the bushes nearby. *Why weren't the neighbourhood dogs barking?* Normally the smallest sniff of a possum or a cat was enough to set off a chorus of dogs woofing. The elderly residents of Penny's estate liked their dogs to be of the small, yapping kind—fox terriers, chihuahuas and Pomeranians. Dogs that needed to compensate for their lack of size with volume.

I shone the phone light towards Penny's screen door and saw that it was open. One of the glass panels in the front door behind it was broken.

'Sayad! Help!' I called.

Out of the corner of my eye something moved in the shadows. Too big for a possum or neighbourhood cat, it glimmered for a second like its coat was made from an oil slick, front paws and head down, hind legs and tail up, crouching.

'What's up?' whispered Sayad, and I turned.

When I looked back, the creature had gone.

'Look!' I pointed at the door, feeling panic rise like the winds ahead of a stormfront.

'Shoot!' he exclaimed. 'Wait for me. I'll grab something from the car.'

Sayad returned with a tyre iron and we pushed the door open.

13

'Gran! Gran!' I called. My heart thumped, and I felt dizzy. Where was she?

The chair Penny kept by the phone in the hallway lay on the ground. The grandfather clock's glass door was smashed. The four clocks hanging on the wall were paused at midnight, the wooden cuckoo frozen halfway out, its beak open as though stunned. I flicked the hallway light switch—*UP/DOWN, UP/DOWN*—but it still didn't work.

'Grandma? Where are you?'

Telemachus brushed against my leg and meowed, so I picked him up. He had a torn ear and was bleeding from several bites on his back and paws. He looked like he had lost a fight with the colony of feral cats that lived in the local park. His whole body shook as he nuzzled into my chest.

'Where is she?' I begged him. Penny loved this cat and would never leave him in such a state. When I accidentally patted him on a sore spot near the tail, Telemachus flinched and stuck his claws into me. 'Ouch!' I yelped, dropping him to the ground, where he fled through my legs and hid under the coffee table in the living room.

I checked the bedrooms, and Sayad did the same for the laundry and the kitchen.

Finally, I went outside. I could hear Sayad checking the bathroom and study. This side of the estate backed on to a large public park and nature reserve. Again, something moved, too large to be a cat, possum or koala, in a nearby gumtree's branches.

'Gran?' I cried again, my voice trembling.

'Charlie?' The croak trailed off somewhere near the fence line.

I shone my phone light towards Penny's voice.

It stood on four legs over her, silver saliva dripping from its mouth. Underneath me, the ground groaned and trembled.

Whoosh! Without warning, the power surged back on.

'WE BRING YOU TONIGHT'S BREAKING NEWS!'

Cuckoo! Cuckoo!

The beast vanished as Penny's house lit up like a football stadium.

'Gran!' I dropped to my knees and cradled her head in my arms. 'Sayad, call an ambulance!'

Her eyes flickered, and she coughed, the breath rattling in her chest.

'What happened?'

'*Tell them that the key to the syneghasts lies with Kepplar,*' she gasped.

'Who's them?' I asked as her pulse weakened, my grief growing from a passing shower to a storm cloud and then a hurricane. *No! No, this can't be happening! We were meant to have more time together*. I laid her back on the ground and began CPR, barely noticing the threads of silver residue that came away from her hair and fixed themselves to my fingertips.

'Sayad, where's that ambulance?' I cried as my grandmother's pulse stopped.

2

'Charlie, five minutes.'

I looked up at Mum from my bed in Penny's spare room. Despite her best attempts, the foundation she'd applied couldn't hide the fact that she had been crying.

Outside, the rain beat its fists against the windows. One of those unseasonal summer storms, where the rain for the last two months comes down in an hour.

'Okay,' I sighed and tickled Telemachus under his chin. The scratches on his back were healing, but the one on his face made him look lopsided. 'She's gone,' I said to him as he purred. 'What happened, Tee?' Every night since her death, he'd slept on my bed. During the day, he followed me, a pale grey shadow that tracked me from room to room and pursued me even to the bus stop.

I roused myself and went through the hallway to the bathroom. Each door handle still bore traces of the fingerprint dust the police had left behind, despite Dad's best efforts at cleaning it off. Dad had wound most of the clocks, but the cuckoo clock remained stuck, the bird trapped halfway out the chalet's doors.

I splashed water on my face. In the mirror my eyes were red-rimmed, and my brown hair glistened with grease. The black dress I wore made my face look paler than normal. For a moment, I pressed my knuckle firmly into my forehead, hoping the physical pain would rouse me.

Grandma Penny, what happened?

Once the doctor had declared that she'd died of a stroke, the police had lost interest. Nothing was missing. The smashed glass pane in the door and the overturned chair meant nothing. Instead, a blood clot had exploded in her head. The pressure in her brain had caused her to stagger through the house, breaking the glass pane and knocking over a chair. No one, not even the power company, had offered an explanation for the blackout.

The unseasonal fog? The creature made from shadows? The syneghasts? A sign of my trauma, they told my parents.

Every night since her death, my sleep had come in shreds. 11 pm bedtime, but I was awake at 12:45 am until the exhaustion drowned me. 4 am, awake again. My eyes were bloodshot as I retreated to the couch to watch infomercials selling Ab-Master Pros, facial creams and life-changing ladders. I hoped that the enthusiastic monotones of these presenters would eventually dull my brain and dreams, but my attempts at self-medication often failed. These days, even my shifts at Happy Jacks became a liquid concrete through which I dragged myself on only four hours of sleep.

'Charlie, I think you should move home for a while,' said Dad as we drove to the church. 'You've barely slept since Penny's death. We're worried about you.'

I wanted to argue, fight back, crash my head into a brick wall, but I knew he was right. The thought of starting university in two weeks without Penny waiting for me back at her house always sent me into tears.

'Only if Telemachus can come,' I replied.

'Fine. Another cat won't make a difference,' Dad said.

≪·✕·≫

The Church of Saint Expedite sat on the intersection of two major roads, one leading to the rolling wheat belt just beyond the city and the other to the bushfire-devastated hills. It had a gothic formality that so many other Catholic churches lacked now, with a disused confessional and a statue of the Virgin Mary surrounded by candles. Up the back sat an organ, although the last competent organist had died in 1992.

To me, it seemed fitting to hold Penny's funeral service at the Church of Saint Expedite—the patron saint of speedy resolutions. She never wasted time on unnecessary words or actions and hated the trash of euphemisms like 'working families,' 'efficiencies' and 'KPIs' that padded so much political speech on television. She hand-washed the dishes after dinner and folded the laundry promptly, unlike at my parents' place where the laundry basket sat in the corner for days.

The current priest at Saint Expedite appeared barely old enough to attend a seminary, let alone, say, a funeral Mass for my grandmother. Under his chin, a few red pimples sat where there should have been facial hair. He grabbed my mother's hand and shook it as we came inside. 'I'm so sorry for your loss. Penelope was much loved in the parish. Many of her fellow volunteers from the St Vincent De Paul society are here today to pay their respects.'

We sat at the front, with my Aunty Margaret, who'd flown in the night before from Hong Kong. Behind us were thirty ageing parishioners, roughly ordered based on their state of decrepitude—those requiring wheelchairs and walking frames seated towards the back and on the end of rows, while those only needing a walking stick sat closer to the front. Most of the men wore ill-fitting suits that smelt of mothballs and resembled those in a movie prom scene from the 1980s. Near the back sat Dan with his parents, as the Fitzpatricks had known Penny for almost as long as they had known Mum.

There was only one person, apart from my family and the Fitzpatricks, whose age lowered the overall mortality rate. He sat in the very last pew near the exit. His shoulders slumped dressed in his tailored black suit with pinstripes. Grief had flatlined him in the same way it had me.

'Who's that?' I whispered.

'I don't know. Maybe someone from the parish?' replied Dad.

A photo of a young Penny in black and white, taken during World War Two, sat on top of her coffin. She smiled in the photo, her hair curled and layered and her neck framed by a set of white pearls. I wiped away another tear as Mum began her eulogy.

'My mother was born on the second of April in 1921 in Oxfordshire. Her father was the village solicitor and believed in girls' education, encouraging in her a love of physics and classical mythology. During the war she worked for the Ministry of Health in London as a typist. My mother survived the Blitz by sleeping in an air raid shelter. She used to say that if Hitler couldn't finish her off, then no one could.'

When I was in Year 9, I'd interviewed Penny about her experiences of the Blitz for a history project. The damp Anderson shelter in the garden at her boarding house. The crowded underground tube stations at night. The lack of nylon stockings. Brown bread without butter and only carrot jam. Lukewarm

19

cups of black tea. The way bombs could destroy nearly every house in a street, but still leave one standing. The young SOE officer whom she loved before Grandad, but who never returned from a mission into occupied France.

'In 1949, Mum emigrated to Australia. She hated how it constantly rained in England. She met Dad at a local dance run by the parish.'

At least she's with Grandad now, I thought. A man who'd died when I was four, but whose photos haunted Penny's house. Them smiling together on their wedding day, him in his army officer's uniform on the Kokoda Track, and a family portrait where Mum and her older sister Margaret wore their best party dresses.

When I was in boarding school, we had talked almost daily. Penny had challenged me when friends or teachers sent me into tears. 'Don't be such a hysteric, darling! It's not worth it,' she told me. Sometimes I slammed the phone down in anger, but she always rang the next day. The Second World War had taught Penny not to waste words, food, paper or rubber bands. She had seen too many bodies brought out on stretchers and laid out in neat rows on the sidewalk with their faces covered by blankets.

Tell them that the key to the syneghasts lies with Kepplar.

Who was this 'them' she'd referred to? How could I give a message to someone or something I didn't know? And what was a syneghast? Was it that dog-like creature I'd witnessed standing over her? At least I knew who Kepplar was, or so I thought. My grandmother had a whole shelf of books by him or about his work in physics, but his equations seemed dense and made from barbed wire. I'd already tried twice to open his books and search for references to syneghasts, but my vision soon became blurred with tears, and I'd had to shut them and promise myself I'd come back to them when I felt less upset.

The 'confused ramblings' of a dying woman is what Mum and Dad believed I'd heard—the blood clot fracturing her thought processes as it killed her. Yet I couldn't forget the creature I'd seen standing over her. Where did it go?

3

Currency Creek, July 2015

I spent the next few months after the funeral back home in Currency Creek, where Mum and Dad treated me like one of Penny's antique clocks—one that had broken down and required repairs. Daily they reminded me to wash my hair, to eat and to exercise. Some days I put on my running shoes and ran for hours down dirt roads, not caring if I twisted an ankle. I ran until I doubled over with my hands on my knees and the air I took in burnt my throat. The words *Tell them that the key to the syneghasts lies with Kepplar* knotted up inside my brain, making it tough to focus on anything but breathing.

I deferred university and archived my plans to study a double degree in Law and Arts. Getting through twenty-four hours each day seemed hard enough, let alone planning essays and exam revision schedules for a course I wasn't even certain I wanted to do.

'Charlie, enough's enough,' said Dad, one night at the dinner table.

For the last twenty minutes I had been pushing a piece of broccoli around my plate, after eating only four bites of steak and two forkfuls of mashed potato. My clothes hung off my frame, and I had started using a narrower notch on my belt. I had spent my adolescence worrying about my weight and the stodgy rice and pasta that formed the basis of most boarding-house meals, but it took my grandmother's death to drop me from a size 12 to a 10.

'You need to come and work for me for a while. This moping about all day needs to stop.'

'But—'

'Charlie,' said Mum. 'When you're not outside running, you spend the day hiding under a doona watching videos with that cat of your grandmother's. It's not healthy. At least if you work for your father, you might develop a proper appetite.'

I sniffled. I wanted to argue, but I recognised the tone of voice Mum used. She had inherited it from Grandma Penny, who liked to employ it on parking inspectors and naughty toddlers. This wasn't a negotiation, but rather a pre-planned ambush.

'And God knows, I could use the help. I've been short-staffed since Simon took that manager's position at the Bunnings in Victor,' Dad added.

I dropped my shoulders and forced down another bite of steak.

<< · ✕ · >>

On the weekends, when I wasn't working for Dad, I went to the footy and watched Dan play. Dan in his blue-and-white-striped Currency Creek Cougars jersey, with his thatch of blonde hair that always flopped over one eye, no matter how much he brushed it. I liked to sit on the bonnet of his ute and watch when it wasn't too cold. When the match finished, Dan would give me one of those grins of his, the one that, no matter what he had done, made his mum laugh, before heading off to the change rooms for a shower. I knew the other local girls looked at Dan and wondered how someone like me had ended up with him. Me with my mousy brown hair, who preferred a night in watching a movie to clinging to the shadows at parties held by people I barely remembered from primary school. In contrast, Dan controlled the centre, with his smile and the stories that made others laugh.

Dan and I grew up together. We'd swum in dams together, ridden dirt bikes, and I was there on the day Dan broke his leg after falling off the shed roof. He'd always been my best friend, and I'd never thought of him as boyfriend material until the night of my Year 11 formal. Dan had gone with one of the other boarders, but we'd spent the whole night giggling and laughing at our own in-jokes. He kissed me for the first time that night on the dance floor.

However, things felt different now. We were both older, and I had changed after Penny's death. Sometimes being with Dan felt like a performance, in which I knew my cues by rote.

Unlike me, Dan had taken his gap year willingly, deferring medicine to work on the family farm for a year. He seemed to revel in fixing fences, shearing sheep and going to the pub with the footy team after training. Me, I felt like an interloper, even though I had lived in Currency Creek all my life. My grief and depression made people my own age wary of me, and it was only through Dan's efforts that they included me at all.

One Saturday evening, I went with Dan to a bonfire party out in someone's back paddock. A recently felled gum tree lay on its side, freshly chainsawed into logs to dump on the fire. Dan parked his ute on the edge of the bonfire, then disappeared to find us some drinks.

I sat on the end of the ute's tray, staring into the fire and thinking about Penny. What would she have thought of me? *Charlie, stop moping about!* Those words, said with the authority of her English accent, part BBC World Service and part the Queen's Christmas Address. I wanted to protest. What had killed Grandma Penny? I shivered again at the memory of that beast standing over her.

'Charlie!'

I flinched.

'Charlie! It's just me. Sorry it took so long to find us a drink. I got distracted by Tommo's new ute.'

I let my shoulders slump as Dan put his arms around me.

'Geez, you're cold. I'll get the picnic blanket.'

Dan draped the blanket around my shoulders and I took a sip of Diet Coke. In front of me, someone threw another log on the fire, which spat and crackled in pleasure.

'Is everything okay, Charlie?'

I nodded and sipped the Diet Coke again.

'You haven't seemed all right since your grandmother passed away.'

Tears filled my eyes. I tried to wipe them away with the edge of my sleeve.

'No, not really,' I said.

'I've tried to give you time and space, but your dad pulled me aside the other day and asked me to talk to you.'

I felt a sinkhole opening up between us.

'I've never seen you this way before, where you just go through the motions. Please tell me what I can do to help?'

Dan squeezed my shoulders, pulling me closer to him. He smelt of wood smoke and the cheap body wash that the footy club kept in the change rooms.

'I'm sorry. Ever since Penny died, I've felt out of sorts. That I failed. That I could have saved her.'

'But she died of a stroke?'

I wanted to remind Dan of what I saw that night, but knew that like my parents, he believed the 'official' explanation.

I sighed. 'She'd been ringing me all night at Happy Jacks. We weren't even busy. I could have finished early and gone home to check on her. Instead I let my grandmother die.'

'Oh, don't blame yourself,' he said, before pulling me into an embrace and kissing me. I knew he wanted this moment to be about us, but part of me felt closed off and separate, like I was watching myself on stage. It was the same part that still believed in what I saw that night, standing above Penny.

<< ·✕· >>

Lamp's Agricultural Supplies squatted between a service station and an empty storefront where, despite the dust, the word 'Haberdashery' was still visible on the front window. Currency Creek had always been one of those country towns where the only places that opened after 7 pm were the pub and the fish'n'chip shop. Lamp's Agricultural Supplies shut by 6 pm on weeknights and only opened between 9 am and 12 pm on Saturdays. Business had been slow since a Bunnings had opened in nearby Victor Harbor. Dad had already let two staff go, and another had resigned, and at least with me, I worked for food and board.

It appealed to me to lose myself in rows of stock feed, fertiliser and barbed wire and fill the space between waking and sleeping with something familiar. Three days a week I was on the floor, with Dad in the back room doing paperwork. The only time I needed

Dad was for those whose accounts were in the red. Those farmers came in and glanced around the store, checking that no one they knew was there before approaching the front counter. Next, they placed a smartphone with a cracked screen on the front counter, followed by a wallet held together with a rubber band.

'Can I speak to your father?' they asked in low voices, their eyes fixed on the chipped woodwork of the front counter.

'Dad?' I'd call out before heading into the nearest aisle and start to tidy up our displays of wire-cutters, hammers and nails.

I only hated working in the store at closing time. Occasionally Dad expected me to do it by myself: lock the doors, clean up and balance the till while he attended a Southern Fleurieu Rotary Club meeting or went to CFS training.

That July, it was dark by 5 pm. We were at the other end of the main street, a good eight hundred metres from the fish'n'chip shop and the pub. If I looked down the street, I could just make out the outlines of the cars parked in front of the pub and hear their doors opening and slamming shut. Without the clouds of rain overhead, the days and nights rarely snuck above ten degrees. I spent much of the day wearing a black down jacket that my parents had bought me for a school ski trip. In the mornings, I broke the ice on the ute's windscreen by pouring tap water over it before driving into work with Dad.

'Charlie, is it okay if you close tonight? There's a Rotary meeting in Victor and I need to do some shopping beforehand,' said Dad. 'I'll pick you up around 8 pm.'

'Okay,' I sighed, even though I had been counting the minutes until closing time. I wanted to go home and curl up under my doona, and watch videos on my laptop, with Telemachus by my side. I knew closing tonight would take some time, as the bins needed to be put out for collection. This meant mopping the floors and cleaning the staff kitchen and bathroom.

Dad departed at 4 pm, which left an hour to closing. Between 4 and 5 pm was often our quietest period of the day. Most of the farmers preferred to do their shopping in the morning, after the school and grocery run. Despite it only being ten degrees outside, Dad refused to close the shop door as to him, an open door meant 'Welcome,' so I spent this hour scrolling through my phone while trying not to lose my fingers to frostbite. Lynn had shared a photo of their first drink post-exams, and Annabel was out at an Asian fusion restaurant, whereas I sat on a vinyl-covered stool where duct tape covered over the cracks. I let myself tumble into the rabbit hole of random online videos: trailers for the upcoming seasons of my favourite shows and the latest superhero movie, followed by viral clips of cats sitting on robotic vacuum cleaners and Jack Russells jumping over childproof gates.

Bang!

The shop front door slammed shut, making the front window rattle. The calendar pinned to the noticeboard behind me crashed into the floor.

I flinched. What was that? The wind?

Normally a thirty-kilogram bag of chicken feed kept the door propped open. These bags were so heavy that I preferred to move them around using a sack-truck. I went outside, where the flag in front of the war memorial hung from its pole, unmoved. The litter wrappers and dry gum leaves sat stiff as corpses in the gutter. Only the bag of chicken feed had changed. Something had slashed it open, letting the pellets bleed out across the pavement. Huh? What had done this?

Even the birds that normally sat on the powerlines and

stained the war memorial with their droppings had fled the cold. I looked closer again. Perhaps, I rationalised, the bag's weave was faulty. What else could it be?

I grabbed a dustpan and broom and started cleaning up the mess. The movement warmed up my stiff, frozen joints, making me feel less jittery. Afterwards, I shut the shop door and turned over the *Closed* sign. The next two hours were a blur of vacuuming, mopping and dusting, apart from a phone call to Mum, who promised to put a few lamb chops aside for me, and a text from Dan about catching a film on the weekend.

I had just finished mopping when the power died. The outlines of shovels, price tags and bags of seed dissolved into the blackness. My breathing quickened as the hair on the back of my arms rose. Even the one streetlight positioned at our end of the street was out. I looked at my phone, but it said *No Service*. Surely it couldn't be another blackout like the night Penny died?

Stop being an idiot, Charlie. I fumbled around under the front counter, trying not to stick my fingers into a mouse or cockroach trap. Eventually I found the emergency torch, which glowed for a second before dying. I shook it and smacked it on the back, but Dad had forgotten to replace the batteries. Only my mobile phone's flashlight app worked, yet its quavering beam just heightened the shadows.

I paused and took a deep breath to steady myself. 7:45 pm. I expected Dad in the next fifteen minutes. Should I wait for him before putting the rubbish out? There would be a working torch in the ute. Yet the rational part of me reasoned it was only a blackout, and nothing like that night in January with its unseasonal fog. I had walked the aisles of this shop since I was a toddler. How would I explain to Dad that I hadn't finished all the chores? A blackout?

I already felt stupid enough. Taking my phone in one hand, I grabbed the garbage bags, which stank of dead possum; Dad had removed one from the roof cavity earlier that day.

Outside, it seemed even blacker, with the only light coming from a tiny sliver of silver moon. The bins were by the back fence, past the storage shed.

Dogs barked near the pub. Leaves rustled in the gum tree above me. *The creature standing over Penny, dripping silver saliva.* My heart battered against my chest as I white-knuckled my phone and strode forward. The gravel crunched behind me, followed by a low, deep growl. A claw raked across the side of the skip bin. Then another growl. Too low for a possum—could it be a fox? Yet you never saw foxes in town, as they preferred dawn raids on chicken coops.

I shone the beam of my phone towards the sound. A hiss. I took in a sudden breath as I felt the ground shudder for a second beneath me. The footsteps circled me, panting, but stayed outside the edge of the phone's light. A louder growl. Something cold and bulky brushed against my right leg. I tripped and dropped the rubbish bags, my shoulder slamming hard into the shed's sliding door as I fumbled for the solar-powered bug zapper switch that hung above it.

Buzz! A blue beam of UV light shot across the ground and smashed into another one of those creatures, like the one I'd seen at Penny's place. For a moment, two eyes glared at me before it shattered into ash.

'Charlie?'

I heard Dad just as all the lights surged back on. The rubbish bags sat about a metre from the skip bin. One was torn open, exposing the rotting possum corpse and white maggots writhing across its fur. On the left side, scratched into the blue paint of the skip bin, was a claw mark.

'Are you okay?'

'Yeah—just startled,' I said, rubbing my shoulder.

Dad examined the side of the skip bin. 'Gosh, that's a big scratch. Did you see it?'

'Some sort of gigantic dog?'

'A farmer at tonight's meeting said there's a pack of wild dogs running around attacking livestock at the moment. It's strange they'd be so close to town.'

'Yeah, but look at the size of those paw prints.'

Dad let out a short whistle, as he bent down to get a closer look at them. 'They're almost as big as my hand span,' he said, laying his hand inside one. 'Tomorrow, I'm going to leave you with the shotgun, Charlie, in case that monster of a dog shows up again.'

'Okay,' I said, and swallowed hard, trying not to gag. My stomach was churning and nauseous. Had I just seen another one of those creatures?

4

It was six months after Penny's funeral before Mum and I could face cleaning out her place. Despite monthly visits from a gardener, the weeds still sprouted from the cracks in her driveway. On the day we arrived, a soggy mess of political flyers, KMart brochures and council newsletters tumbled out of her letter box. At the front door, I stopped. Mum and Dad had fixed the broken glass, but the colour was slightly off compared to the other panes. *You can do this, Charlie*, I told myself while gulping in air like a recently rescued swimmer—breaths that plummeted down my throat, missed my lungs and hit my stomach instead. For a second, I clutched the doorframe, feeling faint and dry retching, until I heard Mum calling from inside. *C'mon, Charlie*, I demanded and forced myself to stand up straight and walk forward.

Inside the house, I placed Telemachus's cat carrier on the floor and let him out. He came out slowly, his ears back and nostrils flaring. I watched him go from room to room, sniffing the corners, tapping at the doors with his front paws and holding his tail high before disappearing under Penny's bed. When I bent down and looked under the purple valance, his two yellow eyes glared back at me.

I knew I couldn't hide in Currency Creek for the rest of my life, selling chicken feed and sweeping out the aisles of Lamp's Agricultural Supplies. Until now, I had always had a clear map in my head: finish school, get decent grades, go to university and then get my 'dream job'. Although these days, I wasn't even certain what that 'dream job' was. Penny's death had derailed me. I might work eight-hour days, but often I only slept for two or three hours. Mum had taken me to Dr Hawkins, our family GP, who had given me my first vaccinations and stitched up my childhood accidents. Yet my trauma and grief seemed beyond his thirty-two years of experience. He frowned and wrote a prescription for anti-depressants, and suggested herbal sleeping tablets as a remedy for my insomnia. However, as the cold of winter lifted and the days warmed, my mood began to pick up. The farms near Currency Creek started shearing their sheep by the hundreds each day. Driving through the paddocks, I saw thousands of them, pale-skinned and basking in the spring sunlight. My nights were also becoming less angst-ridden, driven by the daily antidote of physical labour in the store.

Before I left for the two weeks it would take to clean out Penny's place, I spent the day with Dan. He fixed fences and tolerated my silences while I read a novel. I packed us a picnic lunch of sandwiches and a thermos of coffee, and we ate it sitting on Fitzpatrick's Boulder, the highest point for kilometres. On a clear day, you could see across the green fields all the way to where the waves pounded against the south coast.

'Are you sure you're going to be okay?' Dan asked. 'I know how much your grandmother meant to you.'

'Yeah, I'm better. A lot better,' I said. 'I've slept through the night every day this week and the week before.'

'It's just these last few months, I've felt like part of you has been closed off from me.'

'Um, yeah, I know. Penny dying knocked me about. Dr Hawkins reckoned I might have had some sort of depression. But the medication he gave me works. I feel like I'm getting better every day,' I said, forcing a smile.

'I'm glad,' said Dan, putting his arm around me.

I nestled into him, recognising my prompt.

《·✕·》

This trip to clean out Grandma Penny's house was part of my healing process. Mum believed that for me and her to move on, Penny's house required emptying. Her clothes still hung in the wardrobe, creams and medications lay along the bathroom sink, and out-of-date crackers and teabags sat in the kitchen cupboard. There were also two linen cupboards stacked high with recycled wrapping paper, glass jars and boxes of deteriorating rubber bands. On the side of the stove sat an ice-cream tub full of animal fat that Penny liked to re-use every time she cooked, despite my warnings about cholesterol. As a child of the Great Depression, Penny had hated waste. She'd told me how her mother kept the pieces of string that shopkeepers used to wrap around the paper that held pats of butter and servings of sugar, and later tied it around old letters and cards that she stored in a kitchen drawer. At Christmas time, my presents came wrapped in recycled paper. If you were lucky, you might even find your own handwriting still on it, wishing you a happy birthday.

There was also the challenge of Penny's books—thousands of them—that lined the walls in the bedrooms and sat on the windowsills in the bathroom, laundry and kitchen. Novels by Tolstoy, Steinbeck, and Austen; poetry by Auden, Eliot and Plath; biographies of tsars, inventors and suffragettes; and manuals on how to repair watches and clocks. However, the ones that confused me the most were the weighty tomes related to physics, particles and quantum mathematics. World War Two had prevented Penny from attending Cambridge, despite her keen intellect. Instead, she'd found an outlet through reading books by and about Einstein, Feynman, Stephen Hawking and James Kepplar. Kepplar even had his own shelf in the bedroom, where sat his memoir, several textbooks and a critical commentary. In the days after my grandmother's death I'd scanned them for references to syneghasts, but only succeeded in making myself cross-eyed until Mum and Dad insisted that I stop. Dockets, torn-off strips of newspaper and yellow post-it notes marked pages where Penny had written cryptic comments in blue fountain-pen ink along the margins. Most would be boxed-up and sent to the local St Vinnie's store. Yet for some reason, I held onto her physics books and their comments about 'resonances,' 'magnetometers' and unexplained 'by-products.'

For two days, we filled rubbish bags and carted them outside to a skip bin Mum hired. Most of that time, Telemachus remained under Penny's bed. He came out at mealtimes to meow and pace up and down the hallway. I scratched him under the chin and below the ears. 'It's okay, Tee,' I whispered. 'We'll be okay.' Sometimes he hissed at me and flattened his ears.

We packaged up Penny's Royal Doulton china set and sent it to Mum's sister in Hong Kong. Mum put the lace tablecloths and bedspreads away, and the smell of sandalwood incense replaced the odour of lavender and mothballs that I always associated with Penny's place.

'Charlie, you were always much closer to Penny than I was,' Mum said, as we started hauling newspapers, dating from the 1990s, to the recycling bin.

Since early childhood, I had understood that Mum had been closer to her father. Other mothers served in the school tuck-shop, walked their children home from primary school and helped with their homework, but Penny worked. Instead, my grandfather took on this role, cooking Sunday Roasts and stitching up holes in his daughters' school uniforms. His early morning shifts meant he finished in time for school pick-up while Penny worked long hours as the personal assistant to the CEO of a shipping company.

'Margaret and I asked her about her past in England and what it was like, but she always avoided answering,' Mum said. 'You are lucky to have been so close to her. It's like retirement and being a grandmother finally gave Penny permission to be herself.'

Penny always kept a supply of Arnott's Scotch Finger biscuits and lemonade in the cupboard and had taught me how to make lamingtons and Anzac biscuits. During the school holidays, we caught the bus into the city and went to the Art Gallery or the movies. For someone who would have been in their eighties by then, her eclectic film tastes ranged from the latest Pixar fare to erotic French art-house films.

'You're like her, you know,' Mum continued. 'The same quick intelligence. The same determination. You even have her blue eyes. Maybe that's why you two were so close?'

'But Grandma Penny never got to know Aunty Margaret's kids. They've always lived in Hong Kong,' I said, as I threw another stack of newspapers with a thud into the recycling bin.

Aunty Margaret had two children my age who lived in Hong Kong with a nanny, housekeeper, maid and chauffeur-driven car. At Christmas when they came to stay, they complained about the wi-fi in Currency Creek and left dirty plates, half-drunk cups and crumbs around the house. I couldn't stand my cousins, particularly on Christmas morning when they whined about not receiving the latest gadget.

'Charlie, look at this! I can't believe Penny kept it all these years.'

Mum was holding a newspaper clipping from the *South Coast Times*, in which Dan and I stood in the local church hall with the parish priest. The headline read 'Currency Creek Primary Students Raise $3000 For Drought Relief.' The fundraising had been my idea, not Dan's, although his charm had helped us convince several local businesses to donate. Most of the casual work for farmhands had evaporated like the moisture from the soil that year, making it hard for parents to even afford Vegemite sandwiches, let alone buy new school shoes. The only places still making money were the pub and the servo that sold cigarettes after hours, which both donated $500 to our fundraising drive.

'Penny must have been so proud of you, like your father and I were.'

I gazed at the photo and grinned. Dan and I looked so happy in our primary-school polo shirts, without the complications of kisses and expectations which now weighed upon our relationship.

'You've always been good at that stuff, Charlie. That's why Penny saw you as a kindred spirit,' Mum said.

Mum was right. I'd mediated the peace between Annabel and Lynne when Annabel's boyfriend had dumped her just before the formal and asked Lynne instead. I had learnt from the best in

Mum and Penny, who could settle a dispute between neighbours or supply a crisis casserole in times of illness or grief. Mum was known throughout the district for her lasagnes, which was a recipe she'd learnt from her own mother.

«·×·»

There was still the problem of the clocks, which hung on every wall and sat on almost every surface. Lantern clocks, carriage clocks, a cuckoo clock and a grandfather clock that looked naked without its glass front panel. The pièce de résistance was a Victorian mystery clock, where a woman dressed in long, flowing robes held the clock up like a lantern. No one had wound them in months, and now each one told a different time.

'Time should always be precise,' Penny would say, as she wound each clock at 4 pm every day. Penny didn't have any digital clocks that ran on batteries; rather, her clocks comprised mechanical gears and pendulums that swung to keep the time. Her father, an amateur horologist, had restored and maintained his own clocks, a skill Penny had learnt from him. I loved watching her at work. On the kitchen table, she would unroll a bundle of tools: precision screwdrivers, pliers, tweezers and a magnifying glass that she attached to the front of her glasses. As she unscrewed the case of a wristwatch, Penny labelled the parts out loud for me: 'The outer rim of a watch is called a bezel. The crown is the knob that we pull out to adjust the time. Remember Charlie, anything that a watch does beyond telling the time is a complication.'

Penny had owned a small collection of valuable wristwatches, including a Rolex Submariner, an Omega Sportsmaster, a

Blancpain Fifty Fathoms and a bejewelled gold Cartier, which were now stored in a bank's safe deposit box. The Rolex and Cartier she had inherited from her father. Yet none of these had been my favourite, because as a child, I'd preferred the Tempus Imperium. According to Penny, the Tempus Imperium was a chronometer. A special type of watch, renowned for its accuracy. In Switzerland, she had said, a lab existed solely to test the accuracy of watches at different temperatures and times of the day. The Tempus Imperium contained a genuine diamond and quartz movement, waterproofing to ten metres and a cracked leather band. I loved the detail of this watch—its outer bezel of adjustable numbers that went up to one hundred and eighty degrees and its two inner complications, one measuring up to ninety degrees and the other for setting the date, month, day and year. It's the only vintage wristwatch I've ever seen with the ability to set the year. Three years ago I'd googled the brand 'Tempus Imperium' after spending too many afternoons watching *Antiques Roadshow* with Penny. To my surprise, it had no digital footprint; the other watches, the Rolex, Omega, Blancpain and Cartier, appeared in the online catalogues of well-known auction houses and collectors' websites. But no one, it seemed, had ever heard of a Tempus Imperium. She'd told me that the SOE officer had gifted it to her before his last mission.

Now, Mum and I had the job of sorting out these clocks and watches amongst the many other objects in Penny's house. Her will divided the small fortune she had saved over many years equally between Aunty Margaret and Mum, whereas her two-bedroom house would remain unsold for now, instead becoming a place for me to stay while studying and accommodation for Aunty Margaret and the cousins when they returned to Australia.

Yet the minutia of Penny's estate—the clocks, wristwatches, the china, and furniture—still required Mum and me to divide it up, or so we thought.

Once we removed the newspapers and out-of-date magazines, we started checking the state of Penny's Queen Anne furniture. Many chairs, sideboards, lamp tables and chests of drawers crowded the rooms of the house, made from walnut and oak, their legs squat and patterned with carved scallops and shells. I bent down to get a better look at the base of a dining chair and found, *For Margaret, the dining table set* painted underneath. Mum checked a lamp table with a marble top and found *For Helen, the matching lamp tables*, and then glanced under the base of a carriage clock where *For Charlie* had been etched.

'When will you check the wristwatches, Mum?' I asked.

'Not today.' she replied. 'I'll go to the bank sometime later this week.'

《·✕·》

After three days of cleaning and clearing, we tackled Penny's desk, a heavy oak desk in the spare room with a roll-down lockable top. It took several days to find the key to unlock the desk drawers. Inside one sat a stack of yellowing papers and several leather-bound diaries and journals with split bindings. I also discovered a set of recipes for fruit cakes, bread and butter pudding and lamb shanks written out in Penny's cursive. In another, I spotted a series of handwritten letters that my grandfather had written to Penny from mine sites in Ghana, Indonesia and Broome. In the bottom right-hand drawer, I found a leather folio with the initials *C.B.* monogrammed on the front, filled with typewritten reports about projected epidemics and disease, gauze supplies, petrol rationing for ambulances and the nutritional qualities of army rations.

'Are you going to chuck that, Charlie?' Mum asked, brandishing a plastic crate filled with ten-year-old phone and power bills. Only my grandfather's letters were safe from the cull.

'These should really be in an archive somewhere, Mum. I mean, look at this. These are official Ministry of Health Reports from the Second World War. I think I'll hold on to them for now.'

As I replaced the folder on the desk, a couple of envelopes spilled onto the carpet: an aerogram and another one containing a set of photographs. 'Mum, look at these,' I said, flicking through the photos. Penny was sitting on a rock with a snow-capped mountain behind her, with a young man's arm around her waist. Unlike Grandad, with his receding hairline that showed from an early age, this man had a full head of hair, a solid jaw, and a crooked nose. For some reason, he reminded me of that stranger in the pin-striped suit at Penny's funeral. Yet, that wasn't possible. In the photos, the young man looked the same age as Penny, whereas at the funeral he looked in his late fifties.

'Huh? That's not Grandad!'

'Let me see,' said Mum, coming over. 'Maybe it's the SOE officer who died in occupied France?'

I turned the photo over. Someone had scrawled in pencil, 'May 1925' on the back. 'May 1925? Penny was only born in 1922. She looks about twenty-six in that photo!'

'It must be a mistake.' Mum tapped her finger on the date. 'Look, that two could easily be a four, the pencil's so smudged.'

I looked through the rest of the photographs: Penny with the same young man sitting at a table in a cafe; Penny standing

41

alongside a control panel with a Chinese woman dressed in a lab coat; that same young man and Penny standing in front of the Eiffel Tower. 'Where's Grandma Penny in this photo?' I asked Mum, pointing at the one of her in front of the control panel.

Mum looked over my shoulder again. 'You know what your grandmother's like, Charlie. Her interests were eclectic, to say the least. Maybe it's a factory she visited when she worked for the shipping company?'

Lastly, I turned my attention to the aerogram addressed to the 'Packing & Supplies Co-op, PO BOX 101, Charing Cross, 38 The Strand WC2N 5JB, United Kingdom' in Penny's cursive. The envelope was outlined in the distinctive blue and red border that meant international postage, and the back lip firmly stuck down to the body.

'Do these even still work, Mum?' I asked. 'And who on earth was Penny writing to at a Packing and Supplies Co-op in London?'

'It looks like she meant to post it before she died,' Mum said. 'Why don't we do that for her?'

I smiled.

'I'll put it in the post tonight, Charlie, after I go to the supermarket.'

≪·✕·≫

Later that evening, as Mum and I sat eating Thai takeaway, she handed me the Tempus Imperium.

'Charlie, I looked at the wristwatches in the vault again. This is for you.'

Here it was—the front casing scratched, and the brown leather band speckled with cracks.

'Turn it over.'

On the base of the watch were etched the words, 'For C. L.' in Grandma Penny's handwriting.

'You'd be the only C. L she knew, Charlie. The Rolex, the Omega and the Cartier had your cousins' names on them.'

The Tempus Imperium vibrated in my hand, one movement for each second.

5

By February 2016, I'd stuck myself together with plaster and glue. I re-enrolled at university and started working at Pizza Shack again. Telemachus slept on my bed most nights; a purring hot water bottle that woke me every morning at 5 am, miaowing to go outside.

I now wore the Tempus Imperium on my wrist. It was big, heavy and unfeminine, in a world where wristwatches were a waif-like fashion statement or mini-computers that told you your heart rate, GPS location, and answered phone calls. The function of the inner dial where one hundred and eighty degrees sat in the place of a twelve, and the outer rim, which Penny called the 'bezel', still mystified me. There was also that button that sat halfway between 10 and 11 o'clock. Sometimes when I fidgeted, I rotated the outer bezel of the watch and flicked that button on the left, on and off, yet nothing happened. Several times I googled 'Tempus Imperium' and even consulted a jeweller in the city.

'I don't know this brand,' the jeweller admitted. 'But look here. This face has been hand-machined, and the internal movement combines both gold and diamond rather than steel and quartz. This watch has been handmade by a master craftsman. Where did you get it from again?'

'I inherited it from my grandmother.'

'If you ever decide to sell it, let me know,' he saw. 'I know plenty of collectors who'd be interested in such an unusual one-off piece. They'd pay a good price.'

'Oh no, it's not for sale,' I said, and left.

«·✕·»

One evening, while I waited for a bus back to Penny's place, I played with the Tempus Imperium, pushing the button up and down and adjusting the bezel several clicks to the right and then two back to the left. Earlier, I went with Dan and some friends to the cinema and saw a film about people with superpowers clad in costumes, where power always came with responsibilities.

In another couple of days, university started. I had bought my textbooks, chosen my electives, and received a new backpack for Christmas. To me, these plans were as solid as the concrete footings on which they built houses. My doubts about my choice of degree, I drowned out with deliberate optimism. *The Careers Counsellor was right! You got the marks and are smart enough to do Law!* I envied Dan's certainty about medicine and his plans to be a country GP.

The bus was late. Dan had wanted to wait with me, but I told him not to worry. I'd call him tomorrow morning. The stop for the 257 that went to Penny's place lay across the road from the main restaurant strip of the city and backed on to the parklands. During

45

the weekend, families filled these parks with prams and scooters, kids tested themselves on slides and swing sets, while old men played bocce and talked of Sicily. However, at night, it became a tangle of trees, where the footpath lights only deepened the shadows. I checked the time—9:33 pm—as tiny pin pricks of anxiety crept across my skin. The bus should have arrived five minutes ago.

Behind me, something moaned. I flinched. *Don't be silly*, I told myself, *it's only a homeless person*. Most nights, a rag-tag group of homeless people slept under the porch of the nearby public toilets. During the daytime, they stored their shopping carts and bedding made from blue tarps and blankets near the back storage door. At night, they drank cartons of wine, sang songs and bummed cigarettes from anyone who walked past.

That moan again, low and deep, as though someone was in pain. Part of me wanted to check whether this person was okay, but the thought of stepping away from the streetlights and into the blackness of the parklands scared me.

Where was this bus?

A dog howled in the distance and I heard the gravel crunch on a nearby pathway. Two of the footpath lights fizzed out. *It's nothing*, I told myself, as I turned around. My eyes darting up, down and across, but failing to dent the darkness.

Hee-oowwwl... There it was again, that moan, but I still saw nothing.

Was it a stray dog? A family pet escaped from the backyard? Surely not. Perhaps an oversized possum or a stray?

I turned back to the well-lit road in front of me, watching the cars flash past. I could just hear the tinkle of voices coming from a nearby pub, above the traffic noise. Across the six lanes, the city grid glowed.

Maybe I should cross and catch a taxi? Beneath me, the bitumen seemed to tremble, making me feel weak and unsteady on my feet. *What was going on?*

Another footpath light flickered off as the panting of the creature came closer. A low, deep growl, like the one I heard that night at Penny's place and later in Currency Creek. The hair on my arms stiffened and stood on end as goosebumps pimpled my flesh. I shifted from foot to foot and rubbed my arms for warmth. *How did it get so cold?*

I punched the crossing button of the traffic lights next to the bus stop. Yet, the little man remained red, and the ticking evenly spaced. I hit the crossing button again, but the man refused to change. *Should I cross?* The lilt of the voices and the pub lights enticed me.

The nearest footpath light to me fizzed and went dark. I looked right, then left, and then for a second behind. A dog, the size of a Shetland pony, silhouetted under the streetlight. I froze, and it growled again. I held my breath, despite the pounding in my ears. *What should I do? Run?* The panic flailed in my mind, like a toddler beating the ground during a tantrum, until the hum and clang of the 257 bus splintered the silence. The bus's headlights smashed through the darkness, illuminating where I stood. A crowd of shift workers got off: nurses, security guards, and cleaners, before I jumped on. My hands shook, and I dropped my ticket.

'Are you okay?' asked the driver. 'You look faint.'

I grabbed one of the metallic poles inside the bus and steadied myself, and this time scanned my bus ticket.

'Yeah… Um… Just tired,' I replied and headed down the aisle, taking a seat near the rear left wheel.

As the bus pulled away from the kerb, I looked at the place where I saw the silhouette. Nothing now, except the orange glow of a streetlight.

Behind me on the bus, someone coughed, and I turned around. A nurse with black rings under her eyes sat messaging on her phone, next to a teenager gazing at a YouTube video, but two rows to the left of me sat a man in a well-cut pinstripe suit with salt and pepper hair.

Where had I seen him before?

He looked older than my parents—mid-fifties, yet too well-dressed to be from Currency Creek. His suit tailored so that the jacket didn't gape open as he sat. The navy-blue fabric soaked in the light, rather than reflecting it like the cheap nylon suits that men my father's age wore to funerals, weddings, and job interviews back home. Even his tie matched his suit rather than the technicolour creations that men at home felt obliged to wear, having received them as Christmas gifts.

He nodded and met my gaze. I rubbed my eyes. *Who was this man?* The phone in my pocket buzzed. It was Mum calling for a chat. I turned back and answered.

6

Last night, those dreams had reared their ugly heads again. It seemed every hour I slipped into a half-sleep, but black dogs circled me as I turned and twisted in my bed. By morning my limbs felt leaden, and the sheets were damp and knotted. I poured cold water into my coffee and forgot to butter my toast.

8 pm, then 9 pm, each minute of my shift chiselling away at my patience. My nerves felt stretched as tight as a rubber band. I yelled at a driver for dropping a bottle of Coke on the way out. I slammed the walk-in freezer door several times. I made Sayad turn down the Fresh FM Party Remix on the radio when before I would have pirouetted around the kitchen with him to Sia's 'Chandelier.' 'The cheese goes before the pepperoni!' I snapped at a fourteen-year-old kid who'd only started at Pizza Shack three days ago.

By 10 pm, I'd had enough. I needed to take my break and recalibrate. Out the back of Pizza Shack was a gravel car park with a crumbling toilet block and two skip bins. By the back door squatted three flipped-over milk crates and an ashtray, lit by a single LED globe. I sat down. Meditate, I ordered myself.

Concentrate on your breathing like they taught you at school.

Inhale… one… two… three… four… five…

Exhale… one… two… three… four… five…

The bulb above me brightened, then fizzled out. I opened my eyes but couldn't see anything. Clouds smothered the moon and none of the carpark lights were working. The noise of the Pizza Shack was muffled behind a closed door.

A growl to my left, and I turned just as two paws landed on my chest, knocking me over.

Yellow, pus-coloured eyes glared at me. I tried to move but couldn't. The gravel carpark twitched and shuddered under me. My brain kept telling me to stand, but fear squeezed the air out of my lungs. *Is this what happened to Penny last summer?* The beast breathed, and a chill soaked through my Pizza Shack polo shirt. I recognised this cold, as Penny's skin had felt this way when Mum and I dressed her body at the funeral home. The iciness made me sleepy, despite it being a hot February night. I knew now what those Everest climbers experienced when the oxygen ran out and they were too exhausted to climb down the mountain-side.

A beam of blue light shot through the gloom, knocking the beast off me. It whined and dissolved into ash. The bulb above flickered, spilling light all over me again, and the creature was gone apart from a black oil-like stain on the ground.

'Are you okay?'

Above me stood the man from the bus, still in the same suit and shoes. I took his hand and stood up, but almost fell over. Tremors rippled through my body in waves, making me feel woozy.

'Here, put this on,' he said.

He passed me a silver emergency blanket, the kind they give people who've survived bus crashes, earthquakes and avalanches, and I pulled it around my shoulders.

'Don't worry, you'll warm up soon,' he said, and sat down next to me on an overturned milk crate.

'What was that?'

'A syneghast.'

'A what?'

'A syneghast. A beast formed from dark matter.'

'Dark matter? Isn't that just science fiction?' I spluttered, thinking I must have hit my head when I fell.

'Look, perhaps I should introduce myself first. Odysseus Clay, adjudicator of the Temporal Sinistrum,' he said, offering me his hand.

I shook it. The hand seemed solid enough.

'The Temporal what?'

'The Temporal Sinistrum. It's an organisation responsible for maintaining the historical continuum. I worked with your grandmother.'

'Sinistrum? That sounds awfully close to the word, sinister.'

'It's from the Latin, where 'sinister' means left-handed. Julius Specter believed that because of the work Temporal Sinistrum did, they existed on the periphery, like left-handers do in a world of right-handers. He was left-handed himself.'

I looked at him again. He was the man I'd seen at Penny's funeral, but something still bugged me about the way his nose sat askew, as though it had been broken a long time ago.

'I see you are wearing her Tempus Imperium.'

Penny's watch sat on my left wrist. I hadn't taken it off in months. Like me, he wore his Tempus Imperium on the left. However, his watch looked almost new, whereas the glass on mine appeared dull and scratched.

'How did you kill that thing?'

'Sunlight or UV light from a torch or lamp is quite effective.'

The bug lamp I'd switched on that night in Currency Creek projected UV light.

'I think one of them killed my grandmother. I saw it in the backyard, the night that she died.'

'Yes, that would fit with what I've learnt so far.'

My mouth gaped wide open. I couldn't speak, the words stunned on my tongue by the fact that someone finally believed me about the creature.

'I think Penny found a clue about their origins. The Sinistrum hadn't heard from her in thirty years until we received a letter. Then the emergency beacon went off on her Tempus Imperium. But we were too late. The fact that she left you her watch is significant. Somehow, you are involved in this.'

'Really? But Mum and I went through her papers. There was nothing but bills, old photos and a folder full of reports from her work during World War Two.'

Tell them that the key to the syneghasts lies with Kepplar. Was this Temporal Sinistrum the 'them' Penny referred too? Could I trust this man I barely knew, even if he had saved my life? These stories of time travel, of working with Grandma Penny, seemed about as believable as two plus two equalling three.

'You need to come with me to the Sinistrum. You won't be safe here.'

Part of me wanted to laugh. Me leaving with a complete stranger? Hadn't he ever heard of 'Stranger Danger'? The laugh would be high-pitched and made of glass, ready to shatter like my current emotional state. He might have saved my life, but normally men in pinstripe suits didn't talk to teenage girls unless they were related, or were their high-school physics teachers. Men that age, unless their jobs demanded it, treated girls my age like bottles of red wine before interacting: wait and let it mature. Whereas for me, when a man that age spoke to you, visions of serial killers, paedophiles, politicians kissing babies and 'touchy-feely' employers who liked to hug too long sprung to mind.

'Seriously? I barely know you! You might have saved me from that syneghast thing, but how do I know I can trust you?'

'Because your grandmother did. This isn't some horror film, Charlie. These syneghasts will kill you if they get the chance.'

I looked again at Odysseus's bent nose. Where had I seen it before? But my brain still felt dazed, like I had suffered a concussion. Nothing was making sense, except the way my heart flailed inside my chest.

'But I can't. I start law lectures tomorrow, and Mum, Dad, and Dan would be so upset if I disappeared,' I said.

'But the syneghasts will keep coming, Charlie,' said Odysseus.

The thought of leaving with this stranger in his navy pinstripe suit scared me. My parents had spent the last year worrying about me as I moped around Currency Creek and worked in the store. They'd cooked my favourite lamb roasts, made me cups of tea and insisted that I get out of bed in the morning. By starting university this year, I had intended to show my improvement. I just couldn't let them down by disappearing.

'I'm sorry. I can't. It's just not possible.' I said, rubbing my head again and searching for a bump.

'Look, take this,' he said, handing me a flashlight with a blue globe. 'It's a UV torch that'll help keep you safe. If you change your mind, push down this button on your Tempus Imperium three times in quick succession, and I'll come straight away.'

'Okay,' I said, as he turned around and walked into the night.

The door opened behind me. Light and music spilled out from the Pizza Shack kitchen.

'Charlie, you've been outside for ages?' said Sayad. 'Is everything all right?' His eyes fell on the silver emergency blanket.

'Yeah, um, I was cold, so I grabbed this from my car's first aid kit,' I replied as I folded the blanket and followed him inside.

'Well, hurry up! They're about to play Pharrell's 'Happy' on the radio. You've got to come in and dance. That'll warm you up.'

'Sure,' I replied, and followed him back inside.

7

That night I slept deeply, although my dreams were frozen in ice. In one, I saw myself trapped like a prehistoric man inside a glacier. In another, I swam underwater in a frozen-over lake and tried to come up to breathe, but the ice wouldn't break above me.

I devoted the next day at university to introductory lectures on torts and contracts and writing notes in an A4 exercise book. At lunchtime, the sun shone on the Cloister Lawns where Dan and others ate lunch and played frisbee, and my phone buzzed: *Hey C, why don't you come and join us? The weather's great and I'm getting my ass kicked at frisbee. XOX Dan*. Part of me wanted to forget Odysseus Clay, syneghasts and an organisation called the Temporal Sinistrum, but I couldn't. I withdrew to the library's Reading Room, with its wooden pews and desks carved with *Angus loves Rose, 1958*. I had already tried Penny's books again after I'd finished at Pizza Shack, but Kepplar's dense explications about Unified Field Machines and particle resonances didn't seem to have any relation to time travel or syneghasts. I'd then moved to the internet, but my searches soon turned into a vortex of conspiracy theories and paranoid rants, so I'd decided to head to the university library. The theoretical physics section sat in the shelves on the left side of the room. There were books by Albert Einstein, Richard Feynman, James Kepplar and Stephen Hawking, but my interest lay in those on quantum particles and time travel paradoxes. I made a pile of books with titles like *A Brief History of Time*, *Quantum Paradoxes Explained*, *The Mathematical Justification for Time Travel* and *A Chronicle of Theoretical Physics*. I scanned through them, testing the limit of my high-school physics and mathematics, reasoning that if time travel was possible, surely someone had written an argument for it?

In a short philosophical paper that Einstein had co-authored with his student Julius Specter, he stated:

> Time is only relevant to those atoms that exist at this very moment along a continuum. A continuum in which pressure redistributes atoms from one moment in time to another. The particular resonances of the atom acting as a map for such re-distribution. Therefore, if enough power is harnessed, time travel is a given.

So it was possible, I pondered, if they could produce enough power? Where would you locate such an organisation? Such a redistribution of atoms would require an immense amount of power, which meant that the Temporal Sinistrum wouldn't be able to hide from the rest of the world and its internet sleuths and conspiracy theorists for long.

My brain ached under the weight of such thoughts as I fiddled with the Tempus Imperium on my wrist. It felt so big and heavy compared to the smart watches and Swatch watches the other students wore. I still hadn't worked out what each part of the watch did. Part of me wanted to press that button three times and signal Odysseus Clay. Those syneghast creatures had killed my grandmother and now they were after me. No one had believed me last year, not even Mum and Dad. Yet here was a man who'd already saved my life once and who claimed to have worked with my grandmother. I didn't know what to do.

«·✕·»

These thoughts hung above me as I walked to the bus stop at 4 pm. On the horizon, a storm blew towards the city. A mass of black clouds consumed the hills in the distance before spreading like a pestilence across the outer suburbs. The winds whipped up the surrounding ground, tossing up and tumbling papers and dry leaves as I trudged to the bus stop. Six people crowded under its green roof: two women hidden under raincoats and headscarves, a man panicking into a mobile phone and three schoolkids insulated by headphones. Two minutes later the bus pulled up, windows moist and fogged. No one got off; instead, I and the six others crammed inside.

As we wound away from the main roads to a confusion of side-streets, the first drops of rain smashed into the ground outside and pummelled against the side windows. Soon, golf-ball-sized lumps of hail began to hit parked cars and smash into their windscreens.

'It's too dangerous. I can't drive in this!' said the bus driver as he pulled over and parked by the side of the road.

I looked outside. The hail had stopped, but now the rain

pelted down instead. We were only one stop from where I normally got off. I pulled the hood of my sweater over my head and secured my backpack straps, and made a dash for it at the first break in the rain. I skidded across the pavement, where the hail lay as thick as snow, but stayed upright. Only five hundred metres to Penny's place, as long as I avoided breaking an arm on the way.

At the top of Penny's driveway, I halted. The front door was open, banging in the wind. I knew I hadn't left it that way. However, the rain soon soaked through my doubts and I rushed inside. Water from an open window streamed across the kitchen floor, and leaves blew throughout the house. Anxiety surged inside of me, flooding my body, making my heart pound and my breathing shallow. Something had lacerated the couch and armchairs, disembowelled the cushions and left long scratches on the walls and teeth marks on the kitchen cupboard doors. Penny's books lay scattered throughout the house. Paw marks the size of saucers stained the beige carpet. I tried to flick on the lights but failed. Was it another syneghast?

Telemachus howled, but I couldn't find him.

'Telemachus? Telemachus!' I called.

A scratching against the linen cupboard door answered me. I opened the door and Telemachus tumbled out. He meowed and jumped into my arms. 'How did you get in there, Tee?' I asked, hugging him tight. 'What was it? Did you try to hide and get trapped?' The cat just looked at me and meowed, his body shaking in my arms until I started stroking him. *One...two... three... breathe in, Charlie. Three... two... one... breathe out...* When both our heart rates had slowed, I placed the cat on the ground, where he skidded into my bedroom and under the bed.

I pulled Odysseus Clay's UV torch from my backpack and

gripped it until my knuckles turned white. I tried to say the Hail Mary under my breath. For many years, I had avoided religious education classes in my Catholic high school and dozed during Mass, but now the words formed on my lips: 'Hail Mary, full of grace, the Lord is with thee.'

'That won't work.'

I turned; behind me stood Odysseus Clay.

'These syneghasts aren't werewolves or vampires. They don't fear the Cross, Christ or God, just fire, sunlight or a UV torch.'

I gaped and gripped the torch tighter.

'Come on,' he said. 'It might be outside still.'

Outside, the rain diffused the edges of Penny's backyard into an impressionist painting. 'Pan your torch horizontally from the left. I'll take mine from the right. We'll meet in the middle.'

Our two blue lights speared into the gloom, catching two garden gnomes fishing despite the rain.

'Nothing! Damn it!' said Odysseus.

Inside, I flicked the hallway switch again; a *crackle*, and I could see again.

We went into Penny's kitchen, as it seemed to be the least wrecked room. 'What do they do to the lights?' I asked.

'Because syneghasts are creatures of dark matter, their very existence destabilises light particles and makes the ground shake. The only things impervious to them are fire, UV spectrum lights and lithium batteries, like the ones used in your mobile phone.'

'What do these syneghasts want with me?'

'Your particulate, which is especially strong,' Odysseus said, gently placing Telemachus on the ground.

'Particula—what?'

'Everyone has one. A particulate. Because syneghasts are

made from dark matter, they constantly need to feed on light particles, and that is what makes up a particulate. Humankind has given these particulates many different names over history, such as the Christian *soul*, the Hindu *Ātman*, the Jewish *Nefesh* and the Shinto *Ichirei shikon*. Paragnosts like yourself and Penny have especially strong particulates.'

'Para-ghosts?

'No—paragnosts, people with a gift for visions or prophecies.'

'Me, a paragnost? That's absurd, there's nothing extraordinary about me. I make pizzas and go to university.'

'That's not what my Tempus Imperium tells me,' he said, pointing at his watch, whose face now glowed a strange green. As he brought it closer to me, the glow grew brighter.

'But mine, I mean my grandmother's, doesn't do that,' I said.

'You just haven't switched on that feature,' he said, pointing at one crown. 'Centre the arrow at 6 o'clock and you'll see.'

I clicked the crown around, and my Tempus Imperium's face glowed even greener than the one Odysseus wore.

'You see. Penny clearly saw this in you, Charlie. That's why she left you her Tempus Imperium. Can I ask you a question— have you ever had a vision or even a sense of déjà vu where you realised something had had happened before? You might even call it a premonition.'

<< · X · >>

When I was in Year Nine, my science teacher had scheduled an excursion to the zoo. The night before, I'd dreamt of a tiger padding around the zoo pathways, his chin wet with blood and teeth gripping a child's arm. I told the Boarding House Supervisor, but she forced me to go to school that morning, since it was 'only a dream'.

By recess I had an idea. I have a low tolerance for dairy, especially flavoured milk, so I went to the school canteen and bought two chocolate milks. I drank these quickly, so that by the time we boarded the bus I felt sick. Inside the bus the air stank of the rowing team's sweat from that morning's training session. My head spun, the nausea punching its way out of my stomach in an acidic stream of chocolate milk and Weet-Bix. I drenched several rows, two fellow students and most of the aisle. They cancelled the excursion. The rest of the class went back to school to watch the same David Attenborough documentaries that we had already seen in Year 7 and Year 8, and I spent the rest of the day in the infirmary reading a novel and faking a stomach-ache.

Later that night, during study period in the Boarding House, messages started cluttering up my phone screen. When the supervisor wasn't looking, I checked. My friends were congratulating me on my well-timed vomit and sharing a link to a local news story about a tiger that had escaped and mauled two vets and a child from a primary school.

The only person I ever told about these visions was Penny.

'Oh Charlie,' she said. 'You poor thing. I'd hoped it skipped your generation, like it did your mother's.'

≪·✕·≫

'Yes,' I said, looking straight at Odysseus Clay. 'Yes, I do on occasion.'

'You've inherited your grandmother's paragnostic ability, it seems.'

Telemachus had emerged from under my bed and began

61

brushing against Odysseus's shin. He bent down and picked the cat up, and it nuzzled into his chest and purred. Odysseus scratched him under the chin to the left, in a spot that I thought only Penny and I knew about. Who was this man? Even the cat seemed to know and trust him.

'Grandma Penny had them as well?'

'Yes—it's how she avoided that bomb during the Blitz, the one that destroyed the Ministry of Health. I recruited her the day after.'

I had always thought it was luck that Penny went for supper just before the German air raid started.

'How does this fit with your Temporal Sinistrum?'

'In the past, we used to employ these premonitions to help us avoid Continuity Errors. Nostradamus and Joan of Arc are both examples of paragnosts we've consulted in the past. These days we utilise a more reliable approach in our Timeline Exchange Centre.'

'How do I fit into all this, then? My visions aren't exactly frequent or reliable,' I said, but then froze. The memory of the night before Penny died flashed in my mind. I remembered how I'd woken, startled, at 4 am, the last traces of a nightmare about hell hounds and death dissipating before I could make sense of it. My jaw had been sore from grinding my teeth while I slept. I had blamed it on the film about wolves circling the survivors of an Arctic air crash that I'd watched before bed.

'Charlie?'

I flinched and shook my head, realising now the purpose of that nightmare. 'It's my fault Grandma Penny's dead,' I said as I tried to wipe away my tears. 'I dismissed a nightmare I'd had the night before about those syneghast creatures.'

'Did your grandmother feature in it?'

'No.'

'Well, don't blame yourself then, Charlie. How were you to know about the syneghasts back then?'

'But I could have told her!' I said, wanting to punch a wall.

'What's done is done, Charlie. There are some things we can't change at the Sinistrum, like an individual's person's date and time of death, unless it's a pivot point. Otherwise we'll cause a Continuity Error. The Sinistrum learnt that the hard way when they failed to stop Brutus from assassinating Julius Caesar. His death was a pivot point that resulted in the eruption of Mt. Vesuvius.'

'No,' I said, looking down at my damp sneakers. I wanted to tell him about Penny's last words: *Tell them that the key to the syneghasts lies with Kepplar.* Was this Temporal Sinistrum the 'them' that Penny had referred to as she lay dying in my arms over a year ago? Despite him having saved my life last night, part of me couldn't trust him yet.

'Charlie, I really think you should come with me. It's not safe.'

'B-but—' I stammered. 'I—I don't even k-know what this Temporal Sinistrum does!'

'The Sinistrum exists to help maintain history's continuum and avoid Continuity Errors.'

'Well, what's a Continuity Error then?'

'If Lee Harvey Oswald hadn't killed Kennedy, for example. In the original timeline, Kennedy survived the assassination attempt and launched a nuclear assault on the USSR. He became a fascist dictator determined to destroy the Communist threat, but all he achieved was bringing on the Fulcrum earlier. From our research, we knew that Kennedy's assassination was a pivot point. We had an adjudicator give Lee Harvey Oswald that rifle. We also placed a second shooter on the grassy knoll so as to ensure that he succeeded and nuclear war was avoided. However, now our adjudicators are dying in syneghast attacks like what happened to your grandmother, and Continuity Errors are happening across the entire historical spectrum leading to the Fulcrum.'

'Fulcrum?' I stared at Odysseus.

He looked back at me. 'Yes—an extinction-level event. The next Fulcrum begins in 2025 and it will take approximately three hundred years for humanity to die off.'

I inhaled sharply, feeling the breath whistling between my teeth. '2025? That's only nine years away!'

Nine years from now, I expected to be twenty-six and working long hours at a law firm, drinking too much coffee, watching the latest streaming series and going for evening walks on the beach. If Odysseus was to be believed, this pragmatic reality was nothing more than a fantasy that would dissipate like smoke when the wind blew.

I poured myself a glass of water from the sink and tried to drink, but my hands were shaking so much that most of the liquid splashed down my chest. My legs felt weak, and the blood pounded in my head. I sat down at Penny's kitchen table and tried to slow my breathing.

Breathe… one… two… three… Breathe… one… two… three…

Odysseus put Telemachus down and opened a cupboard, where he pulled out a tin of cat food. He spooned out the seafood medley onto an old saucer of Penny's and placed it near the back door for the cat. It was the stench of the cat food that did it— the odour of fish and jelly that let in an uninvited memory. A crack of light spilling from an open door; me aged nine, sleep-fogged, eyes blurry and thirsty for a glass of water. In the kitchen, Penny was talking to a man I didn't know, who opened that same cupboard door and served out the same cat food, the smell strong as a fisherman's bucket of live bait, sitting by their feet on the jetty. A waft caustic and electric at the same time, which always made my nose twitch.

Breathe… one… two… three… Breathe… one… two… three…

I steadied myself, counting each breath in and out until my heart rate slowed and my mind stopped flailing.

'Can the Fulcrum be stopped?'

'Possibly. The whole point of the Temporal Sinistrum is to stop it. But we will need your help.'

'What about deciphering these premonitions?'

'Yes, we still have that capability, despite Hinze's Timeline Exchange Centre.'

I looked Odysseus over again, from his grey hair to his black shoes. Could I confide in him? Under the bright fluorescent lights of the kitchen, the bend in his nose stood out. Where had I seen it before? Was Odysseus the same man I'd seen in the kitchen that night? But my memory lacked definition, a dark outline based on movement not detail.

Think, Charlie, think.

'Aha!'

'What's up, Charlie?' Odysseus asked.

I opened my backpack, pulling out the envelope of photos I'd found along with Penny's Blitz notes. I took out the one of Penny and the young man sitting in front of a snow-capped mountain and held it up to the light and then looked at Odysseus again. The same nose bent to the left, the same thick jaw and brown hair, although now it was a salt-and-pepper grey. Under the bright fluorescents in Penny's living room, I saw the resemblance.

'It's you!' I said. 'You're in this photo with Penny?'

Odysseus took the photo from my hand. 'Ahh, the Matterhorn, April 1925. I remember that day. Penny and I watched a team of climbers ascending the summit.'

Several calculations whirred through my mind. 1925 was over ninety years ago, and this man looked in his late fifties!

'That can't be possible. The math doesn't work.'

'Perhaps this will help,' said Odysseus, pulling an envelope from his pocket. An envelope I recognised, with the markings of an aerogram and the address for a PO Box in London. Odysseus opened the envelope and passed me a sheet of paper that still smelt of Penny's perfume.

> *20ᵗʰ December 2014*
>
> *My dearest Charlie,*
>
> *If you are reading this, then something has happened to me. By now, you would have realised that my life prior to meeting your grandfather was not as straightforward as it seemed. I am sorry for not telling you about my role with the Temporal Sinistrum earlier, but unless you live a life where time is malleable, it is difficult to understand.*
>
> *Like me, you have the talent for premonitions, and this makes you a target for the syneghasts. This is why in my will I left you my Tempus Imperium. I've written to Richard Hinze, the Controller, about you and know that if you are reading this letter that he has sent an adjudicator to find you.*
>
> *With love,*
> *Grandma Penny X O X O X*
>
> *P.S. Don't forget to wind the cuckoo clock at 11 am once a week on a Saturday and feed Telemachus.*

Remember Telemachus prefers the Whiskas dry food,
but only feed him once a day or he'll overeat.

I held this paper written in Penny's own hand and read it again, my thoughts tumbling like lemmings off a cliff. *Oh, Grandma Penny, why didn't you tell me?* She had even lied to me back on one rainy August evening in 2011. The Temporal Sinistrum? Time travel? This man who stood in front of me, whose arm in that photo rested around Penny's waist with a familiarity I recognised. Even the reminder about Telemachus and his penchant for overeating was so Penny, but the detail about the cuckoo clock was wrong. Ever since I'd been old enough to help Penny with the winding of her clocks, we'd always done the cuckoo clock at the same time as the others: 4 pm, daily. Perhaps in her confusion about the syneghasts she'd made a mistake? I remembered how frail my grandmother had become in the weeks leading up to her death, and I pushed this detail aside like a loose branch and walked past.

'You realise we've met before, Charlie?'

Near the back door, Telemachus chewed on his food in short, sharp bursts. The cat clearly knew Odysseus, because he'd been happy to be held by him, despite his earlier fright. Odysseus even knew which cat food was his favourite and where Grandma Penny kept it.

'It was when you were about nine, if I remember correctly. You stumbled into the kitchen one night, wearing Hello Kitty pyjamas and asking for a glass of water. Penny tried to introduce us, but you just kept yawning and rubbing your eyes until she herded you back to bed.'

Could I trust him? Telemachus clearly did, and so did my grandmother. He even remembered what I'd had on my pyjamas when I was nine.

'Penny did say something as she died.'

'Like what?'

'*Tell them that the key to the syneghasts lies with Kepplar.* I think she meant that physicist, James Kepplar, but I looked at his books both here and at my university library and there was no mention of these syneghast-things anywhere.'

'Kepplar?' Odysseus fixed his gaze on me. 'James Kepplar?' A smile dawned, Odysseus said slowly, 'Charlie, this might be the breakthrough we've been looking for. But if Penny thinks that Kepplar's research holds the solution, then we will have to look beyond his published work.'

For the first time, Odysseus had smiled at the mention of Kepplar's name. It was the duplicate of the smile that appeared in Penny's photos on a much younger face. Telemachus had finished his meal and was now pawing at Odysseus's leg, hoping to be picked up again. The letter, that photo, a night in this very kitchen, and Telemachus's obvious preference for him. Was it enough to be certain?

Despite the chaos, Penny's living room still felt like home, with the prints of Monet's *Water Lilies* on the wall and my phone full of messages from Dan and my friends. Part of me wanted to shove Odysseus out the front door, make a cup of tea and sit down and watch TV. Australia was playing a T20 match in Perth, and the crooning of the commentators would be just enough to soothe my jangled nerves. However, I'd now seen three of these syneghasts and only just survived the attack at Pizza Shack. There was also this Fulcrum to contend with, and what that might mean for my future and that of everyone I cared about.

Odysseus scratched Telemachus again in that spot to the left and under his chin. 'He always did like to be scratched in that spot, even as a kitten,' he said.

With a shrug of the shoulders and a sigh, I gave in, 'All right, I'll come. Just give me a few minutes.'

I topped up Telemachus's outside bowl to the brim with dry food and then filled two more bowls with water. As I gave him one last pat along the back I whispered, 'Sorry, boy, but I need to do this,' before putting him outside.

'I'm ready now,' I said, then sucked in my breath like I was about to dive into a cold pool.

'First, we'll need to set the coordinates on your Tempus Imperium.'

'What if something goes wrong? Can't I just travel with you?'

'No, not this time. Mine's almost out of power. A Tempus Imperium needs to be fully charged to move two people.'

'But—'

'Shhh, Charlie, and listen. First, I want you to set a zero for the day, month and year on your Tempus Imperium. Midnight for the time. And then shift the outer bezel to zero for the longitude. You must use the middle crown to the right of three o'clock to adjust the inner complication, the one with ninety degrees. Please set it for a latitude of zero. Now, when I say to, press the outer button halfway between seven and eight o'clock. The red hand only will spin, one repetition every second, and on the fifth second, it'll happen.'

I shifted my weight from one foot to another.

'Do it now.'

'What will happen?' I said, pushing the pin down.

'You might want to hold my arm,' he said, as a white light radiated outwards and swallowed us.

PART 2

London, December 1940

Penny flinched as the Anderson shelter rattled.

'By golly, that was close,' whispered Maureen in her ear.

Penny pulled her father's silver fob watch from the pocket of her coat. 2:15 am. Her stomach rumbled. Nearly eight hours since dinner. They had been midway through one of Mrs Symes's ration-book concoctions—a shepherd's pie filled with scrambled eggs and dripping—when the air raid siren started. Penny had been so hungry that she'd taken three more mouthfuls before she scurried down to the shelter in Mrs Symes's back garden. She'd only had time to grab her coat, Agatha Christie's latest mystery *Murder is Easy*, and a blanket.

The shelter sat half-submerged in the bottom of Mrs Symes's garden, with walls made from corrugated iron and reinforced by sandbags and a roof covered by a layer of dirt. There were only four bunks, despite Mrs Symes having five boarders: Penny, Maureen, Mr Devitts, Helen Sainsbury, and her son, five-year-old

Theodore. Penny and Maureen shared a bunk, and so did Helen and Theodore. They lit the shelter with two oil lamps that danced in time to the battery of ack-ack guns nearby.

'Yes,' Penny replied. 'Where do you think it landed?'

'It sounds somewhere to the east? Maybe Hackney?' said Maureen.

'I hope the King and Queen are all right,' said Mrs Symes. 'Apparently, they and the princesses only just survived the bombing of Buckingham Palace.'

'I'm sure they're fine,' said Mr Devitts. 'Hitler might try to outdo the Kaiser, but he won't win.'

'This time we need the Americans to enter the war earlier than the last one. With the loss of the Channel Islands, the Germans are practically on our front doorstep.'

'But when will that happen?' asked Maureen. 'A girl at work reckons the Yanks aren't interested in Europe.'

'I'm sure that they'll see sense. Hitler's too dangerous. If he takes England, where will he stop next? Canada? Australia?'

'Shush!' said Mrs Sainsbury. 'I'm trying to get Theodore to sleep.'

On the bunk below Penny and Maureen, little Theodore lay curled into a ball, his knees against his chest and his eyes squeezed shut. His mother had pulled up his blanket and placed her coat on top of it. She stroked the hair on his head as the shelter rattled again. The poor boy, thought Penny. How on earth could he sleep through this? These bombs would keep even the Devil himself awake.

'That must have been down near the docks,' said Maureen.

'I'm going to try to get some sleep. Sir Charles still expects me at my desk by 9 am tomorrow morning typing up reports,' said Penny.

She pulled up her blanket and shivered. The days were so short that even the sun seemed ready for bed by 4 pm, and the chill—whether in the form of pounding rain or the ice that coated the bucket of water Mrs Symes kept in the shelter's corner—made it hard for her to sleep. She hadn't had an unbroken night's sleep since September. The only warmth came from the big male tomcat that had adopted the Anderson shelter two weeks ago as its new home. Mrs Symes had tried to chase him away with her broom, but he'd hissed and flattened his ears.

'He's as stubborn as the Prime Minister, this one,' said Mr Devitts at the time.

'Yes, and with his ears back, he almost looks like him,' said Maureen.

'We should call him Winston, then,' said Penny.

Penny rubbed Winston under his chin and he purred. Despite the rattle from the bombs, the *thwack-thwack* of the anti-aircraft guns and the bells of the fire trucks, the cat slept. He only opened one eye occasionally to check that Penny and Maureen still lay on the bunk with him.

In the air raid shelter, Penny often dreamt of the white cliffs of Dover tumbling into the sea. She felt the ocean's icy embrace around her, the spray kissing her face as the limestone fell away to reveal ancient creatures—ichthyosaurs and plesiosaurs—frozen into place by the sediment of millions of years. As a small child, she had loved the Natural History Museum and its prehistoric creatures. She'd delighted in the strange syllables of their names: 'dip-lo-do-cus,' 'tri-ce-ra-tops' and 'ich-thy-o-sau-rus'.

Yet tonight was different, because the snatches of sleep that Penny took felt like gasps for breath. Every time the ground around the shelter rumbled and the kerosene lamp swung from the roof, she awoke gulping for air. She kept seeing the same thing: the clock that hung on her office wall, smashed, the time stuck at 6:11 pm, and the filing cabinets spilling their papers into the orange flames.

« · ✕ · »

'Wake-up, sleepy head! It's 6 o'clock, the all-clear's gone. Jerry's flown home,' said Maureen as she shook Penny awake.

'It'll be toast and marmalade for breakfast, if Hitler's left the larder intact,' said Mrs Symes. Two weeks ago, a bomb had landed five houses down, shattering all the jam and marmalade jars and leaving nothing but stale bread and butter for breakfast for several days.

Penny dragged herself inside. She needed a cup of tea, a face wash and a change of clothes before making her way to the Ministry of Health in Whitehall. The other boarders in the grey morning light looked just as tired as her: Mr Devitts limping to the house with his bad hip, a still-sleeping Theodore carried by his mother, and Maureen, whose red hair definitely needed a brush. Only Mrs Symes seemed to have any energy, bustling about the kitchen making breakfast.

'Mrs Kingsley next door says that they hit the Bakerloo and Piccadilly lines last night,' said Mrs Symes. Penny groaned; it would take her an extra hour at least to get to work on the bus.

On the way to the bus stop she passed several older men coming home, their faces marked with soot, shirt sleeves soaked and trouser knees blackened with ash and dust. She recognised Mr Wilson from across the road. He worked as a stationmaster but spent several nights a week on Fire Watch at St. Cuthbert's, a church three streets away.

'Did St. Cuthbert make it through another raid, Mr Wilson?' she asked.

'Oh, Penny dear, only just,' said Mr Wilson. 'Several incendiaries landed on his roof, and the stirrup pumps stopped working. It reduced us to running bucket after bucket of water up the stairs, but we saved the old boy.'

'You did well then,' grinned Penny. 'I'm sure Molly's already got a cup of tea on the table and some breakfast waiting for you.'

Penny turned to go, but Mr Wilson stopped her. 'Lassie, take care,' he said. 'There was a direct hit four streets over, and they're still digging the bodies out.'

'Of course,' nodded Penny.

Young women, shop girls, nurses, ambulance drivers and typists filled the bus. The driver negotiated the broken streets and roads at a walking pace. Houses lay collapsed like rows of dominoes in many streets. Bomb craters pockmarked the roads, gaping like open wounds. Nearby, men with spades dug at the rubble. Penny hated the rows of blankets with feet sticking out the most: a pair of men's leather work boots, a woman's velvet slippers, or a bloodied ankle stump. The worst ones were the bundles even smaller than Theodore.

In the distance, Big Ben chimed.

《 · X · 》

'What time do you call this, Miss Jones?' said Sir Charles Baskerville.

'10:30 am, sir. They bombed the Piccadilly and Bakerloo lines last night. I came in on the bus,' said Penny.

'We will not win the war if we let Hitler's bombs stop us from getting to work on time, Miss Jones.'

'Yes, sir.'

75

'I expect you to stay back past 6:30 pm tonight, Miss Jones. Please make sure each report is properly edited this time.'

Penny paused and swallowed the words she wanted to say before replying 'Yes, Sir Charles,' and returning to her desk and typewriter. *Officious twit!* Penny couldn't help it if two tube lines were down. Before she'd left for London, her mother had warned Penny about her tongue. A tongue that had used to get her in trouble at school, when she questioned why the teachers gave the boys harder problems in science and mathematics. 'Penny darling,' her mother had told her, 'you won't have a job for very long if you question everything. Men don't like women who are too intelligent.' Marriage and cups of tea, that was her mother's solution for everything, whereas Penny had dreamed of attending Cambridge and studying physics until the war intervened.

Above Penny, the office clock ticked. Her desk sat in a room that led into Sir Charles's much larger wood-panelled office. Four metal filing cabinets sat behind her chair. Penny put her handbag under her desk, hung up her coat and got out some paper. Sir Charles's handwritten reports, pages and pages of them, sat on her desk, each of them in his curling script that often took Penny several minutes to decipher.

'A cup of tea, dear?' said Nellie, the tea-lady.

When Penny had first started working for Sir Charles, it had been Nellie who'd comforted her. On her second day, Sir Charles had shouted at her for making a typing mistake in one of his reports. She'd fled to the ladies' bathroom where Nellie later found her, sobbing in a stall. She needed this job if she was to live in London. Her parents resided in a village in Oxfordshire, far from the factories, docks and churches that the Nazi bombers targeted. They wrote weekly, asking her to come home and telling her about how handsome the local boys were in their uniforms. However, Penny wanted to do something for the war effort, even if it meant typing reports for the Ministry of Health about epidemics and the effects of rationing.

Penny smiled at Nellie as she placed a cup of tea on her desk. 'Thank you,' said Penny.

'You look tired.'

'Yes, the bombing kept me awake most of the night. And then it took two hours to get to work this morning.'

'I think it's keeping up most of London as well.'

'True, but I've had to restart this report twice. I keep making mistakes and you know what Sir Charles is like.'

'Sir Charles shouts and blusters a lot, but he's not an ogre. He just worries. He lost his youngest son at Dunkirk. Sometimes he forgets himself.'

'I know, I know,' said Penny. 'I just don't want to disappoint him.'

'You won't,' said Nellie, placing two biscuits in front of Penny. 'The last girl got so frightened by the bombs she returned home to Shropshire. The one before left to drive an ambulance after only two months. He knows he won't be able to get anyone else.'

Nellie pushed the tea trolley into the next room.

Penny looked at the clock again. 1 pm, only five and a half hours to 6:30. Only five hours and eleven minutes to 6:11 pm when the clock had lain shattered on the ground in her dream. *No, that's not possible*, she told herself. None of Hitler's bombs had come this close to the Ministry building yet. Big Ben still chimed every hour. The King still stuttered on the wireless. The Germans' bombs landed near wharfs and on factories making parts for Spitfires, not on the public service.

'Miss Jones, in here now!' said Sir Charles. 'Miss Jones, when will you learn the correct placement of a comma versus a full stop in a sentence? Look at this. There should be a comma between 'epidemic' and 'the', not a full stop, as these two clauses belong in the same sentence. How am I meant to submit this to the Minister with such errors in it?' Sir Charles peered over his reading glasses at Penny as his pen tapped at the offending section of the report.

Don't cry, don't give him the satisfaction, Penny told herself, even as her eyes welled with tears.

'And Miss Jones, where are we getting this ink from? It blots too much for my fountain pen and clogs up the nib.'

'Whitcoulls. The clerk said it was locally made. They can't get the imported ink anymore. War shortages.'

'Humph!' said Sir Charles. 'I want you to ring around every stationer in London that's still standing and see if they have any supplies of the imported ink left. I also want—'

A man coughed behind Penny, and Sir Charles stopped.

There were two army officers in khaki uniforms and caps standing in the open door—an older man with a greying moustache like Kitchener and another much younger one, carrying a folio and a fountain pen.

'Ahh, Colonel Wiltshire, you're early. Miss Jones, please get the Colonel's assistant the latest version of the report on *The Potential Consequences of Weaponised Pathogens in Civilian Areas*.'

The young man followed Penny back to her desk.

'Here you are,' said Penny, passing him the finished report.

'Thank you, Miss,' he grinned, and his eyes glimmered above a crooked nose.

Silly girl, Penny told herself, *he's part of the Special Operations Executive*. It was one thing to date someone from the Army, Navy or Air Force, but SOE? There were whispers about this unit, whose members parachuted in behind enemy lines and took the fight to the Nazis using tactics her father would describe as 'unbecoming of a gentleman'. But Penny saw the daily statistics for deaths and injuries from the bombings as part of her work; the real numbers were too horrendous to print in the newspapers. Hitler wasn't playing cricket in whites on a village green. Instead, he firebombed London, Leeds and Liverpool. She hated to think why the officers from the SOE were discussing weaponised pathogens with Sir Charles, but as a secretary, her role was to finish those reports and find Sir Charles his ink.

≪ · ✕ · ≫

Despite spending two hours calling every stationer still standing in central London, Penny couldn't find Sir Charles's preferred ink. She would never make it back to Mrs Symes's by 6 pm for dinner and her favourite bread and butter pudding, which, even without the raisins, still tasted marvellous; she still had two reports to finish, along with the *Report of the Sub-Committee into Projected Epidemics and Disease*—the one where Sir Charles had already complained about her semi-colon placement. Yet her stomach rumbled, and she almost fell asleep at 4:30 pm. Thankfully, Sir Charles hadn't caught her.

The thought of a cup of tea and sandwiches tantalised Penny. The tea-rooms on the corner stayed open late. She placed the reports in Sir Charles's red leather folio alongside a lead pencil and took her handbag, planning to edit them while having a quick sandwich. Last night's dream still felt tumorous inside her head— the vision of a clock smashed at 6:11 pm.

'Just heading out for supper,' Penny told Tom, the night porter and fire watchman, who sat by the front entrance reading *The Times*.

Halfway through her fish paste sandwich, Penny heard the air raid siren. At least she'd had time to finish most of her dinner. Outside on the street, an Air Raid Warden stood directing people.

'This way, Miss,' he said. 'The nearest public shelter is at the end of the street.'

The size of five Anderson shelters hammered together, this one stood above ground, its walls and roof reinforced by hundreds of sandbags. A few regulars sat in the corners on rectangles of newspaper, but most just stood. They were stragglers like Penny from the many Ministry buildings that lined the streets near Westminster, the early air raid siren at 5:30 pm catching them still at work.

Penny heard the familiar dissonance of the Luftwaffe's engines. Unlike the Spitfires that ran as smooth as a lion's purr, the sound of the German bombers was phlegmatic. Soon, the rapid *thwack-thwack* of the anti-aircraft guns near the Thames began. The shelter shook and Penny stumbled, and a man in a khaki uniform caught her. 'It's all right,' he said, and winked as Penny straightened herself. She recognised the man's square jaw, thick brown hair and crooked nose from earlier. She was about to say thank you when the door to the shelter opened to an Air Raid Warden silhouetted against the glow of fires in the distance.

'We need to evacuate this shelter. A parachute mine's landed nearby. You must head across Westminster Bridge towards Waterloo Station and take shelter there.'

Penny grabbed her handbag and Sir Charles's folio and followed the crowd. On a nearby lamp-post hung the tangled-up mine, the parachute's fabric glinting like mercury in the moonlight. She walked past the Houses of Parliament and Big Ben, but paused on

Westminster Bridge and looked down the river towards the Tower of London. On each side of the Thames fires crackled, turning warehouses, factories and dockyards into kindling. She saw firemen holding hoses that snaked into trucks and then back out again and down towards the river where they sucked up the brown water.

Penny followed the young man in his khaki army uniform down into Waterloo Station. The same chill that dampened Mrs Symes's Anderson shelter pooled inside the tube station. She turned up the collar of her coat and did up the buttons before finding a section of floor against a wall to sit on. On one side was a family—a mother, and two twin girls. The twins slept on a bed made of newspaper, covered in a thick woollen blanket. On the other side of Penny sat that same young SOE officer, head bowed, engrossed in a pocket-sized volume of Wordsworth's poetry. She wanted to say something, but the words remained stuck to her tongue. *Penny*, she told herself, *that's not like you to be so silent.* But there was something about his smile and crooked nose that felt familiar. Confused, Penny retreated into correcting Sir Charles's reports with the pencil from her handbag.

'Oh dear!' she said as the lead snapped.

'Here, let me,' said the young man next to her. He pulled a penknife from his trousers and whittled away at the tip of the pencil, removing just enough wood to reveal the lead tip.

'Thank you so much. Sir Charles is expecting these reports by tomorrow.'

'You are welcome. Lieutenant Stephen Clifford,' he said.

'Penny Jones.'

'Lovely to meet you,' he said.

She looked at him. There was something in the way he smiled that pleased her. Those eyes were the colour of a lake on

81

a clear summer's day. Although she knew the dangers of falling for soldiers who promised engagements and then died in battle: Maureen's cousin had lost her fiancé to the Luftwaffe, and four months later a baby girl was born.

The station lights flickered above her. Another direct hit, somewhere nearby.

Penny thought about Balham Station on the fourteenth of October. Dozens of bodies covered by blankets had been laid out on the footpath the next day when she'd passed on the bus. She remembered a woman in curlers and a dressing gown holding a small child whose head lolled like a rag doll's.

'You needn't worry. This station won't be hit tonight,' said the SOE officer.

'How could you know that?' she asked.

'I just do,' he replied.

Penny laughed despite herself at this confidence. Then a sudden *whoosh* of air forced her to grab onto Sir Charles's papers, as a train pulled into their platform. By the time she looked up, the SOE officer in his khaki uniform had gone.

《 · X · 》

By 5 am, the all-clear siren sounded. Just enough time for a quick trip back to Mrs Symes's place for a wash and a change of clothes before work, Penny thought. Hopefully, Sir Charles wouldn't be too angry with the delay. Surely he understood that the Luftwaffe had disrupted everyone's plans? The family next to her had already gone.

Despite her tiredness, Penny pinned back her hair and swept the dust off her coat. She did like that officer and the way his eyes had followed her.

On the street outside Waterloo Station, people emerged. Some held mops, brooms or buckets, while others were dressed for work. Penny knew that despite how exhausted the bus driver felt, he still drove the bus the next day. Likewise, the postman still delivered the letters, and the BBC still played *It's That Man Again* every week.

Penny arrived at Mrs Symes's place at 7 am. Mrs Symes, her hair pinned-up in curlers and in a dressing gown, stood holding a broom and talking to Mrs Kingsley over the fence.

'Michael said that Westminster took it quite heavy last night. Even the Deacon of the Abbey was up on the roof helping the Fire Watch,' said Mrs Kingsley.

'Gosh! They've gone after the government rather than the poor East End for once,' said Mrs Symes.

Penny stopped, her heart pummelling against her chest. She needed to get to the Ministry of Health as soon as possible.

'My dear, are you all right? You've gone as white as a sheet!' said Mrs Symes. 'I was worried when you didn't make it back for dinner before the air raid sirens started.'

Penny swallowed. 'I'm fine, Mrs Symes, just tired. I got caught at the Ministry when the sirens sounded and spent the night at Waterloo Station.'

'You poor thing, that must have been exhausting. There's a freshly boiled kettle on the stove and some bread on the table. Help yourself.'

'Thank you, Mrs Symes. I think I will,' said Penny as she headed inside.

‹‹ · ✕ · ››

Many of the streets surrounding Westminster were closed. Penny walked from Trafalgar Square, where Nelson still stood on his column, his base fortified with dozens of sandbags. Nearby, firemen sprayed water across still smouldering houses and shops with caved-in roofs. One building stood sawn in half like a life-sized crumbling doll's house. Inside were beds with pillows, a sitting room with a settee, and a kitchen with four chairs and a table in the centre. On the table were four plates of stew and a half-finished mug of tea coated with dust. An old man in a cardigan and slippers stood smoking nearby, watching a rescue team pick through the rubble. The scent of gas made Penny cough and splutter.

'Miss, you'll need to move on,' said a policeman, his arm touching her shoulder. 'There's a burst gas main and we need to clear the area.'

Penny turned down a side street, despite knowing it would add another ten minutes to her journey.

'Have you seen Silky?' A grubby hand pulled at her arm.

Penny looked down at a small boy, no older than nine, and a snot-nosed girl who stood next to him.

'Who's Silky?'

'Our cat. She disappeared when the bombs started last night, and we can't find her anywhere, Miss.'

Penny shook her head, and the children ran away.

Penny tried to take several short-cuts, but each time a policeman or an Air Raid Warden blocked her way: 'No, not through here, Miss. They're defusing a bomb,' or 'They still haven't got the fire out,' or 'Only ambulances and rescue workers allowed'.

Finally she made it to the tearoom from the night before, where, inside, a woman swept up the remains of teacups and saucers. Up and down the street lay broken glass, a million tears catching the morning light. All that remained of Whitfords Booksellers was a brick wall and the pages of novels that blew through the air. Yet it was the sight of the Ministry of Health office that caused Penny to nearly faint. Brick, masonry, split wooden beams and glass in a stew of rubble, dust and ash. Sir Charles? Old Tom, the porter? Only last week Tom had showed her photos of his grandchildren, recently evacuated to a manor house in Sussex.

'Miss! Miss, you can't come any further,' a policeman stood in front of her.

'What happened?'

'A direct hit just after six last night, Miss. Only two deaths so far. They're searching the rubble now.'

The policeman gestured towards the left, where two bodies lay covered: a pair of black leather shoes at the base of one blanket, and some dusty brown ones under the next. The same black shoes she recognised from avoiding Sir Charles's gaze. And poor old Tom must be the man next to Sir Charles. Near them lay the clock from Penny's office, its hands frozen at 6:11 pm.

Penny tightened her grip on her handbag. Inside it sat Sir Charles's leather folio with the draft reports. Her gut twisted; all night she had worried about those stupid reports.

'Are you all right, Miss Jones?'

Penny turned. That same SOE officer stood behind her, but he wasn't smiling this time. Penny's entire body shook. She had left the building at 5:30 pm. If she hadn't taken a dinner break, her nylon-stockinged feet might have been next to Sir Charles's black shoes.

'Here,' he said, putting his arm around her and leading her away from the bomb site. 'You look like you've had a real fright. Can I buy you a cup of tea?'

They found a tea shop with intact windows, two streets away.

'If I hadn't taken a dinner break at half-past five, I'd have been dead too,' Penny told him. 'I dreamt I saw my office clock lying in that exact place, frozen at that exact time. I reasoned with myself, told myself it would not happen, but I was wrong.'

'Do you have these visions often?' he asked.

'Sometimes.'

'Good, because I have a job offer for you,' he said, his blue eyes watching her. 'I work for a special agency tasked with maintaining history's continuum, and we want someone with your unique talents for prophecy.'

'Prophecy? You think my dream is a prophecy? Like Joan of Arc or Cassandra?' Penny laughed. There had been rumours in the press of Hitler's interest in astrologers and the occult, but a division of the British Army engaged in such things? A precipice opened before her—tiredness, grief, and hysteria dancing on the edge—before she steadied herself and asked, 'Is that what the SOE really does?'

The steadiness of his words surprised her. 'You might say that we have some connections to the Armed Forces. Certain shared interests.'

Penny's waivered, 'But why me? I'm only a secretary in the Ministry of Health.'

'We've been watching you for some time, Miss Jones. We watch everyone capable of premonitions.'

'I beg your pardon. Watch? How?'

'You're a paragnost, Miss Jones. The readings on my Tempus Imperium prove so.' The soldier tapped his wristwatch and then waved his left arm near Penny. 'See, it flashes green if a person has an especially strong particulate and paragnostic ability.'

'But how is this relevant to me? I'm only a typist.'

'History must continue and not be corrupted by the visions

and prophecies of paragnosts like yourself, or otherwise we'll bring on a cataclysm.'

'What? As is in this war?'

'No, something much worse. An extinction.' He said the words slowly, allowing space for Penny to unwrap them, and find what was hidden beneath.

'What? Like the dinosaurs?'

'Yes, like the ones you saw at the Natural History Museum as a child in 1929.'

For a moment, Penny couldn't breathe. The same young man with the crooked nose and square jaw, standing in front of the Diplodocus next to five-year-old Penny and her father. It couldn't be possible, she told herself. She looked at the young man's uniform again. Though he had spent the night in the underground station, it seemed barely worn. The bronze army insignia on his cap flashed under the tea room's lights. Penny felt queasy, and her head spun.

'Here, have some tea. You'll feel better in a minute. One lump of sugar, wasn't it?'

She nodded and gripped the cup tightly. 'I can't leave. I have a job,' she spluttered.

'You had a job. Come and work for us, Miss Jones. Or would you prefer to return to Oxfordshire?'

Penny considered her mother and father eating their dinner each night while bombs fell in London, Coventry and Manchester. She could go home, let her mother make her breakfast and work as a typist at her father's law practice until she married a local lad. Or she could take up this stranger's offer. There was something she trusted in the way he gazed at her. Penny breathed out and asked, 'When should I start?'

9

Sinistrum HQ

A round structure, burrowing into the desert. People dressed in white chanting 'We are the thread that follows the needle.' A pile of handwritten papers from a yellow legal pad waiting for cataloguing and restoration.

The wooden floor felt cool against my head. Solid, it anchored me as my brain rocked back and forth upon waves of vertigo.

'Quick! Let out Vent Two or it'll overheat!'

'It's not working!'

'Use the wrench!'

The voices hovered at the edge of my consciousness, like a police helicopter inspecting a crash.

'Is she all right?' asked a voice to my left.

'Just a bit of interstitial nausea.'

I felt a hand on my shoulder. 'Charlie, sit up and put your head between your legs until it passes.'

I sat up and pulled my knees to my chest.

'Don't worry, I've got you,' said Odysseus. 'This is normal for your first incursion.'

With an effort, I opened my eyes. I sat inside a geodesic dome made from repeated metal triangles that reminded me of a playground climbing frame, though this one glowed and sparked. Outside the dome were half-a-dozen grey computer servers that belonged in a documentary about NASA and the Moon landing. From each one, dozens of pipes and cables snaked up the wall and disappeared into the ceiling. Each pipe had separate gauges for measuring the pressure and the temperature.

'Up you get,' said Odysseus.

I stumbled and only just caught his arm in time.

'This way.' He pointed at a gap in the dome.

Outside the geodesic dome, a small middle-aged woman in a lab coat ran between the computers and checked the gauges. Above her head sat a digital clock, on which the date '14:03 27/04/2025' glowed in numerals the colour of flames and blood.

'How's the Factoreum holding up, Madam Zhao?'

'Ahh, Odysseus, the old girl's still got a few trips left in her. Even if Pipes Two and Three do insist on overheating. We've had two incursions go astray this month alone. One of our adjudicators even ended up in London during the Great Fire of 1666 when she was meant to visit San Francisco in 1906 to observe the earthquake damage.'

Odysseus let out a low whistle. 'Are you going to bring the Dyad online then?'

'No, I don't think we need to resort to any backup solutions yet. I think I've managed to isolate the issue, which should stop any further incursions going astray.'

Odysseus nodded and then gestured towards me. 'Charlie,

89

meet Madam Zhao, our Chief Engineer. She keeps both our Memoria Factoreum and the Unified Field Machine that supplies it with power running.' He pointed at the three one-metre-high copper coils encased in glass behind one of the control panels. 'Your Tempus Imperium draws power from the Factoreum for every incursion—that is, a jump to another time period.' Odysseus moved his right hand in a slow arc, returning to the place I had just landed. 'This dome is where adjudicators enter and leave the Sinistrum when embarking upon an incursion. For safety reasons, these incursions only happen within this dome.' Odysseus paused. 'Finally, the clock above Madam Zhao's control panels is the current date for the Fulcrum. 2:03 pm on the twenty-seventh of April 2025. You'll find similar clocks throughout the building.'

For a second, the numbers of the clock flickered, and I felt Odysseus and Madam Zhao take a sharp intake of breath, but the date of 14:03 27/04/2025 remained fixed.

'Damn!' said Odysseus, 'Nothing is ever simple, is it Madam?'

Madam Zhao nodded as she wiped the grease off her palms before shaking my hand. Unlike Odysseus in his tailored suit, she wore Nike trainers and a lab coat dotted with ink stains and grease smudges, while several loose hairs from a messy black bun fell across her face.

'Charlie? You must be Penny's granddaughter! I've been waiting for this day. Your grandmother recruited me to the Temporal Sinistrum.'

'Really?' I said.

'If it wasn't for Penny, I'd have died during the Cultural Revolution. Your grandmother found me and offered me a job with the Sinistrum.'

What more did I not know about my grandmother? I knew she had worked as a typist for the Ministry of Health during the Blitz and then emigrated to Australia in the 1950s. I always thought her trip to China during the Cultural Revolution was for a local shipping company.

Without warning, I vomited, almost hitting Madam Zhao's Nike trainers.

Madam Zhao patted me on the back. 'It's okay, dear. Get it all out. The first incursion's always the worst.'

《·✕·》

I recovered in a small windowless bedroom. Spartan as a monk's cell, it contained only a bed, a side table and a lamp; instead of a crucifix hanging above the door, there was a coat of arms and another one of those digital clocks with the same 2025 date. The coat of arms contained two images: a flowing river and a picture of a Tempus Imperium, with two Latin mottos written underneath—*Tempus Rerun Imperator* and *Exitus Acta Probat*. I didn't understand them, as my Latin was limited to *Carpe Diem* and my high school's motto of *Beati Mundo Corde*.

On the side table sat a half-empty glass of water that Odysseus had advised me to finish. He'd also told me to rest for an hour until my symptoms subsided. I opened the side table drawer, almost expecting to find a Gideon's Bible—the kind that sits in the drawers of a hotel, whether it's the Ritz Carlton or a highway motel in Pinnaroo. Instead, I found a thick, leather-bound book with the title *Standard Operating and Assessment Procedures of the Temporal Sinistrum* in gold lettering. I opened to the title page where the same coat of arms sat. Below it were the phrases in

Latin again, but this time with translations: *Tempus Rerun Imperator* meant *Time, Commander of all Things*, whereas *Exitus Acta Probat* translated as *The result justifies the deed*. I didn't know the first phrase, but I understood the second one, as I knew its contemporary version—*The end justifies the means*. According to my history teacher Mr Mortimer, this was the logic that the Allies had used for dropping two atom bombs on Japan, believing that a mushroom cloud over the sky of Hiroshima, the flattening of almost every building within the blast radius, the melting skin on those who died and the years of vomiting from radiation sickness by survivors were a 'necessary evil' to prevent a land war in Japan.

My stomach churned. What was this organisation? My doubts filled my pockets with stones as I waded through the manual and learnt about the Sinistrum's history, from its founding in 1941 by Dr Julius Specter, a promising student of Albert Einstein's at the University of Berlin, to its current operating protocol.

≪·✕·≫

I stopped reading and looked again at the grainy photo of Dr Julius Specter standing in front of that geodesic dome downstairs. A short balding man with a pair of wire-framed glasses that sat perched on the edge of his nose, he was the kind of person I'd walk past on the street and not pay any attention to. The photo gave him the demeanour of an accountant or a public servant, not a brilliant physicist. Why, I wondered? What had motivated him to found an organisation that believed in *Exitus Acta Probat*? According to the manual's preface, Specter, a secular Jew, had fled to Britain after the Kristallnacht in 1938 when the Nazis destroyed his lab. He became obsessed with ancient lore and the myths of travellers who could move through the timeline using waypoints like Stonehenge. There were even hints in Roman records of Marcus Aurelius sending members of his own Praetorian Guard on such missions, using a hidden series of chambers under the Forum as a waypoint. Similarly, in the historical records of Japan and Tibet there were clues about such travellers and their journeys. Some of the Sinistrum's historians believed that Buddhism was first brought to Japan through the Torri Gate at Miyajima by time-travelling monks, who'd used a waypoint near the base of Mount Everest to share their faith. Specter's genius was building a machine that could access the time stream in the Memoria Factoreum without needing to use a waypoint.

My thoughts whirled in widening circles. Waypoints? The time stream? Syneghasts? My grandmother as an adjudicator?

Eventually I closed the manual and stood up, waiting for the dizziness to drown me again. Nothing. My pockets still felt heavy with doubt, but I knew that I needed to learn more about this organisation. I sat down again and pulled on my shoes and socks and then headed for the museum down the end of the corridor that Odysseus had mentioned.

On my way there, I passed by a room with the door propped open. A bronze plaque inscribed with *Timeline Exchange Centre* sat above the door. The layout appeared to be a cross between a 1970s computer mainframe room and a mid-century telephone exchange. Operators—*if that was even the right word?*—pulled plugs in and out of consoles while listening to headsets and viewing lines of green code on dark screens. Above their heads glowed the same clock, although unlike the others I had seen, this one was very clearly connected to one of the consoles. What was its purpose? What did these operators do?

The museum was in another large, windowless room at the end of the hallway, with exhibits arranged along the walls. Some comprised black-and-white photographs, while others were artefacts encased in glass. One held a figure made from Plaster of Paris. It was a young man, cowering on the ground. A rag covered his mouth; while his toga was in disarray. The veins on his arms bulging as he coughed his last breath. I had seen such figures before in Year Four, when we'd studied the Roman Empire and looked at pictures of Pompeii. Of statues made by filling gaps in compacted volcanic ash with plaster: a woman and child clutching each other, an elderly man collapsed on the ground and a dog writhing in agony with the studs on its collar still visible although it had died two thousand years ago. The plaque read *Pompeii, Eruption of Mt Vesuvius, 24 August 79 AD*, and in brackets below, *Continuity Error # 16*.

'I thought I might find you in here.'

I turned to find Odysseus behind me.

'What went wrong in Pompeii?'

'An adjudicator failed to stop Brutus from assassinating Julius Caesar, causing a Continuity Error that resulted in the eruption of Mt Vesuvius. It took us two hundred years to repair the time stream.'

I looked again at the plaster figures and shuddered.

'If you look at that wall, you'll find several photographs featuring your grandmother.'

Penny standing with Odysseus outside the Watergate Hotel. Odysseus standing with Mahatma Gandhi. Penny sitting with a group of lawyers at the trial of Nelson Mandela. Soon my eyes turned towards the exhibits: a rifle labelled as belonging to Lee Harvey Oswald, a tricycle that was ridden by a three-year-old child at the exact moment the atomic bomb hit Hiroshima, a series of Chinese letters individually carved from wood, and a publisher's proof of

Silent Spring by Rachel Carson with annotations in Penny's cursive.

'Wow!'

'Yes, amazing, isn't it?'

'I get why you have the tricycle and revolver, but that edition of *Silent Spring*, and the page from the Chinese manuscript—why?'

'These are pivot points, Charlie. Places in the timeline where the future has the potential to dangerously diverge. Our Timeline Exchange Centre identifies these points and then sends out adjudicators to maintain the timeline. In the case of the Chinese manuscript, our adjudicators posed as Arab traders visiting the Chinese Emperor's court, where a printer demonstrated the art of movable type on this very page. Our adjudicators then helped carry this information along the Silk Road to Europe. Without this knowledge, Gutenberg's invention of the printing press would have been delayed by at least a century, also delaying the Renaissance. Whereas the publication of Rachel Carson's *Silent Spring* started the conservation movement with her analysis of the effect of pesticides on the environment. The publisher she pitched the manuscript to was Penny.'

'So throughout history, the Temporal Sinistrum has been adjusting, altering and manipulating events?'

'Charlie, you make it sound so insidious. Think of time as a river, where the Temporal Sinistrum acts like a weir. In a normal river, a weir is a human-made dam that regulates the flow of water and stops it from flooding. Continuity Errors cause this kind of flooding—a particle instability that wreaks havoc on the world and humanity. The Temporal Sinistrum controls its flow through carefully planned action that will ultimately help prevent the Fulcrum.'

'How do you know you are having an effect?'

'First, let me explain to you, Charlie, the reason why Specter founded the Sinistrum in the first place.'

I nodded.

'When Julius first experimented with a prototype Memoria Factoreum, he travelled into the future and saw the Fulcrum firsthand. He arrived at a place where the cities were in ruins, the streets filled with bones, the oceans dry and all life expired, and was so horrified that he founded the Temporal Sinistrum in response. A nuclear war had taken place in 1968 between Communist China and Hitler's Europe, resulting in the Fulcrum. Specter used his Factoreum to help the Allies defeat Hitler and the Nazis in World War Two by ensuring that Operation Mincemeat was a success.'

'Operation Mincemeat?'

'Yes. The Allies hoped to deceive the Nazis by having a drowned corpse with a fake identity and forged papers wash up on a Spanish beach. The hope was that German intelligence would find out what was in the fake documents, and that they would convince Hitler that the Allies planned to invade Europe through Greece, not Sicily. In the original timeline the corpse never made it to shore, but Specter provided the submarine captain with a better location to release the corpse from and ensured the deception's success. Specter's actions adjusted the Fulcrum date to the early 2000s.'

'So it keeps changing?'

'Yes, Charlie. You see that clock above the door? In my time with the Sinistrum, the projected date for the Fulcrum has changed on at least fifteen occasions.'

The clock flickered, but the date of '14:03 27/04/2025' remained, fixed like a rust stain on a bathroom sink.

'But what about the visions, then?'

'Sometimes, for reasons we don't fully understand, people foresee a likely future that has the potential to cause a Continuity Error.'

'What happens to them?'

'Most we recruit, like you and Penny. Even that former Prime Minister of Australia, Harold Holt—the one who disappeared while swimming—now works for us. Although sometimes more decisive action is needed.'

My head reeled, stuck on the word 'decisive'. Was this just a euphemism for murder or assassination? Where the 'greater good' trumped the rights of the individual? I swallowed, unable to respond.

'Charlie, why don't we take a walk outside and I'll explain some more?'

I gulped and nodded.

'Good. However, first we will have to costume you in something more appropriate.'

I still wore the same pair of jeans, Converse sneakers and t-shirt that I had put on that morning for university.

'Let's head to the Anachronism Division and get you a change of clothes.'

10

Adelaide Oval, February 1947

An hour later, I stood in the entrance foyer, the floor beneath me tiled in a chessboard pattern and framed by ash skirting boards. I examined myself in the gilt-edged mirror which sat at the end of the foyer. I wore my hair down and parted on the wrong side, with a pleated tartan skirt that fell below my knee accompanied by a short-sleeved blouse and a set of itchy nylon stockings. For the first time in all my life, I wore a silk petticoat. In the mirror, I looked like the younger version of Penny I recognised from her old photo albums. The same aquiline nose and bright blue eyes, despite the sandy brown hair that I inherited from my father.

Odysseus's suit now matched in cut and style the photos of my grandfather from when he and Penny announced their engagement in April 1950.

'Are you ready for this?' Odysseus said.

I nodded as he pushed open the double oak doors.

Outside, the sun sat in the east. Several vibrations travelled through my wrist as the Tempus Imperium's hands and dials spun frantically.

'Huh? What's going on with the Tempus Imperium?'

'Give it a minute,' said Odysseus. 'It's just acclimatising to this Chrono-sphere.'

'Chrono-sphere?'

'This time period. From the Greek 'Chronos', for the god of time.'

After three minutes, the Tempus Imperium settled on the date: the eighth of February 1947, at a latitude of 34.9 and a longitude of 138.7.

'February 1947, but where are we?'

'Look around,' said Odysseus.

Behind me, the Temporal Sinistrum headquarters sat—a large rectangular white building, three storeys high, that glowed in the mid-morning sun. It squatted between several other similar buildings made from red brick and painted white. On each one was a bronze plaque etched with names such as the *Mawson Physics Labs*, the *George Eastman Classics Building* and the *Lord Justice Downer Law School*, while the one for the Temporal Sinistrum read only *Administration*. Young men in shirts and ties walked in and out of them, carrying thick leather-bound books. I only saw one woman, dressed like me in a skirt and a blouse. No one glanced at the Sinistrum nor attempted to enter it. To them, it was just another building. As I watched, something shifted in front of me, making me woozy, with an acidic taste in my mouth. A glitch dulled the Sinistrum's facade, smoothed out its edges, and pushed it further into the background.

'We're on a university campus?' Then I paused, thinking. I recognised the Mawson Physics Labs, although in 2016 they housed the Student Union.

'It's my university?' I said, 'Except it's 1947.'

'Yes,' said Odysseus, smiling.

A ginger tabby brushed against my leg. Unlike the students who bustled past the Temporal Sinistrum, the cat walked towards it. It sniffed around the front door and pawed at it before heading around the side and disappearing.

'What's going on?' I asked, 'Why are the students ignoring it, but not that cat?'

'The displacement of particles caused by the Factoreum creates this disguise. Think of it as laying a thin filter of grey glass across the building, diminishing it, greying it out. To the Chrono-temps, it's just another building on a university campus, whose function remains a mystery.'

'Chrono-temps? As is in people contemporary to this time stream?'

'You're starting to get it now, Charlie.' Odysseus smiled.

'But why 1947?'

'We tend to avoid locating headquarters much earlier. Otherwise it'd appear as an anachronism in that Chrono-sphere.'

A cheer echoed across the campus. Two of the Chrono-temps stopped and checked their watches. Soon four young men jogged past me and Odysseus, despite their jackets and ties and the summer heat.

'What's going on?'

'Why don't we ask?'

Odysseus called out to the nearest one, a boy with a thin moustache on his upper lip and a fountain pen in his top pocket.

'What's going on?'

'Bradman's batting down at the oval. He might get a century for South Australia before lunch. It's on the radio; they're letting

100

everyone in for free,' said the man, before he ran away.

'Bradman? *The* Don Bradman?'

'Yes,' said Odysseus. 'New South Wales is playing South Australia in the Sheffield Shield. Why don't we go down to the oval and watch?'

'Why not?' This day couldn't get any stranger. Why not watch the greatest batsman ever play? Bradman had died in 2001, three years after I was born.

Odysseus and I joined the crowd that surged towards the oval. I recognised the Member's Grandstand and the hand-operated scoreboard, but nothing else. The light towers, the live replay screens and the three-level stadium seating encircling the cricket ground in 2016 were yet to be built.

We were lucky to find a seat just left of the Members' Grandstand. More and more people were coming in—men, women, and children playing truant for the day. Schoolboys in straw boaters and crimson-striped blazers carried their own cricket bats and balls.

Being at the cricket made me think of Dad and how each summer, at Lamp's Agricultural Supplies, the radio crackled with cricket commentary. In the evenings, Dad often sat in front of the family computer looking up cricket statistics. 'Charlie,' he often said, 'Tendulkar, Lara, and Ponting are all great batsmen, but nothing compares with Bradman's Test average of 99.'

In front of me, Bradman stood at the scoreboard end of the pitch. His cricket whites were saintly and bright in the late morning sun. Unlike modern players with their armguards, boxes and helmets, he wore only cricket pads over his white uniform. On his head was a floppy blue cap for South Australia. The bowler for New South Wales came around the wicket and landed a series of turning off-spinners.

One dot ball and then another. On the third the bowler tried to loft it, but Bradman lunged forward and swept the ball towards the square boundary near the Members' Stand. The crowd cheered as the scoreboard rolled over to 97. Next the bowler spun the ball wildly out of his hand, giving it too much flight. Bradman lofted it back over his head to the boundary with a straight drive for four. The crowd erupted, cheers and applause echoing around the ground. Bradman moved to the centre of the pitch, doffed his cap and held his bat in the air like a king waving to his subjects.

A red-faced middle-aged man and his teenage son turned to me smiling. 'Did you see that? Another century! The Don's amazing.'

'Yes,' I said.

'I'm so glad that Freddy got to watch him play.'

'Me too,' I said, wishing Dad was here.

In front of us, Bradman returned to his crease and the offspinner started his run-up again.

'We should leave at the lunch break,' said Odysseus. 'Hinze, our Controller, wishes to meet you.'

'Odysseus, what does *Exitus Acta Probat* mean?' I said. This Latin motto bothered me, like a sore rapidly festering.

'The result justifies the deed. This is the principle that underlies the Temporal Sinistrum.'

I paused, my mind whirring with questions. 'But then why wouldn't you just go back in time and kill Hitler, or even the Kaiser before him? Think of all the lives that could have been saved.'

'Specter tried, but some things are just fixed in the timeline. You try blowing them up, or in Hitler's case assassinating him with a briefcase bomb placed under a table, but it's just failure after failure. Nothing works, when it's a fixed point in the timeline. Instead, Specter realised he needed to help stop Hitler from winning the war and bringing on the Fulcrum in 1968.'

'Oh.' I shifted from foot to foot.

'That's why the Temporal Sinistrum has a set of rules.' Odysseus stopped walking and looked directly at me. 'One—missions must never be undertaken based on individual desire, as in an adjudicator can never go back and save a loved one. Two—all missions require detailed research and planning because of the risks of the 'Butterfly Effect,' where one minor change could cause huge unintended consequences later. The next two points relate specifically to adjudicators. Three—you must not kill your grandparents or another ancestor, as you will disappear from the time stream. And four—if an adjudicator travels to a Chrono-sphere in which another version of themselves exists, they must not make physical contact because of the risk of a particle paradox that often ends in spontaneous combustion.'

'Spontaneous human combustion?' I gulped.

'Yes. The atoms overheat so much that they explode, killing both versions of yourself. In the early years of the Sinistrum, they lost several adjudicators this way.' Odysseus checked his Tempus Imperium. 'Charlie, we need to get moving again, or we'll be late.'

'Is there anything else I should know?' My mouth felt dry, and I swallowed.

'Well, there's two more things. Firstly, there's the rubber band effect, which limits how long an adjudicator can spend in a specific Chrono-sphere. The further an adjudicator travels from their birthdate, the more time stretches like a rubber band. A snap-back is just as deadly as meeting another version of yourself. It's why these days we restrict such incursions to only the most crucial. Missions to the Roman Empire, ancient Greece, the Middle Ages or even the distant future are severely time-limited because of the risk of a snap-back.'

'What's the last one?'

'Ahh. The Sinistrum limits all interactions with Chrono-temps to only one encounter, especially if it's before the 1800s. Occasionally we will allow a second, but only after a full risk assessment. Any more and a Continuity Error will occur.'

Odysseus looked at his Tempus Imperium again. 'C'mon, we better hurry up. Hinze hates to be kept waiting.'

11

Seattle, October 1918

Richard Hinze watched the gravediggers shovelling dirt into his wife and child's grave. Despite already burying six people this morning, these men worked at a steady pace. They wore gauze masks that covered half their faces. Hinze didn't think their masks met the Chief Surgeon's stipulations for eight layers of gauze, but what could he do? Since the first eleven cases appeared at Camp Lewis, he and the other doctors had played catch-up. Two or three steps behind a virus that spread through a sneeze or cough. A victim might be fine in the morning, and by six-o'clock that evening haemorrhaging from their nose and mouth. Two days after Camp Lewis, they recorded cases in Bellingham and Spokane. Even north of the border, the Canadians were struggling. There were rumours that the Mounties were thinking of closing the road between Seattle and Vancouver.

With each shovelful, dirt consumed the coffins below. Upon his wife's coffin rested Jack-Jack's. She would have liked that, to know that even in death, she still held her baby boy. A tear streaked Hinze's gauze mask. Despite the darkening skies, he watched the two gravediggers and admired their persistence. The way they struck at the dirt with their shovels, and tossed it over their shoulders in a steady rhythm, despite the falling rain.

《·✕·》

Only a fortnight ago, Hinze awoke to Jack-Jack tugging at his nightshirt.

'Papa! Papa! Look at what I've found.'

The boy held a baby bird in his hands, wide-eyed and bleating.

'Careful, son. Give her to me,' he said.

The little bird put its head back and opened its mouth.

'Look, she thinks I'll feed her.'

Hinze felt the soft, downy feathers and twig-like bones in his hand.

'Where did you find her, Jack-Jack?'

'In the garden. Near the big tree.'

'Ok, well, let's put her back in the nest together.'

Outside, the day felt cool and crisp. From September through to June it rained in Seattle, day after day of a drizzle that silvered the pavements and decorated the trees with diamond-shaped droplets. Yet, today would be different, mused Hinze, a quick salve of sunshine before the snow came within the month. Hinze's breath steamed as he reached up to the first branch of the pine tree, where a nest with two other chicks lay. Around him, a much larger bird flew and squawked. Several times she swooped down towards him before pulling up at the last minute.

106

'There she is,' said Hinze, putting the bird alongside her siblings in the nest. 'C'mon, let's go inside, Jack-Jack. I'm sure that your mother has made breakfast by now.'

Inside, Veronica had just finished frying hot cakes, that now sat steaming on two plates, waiting for her son and husband.

'Oh goody! Thanks, Mama!' said Jack-Jack.

Hinze poured syrup on his hot cakes and then some on his son's plate.

'Betty, next door, said that both the O'Driscolls and Partridges have this flu. The youngest O'Driscoll girl might die.'

'Oh dear,' sighed Hinze.

'I wish I could do something for them. Maybe I could get some fish at Pike Street Markets and make a fish pie? What do you think?'

'Make sure you and Jack-Jack wear your masks. And travel around lunch on the trolley, to avoid the crowds.'

He came home that night from the hospital to find the kitchen filled with steam, a kettle boiling away on the stove top. 'It's only a headache,' Veronica told him as she lay in bed, but she felt feverish to his touch. Already today, he had treated five such fevers. Jack-Jack brought his toy trains into their bedroom and pushed them around on the floor, whispering 'Choo-choo' to himself. The fish Veronica bought that day was still wrapped in newspaper and on a shelf in the ice box. By the next day, her chest rattled with a cough that turned her face blue. Two days later, Jack-Jack developed the same fever. He placed the boy in his bed and gave him his toy bear, Ed. 'It's all right, Jack-Jack,' he said as he mopped the boy's brow with a wet cloth. Three days later, he opened the ice box and gagged at the stink of rotting fish and spoilt milk. He put the fish in the trash and tipped out the milk. On the fifth day, he signed both Veronica and Jack-Jack's death certificates, as the family doctor had died the previous week.

«·✕·»

Now, Hinze stood under his umbrella watching the gravediggers. Only Father O'Halloran and Veronica's mother attended the funeral. Her other relatives and friends were too afraid of a disease that they couldn't see, and that targeted the young. Young men like those at Camp Lewis, who survived the mud and bullets of Europe, only to be murdered by an invisible enemy. The disease hid instead in the every-day: the child with a runny nose, the old woman with a cough, or the junior clerk dragging himself to the office to work one more day. Veronica could have caught it at the Pike Street Fish Markets despite her mask, or on the trolley as she held onto a handle and braced herself and Jack-Jack. He would never know.

In the distance, a middle-aged man with a receding hairline and thin-rimmed glasses stood under a tree near two fresh graves. Another survivor like him, he thought, waiting to consign his most precious possessions to a six-foot deep hole.

Father O'Halloran had delivered a well-practised homily on the blight and pestilence of this world and the bliss of heaven with a reading from Corinthians before he departed to attend three more burials that afternoon. Veronica's mother nodded at him, her eyes wet with tears for her daughter and only grandson. She didn't know that in a month, she too would be interned in the same family plot.

Hinze waited, his fingers tracing the tin rivets on Jack-Jack's favourite train in his right jacket pocket. He meant to leave the train under their cross. Jack-Jack already had Ed with him inside the coffin. The boy was dressed in his pale blue sailor suit, his arm hugging the toy bear as he did when he slept. The grave diggers

108

were almost finished, yet still the rain came down. A repetitive *drip-drip* that flooded the non-summer months in Seattle. There hadn't been a break in the rain since the day he put the baby bird back in its nest while Jack-Jack watched. He never told the boy that two days later he found the same baby bird dead on the ground, its neck broken and chewed by a cat.

Finally, the gravediggers patted down the last of the dirt into a neat mound and left. Hinze looked at the white cross, the words: 'Veronica Hinze, Beloved Wife of Richard and Mother of Jack, Age 24', and 'Jack Edward, Beloved Son of Veronica and Richard, Age 4', written across it. Part of him wanted to lie down on their grave and wait for the snow to come. Instead, he turned to leave, his right hand still in his pocket, holding Jack-Jack's train.

Inside their house near the top of Capitol Hill, Hinze wrote his will. Some money for a full family headstone, another amount to pay off his debts, this house to his nephew, and a generous amount for their maid, Ginny. Each room existed in shadow, trapped between daylight and night-time by the drawn curtains. In the kitchen, a stack of unwashed plates mouldered in the sink. He found the last clean mug and filled it with a double-shot of whiskey. He blew the dust off the Victorola record player he'd given to Veronica for their wedding anniversary two months ago and put on Mozart's *Requiem*. On his desk sat an ashtray filled with cigarette butts and a six-shot one dollar revolver bought at the General Store less than a day ago. Alongside it, he placed Jack-Jack's toy train. He brought out a box of bullets and loaded one into the chamber.

Knock! Knock!

Hinze ignored the sound and kept writing his will and suicide note. This time, there was a double rap of knuckles against the door and a voice calling, 'Hello? I-z there-e anyone at home? Hello?'

Hinze got up and went down the stairs to the front hallway. In the mirror that hung outside the door to Jack-Jack's room, he saw himself for the first time in over a week. His eyes bulged out of sunken cheeks and his chin was smeared with stubble. He smelt of whiskey and cigarette smoke. Hinze opened the door to a world becalmed by snow, the first this winter. He thought of how last Christmas, Jack-Jack had stood outside with his head back and mouth wide-open, trying to catch a snowflake on his tongue, his breath steaming as he giggled. A tear trickled down Hinze's cheek. The same man from the graveyard stood on his doorstep clutching an umbrella, his glasses fogged with moisture.

'Dr Hinze-e? Can I come in? We must talk.' He spoke in a thick German accent that hung off the 'z' of Hinze and rolled the 'e' in the words he said.

'No! Can't you see I'm indisposed? Come back another time!' said Hinze, but the man stuck his foot out.

'Ye-*ez*, we-*e* must talk. I am from the *Z*-inistrum.'

'What Sinistrum?'

'The Temporal *Z*-inistrum.'

'I'm not interested in any Temporal Sinistrum. My wife and child have died, and I have their affairs to attend to. Please leave!'

The man refused to listen and pushed his way inside, making the door swing back with a *thud* and cracking the plaster. Hinze sunk to his knees and began to sob.

'We-*e* must talk,' said the stranger, offering him his hand and a handkerchief. 'My name's Specter. Dr Julius Specter.'

In the kitchen, the stranger poured him a glass of water.

'Dr Hinze-*e*, when was the last time you ate?'

'I don't know,' said Hinze as he shrugged his shoulders. He and the stranger sat at the dining room table, despite its coating of dust. Veronica would never have let it get to this state.

'Your work, Richard. May I call you that? Your research on epidemiology and statistical probability i-z outstanding.'

For a moment, Hinze wondered who this stranger was talking about? Did he mean him? The scientist who once developed protocols for mapping disease outbreaks, and systems using index cards to track cases. That version of Hinze had died with Veronica and Jack-Jack. Since the Spanish Flu began, he'd worked on the wards, not in his laboratory. The hospital was so short-staffed because of the virus that even researchers like him with no day-to-experience of medicine since college now administered to the sick.

'That's done with now,' said Hinze.

'I am z-orry about your wife and child. Z-uch a small coffin for the boy.'

'His name was Jack. We called him, Jack-Jack.'

'I understand, but I want to offer you a job opportunity. A chance to prevent such mass z-uffering in the future.'

The stranger's words hung in the air. Hinze thought for a moment about the revolver on his desk, but then refocussed.

'Go on then.'

12

'So Charlie, the Temporal Sinistrum exists to prevent Fulcrums and ensure the timeline continues,' said Richard Hinze as he leant back in his chair and put his thumbs behind his braces. On the wall behind was another digital clock, with red numerals and the same date. Like Odysseus, he wore a suit, but his jacket hung on a coat hanger behind his office door. In his mid-sixties, Hinze combed his few remaining strands of hair defensively against baldness. Every time he looked at me, the whiteness of his teeth gleamed. We sat in the Controller's office, which overlooked the Memoria Factoreum and the Unified Field Machine. Madam Zhao sat at one of the control panels, recording numbers on a clipboard. To the left of Hinze slept the same ginger cat that I'd seen outside in 1947, now curled up in a basket.

'We developed the Timeline Exchange Centre to monitor the time stream and warn us of impending Fulcrums.'

'You mean that room near the museum?'

'Yes, one of my proudest developments. It has meant that we now rely on empirical data rather than just on prognostic visions. The algorithms grow more accurate every day.'

'But where does the premonition part come into it?'

'Over history, there have been people like you or your grandmother, gifted with paragnostic ability that helps us locate these pivot points. Thankfully, these days the Timeline Exchange Centre provides us with such data. We send adjudicators back to ensure that these events occur as they should.'

'Like what?'

'Here, look at this video from 1963,' said Hinze, pointing to his computer screen.

In the grainy footage I recognised a president and his wife waving at the crowd on a Dallas street from their motorcade. Two seconds later, the retort of a rifle echoed, and the president fell forward.

'Everyone blamed Lee Harvey Oswald for the shooting, but we also had an adjudicator on the grassy knoll. Two shots from two identical guns, except in different locations. It's just a pity that the Zapruder footage hints at a second shooter. We prefer to operate in anonymity.'

'Why not just stop Oswald?'

'Because a nuclear war between the USSR and the US would have resulted if Kennedy had lived,' Odysseus interjected.

'But how do you know this?'

'We send archaeologists to these different Fulcrums to find out what has caused it. There was clear evidence in the newspapers and diaries that they found.'

I fiddled with the Tempus Imperium on my wrist.

'Why don't you save those you care about from a premature death? I know Odysseus says it's against the rules, but why don't you?'

'Remember what I said about most people's deaths being fixed? This even applies to mass genocides like the Holocaust and what occurred in Rwanda in 1994. However, Specter's actions in ensuring the success of Operation Mincemeat prevented billions from dying in the Fulcrum of 1968.'

'Oh,' I said, blankly. It was hard to comprehend.

'I know. I lost my wife and child to the Spanish Flu, but we predicate the Sinistrum on what is best for the many, not the individual. The billions over the million,' said Hinze, pointing towards a black-and-white photo on his desk. In it, a much younger Richard Hinze stood behind a woman, his hand on her shoulder. On her lap sat a smiling two-year-old boy in a sailor suit. Next to the photo lay a tin toy train, the paint chipped and the metal dented from use.

'I would have committed suicide if it wasn't for the Sinistrum,' said Hinze, leaning forward. 'Veronica and Jack-Jack were dead, and I had already loaded my revolver when Julius knocked at the door. Since then, the Sinistrum has been my life. We keep time flowing. We stop it from diverging—that crack in matter that would smash the very particles that bind the universe together apart. But at this very moment, our work is in jeopardy because of the impending 2025 Fulcrum. Nothing we've tried has altered this date since the syneghasts first appeared.'

'I'm sorry, but what has this got to do with me?' I said, as I looked around the room.

Above Hinze's desk hung several photos: Julius Specter sitting in a laboratory, and a group of adjudicators arranged as in a class photo. My grandmother sat in the front row to the left of Hinze, and behind her was Odysseus Clay.

'Your grandmother, Penelope Jones, came to us from the

London Blitz in 1940. Her talent for premonitions had already saved her life once. We believe she discovered the reason for the syneghasts and that's why she contacted us via our London PO Box after so many years.'

This image of my grandmother, in which she used a Tempus Imperium and saw visions, seemed incoherent to me. Fragments that I couldn't bring into focus—Penny in the kitchen on Christmas Day, hiding coins in the pudding; her sitting beside me with a cup of tea while we watched the *Antiques Roadshow*—how did this all fit with these tales of time travel? Penny had worked as a typist during the war, or at least that's what Mum and I had believed.

The pipes of the Factoreum rattled beneath me. Two strangers sat next to me who believed in *Exitus Acta Probat*—the end justifying the means. *Tell them that the key to the syneghasts lies with Kepplar.* Penny's last words throbbed like a fresh bruise in my mind. I pushed my thumbs into my forehead and tried to knead the headache away.

'Are you all right, Charlie?' asked Odysseus.

'Yeah, just too much information making my head hurt,' I said, rubbing my eyes.

'I understand; it's a lot to take in,' said Odysseus.

'Why did my grandmother leave the Sinistrum?'

'Most people don't leave. Once they see what is to come, they are committed for life. But after eight years, Penny wanted something more—something historically inconsequential, but personally important—a family.'

I nodded, as this fitted with my view of Penny, who kept bottles of lemonade in the fridge for when her grandchildren visited.

'Yet after thirty years of silence, your grandmother wrote to us through our London PO Box. We think she found a clue to the syneghasts.'

'Those creatures? The ones that killed her and attacked me?'

'Yes, the syneghasts. Creatures of dark matter that need to consume particulates to survive.'

'But where do they come from?'

'That we don't know. According to Specter's diaries, they've always existed in some form. They even appear in Ashkenazi folk tales as shape-shifting wolves. Yet in the last thirty years, more and more have appeared. One here or there was manageable, but now a syneghast attack is a real risk on every incursion. This month alone, we've lost three adjudicators. The Sinistrum's down to only four operatives, including Odysseus here,' said Hinze.

'What are they made from?' I said. 'Their coats looked black enough to absorb light.'

'You've heard of a black hole in outer space, made from the remnants of a collapsed star? The gravitational pull is so strong that the hole sucks in everything, including the light of nearby stars. The syneghasts are like that—a magnetometer that sucks in and snuffs out the surrounding light. That's why they find a person's particulate especially attractive. Particulates are a form of energy that syneghasts need to devour in order to survive. The more syneghasts there are, the more damage to the very particles that bind reality together; hence the Fulcrum. These creatures have put the entire project of the Temporal Sinistrum at risk.'

I shuddered. Even the mention of these syneghasts made my skin prickle.

'So there's a lot more of those things?'

'Yes.'

I bit my bottom lip, before asking, 'But aren't you afraid they'll attack this place?'

116

Odysseus put his hand on my shoulder and smiled. 'Don't worry, Charlie. The Sinistrum is the safest place to be. We have the Palladium, an electromagnetic shield that prevents the syneghasts from entering. And as long as the Factoreum's switched on and running, we have enough energy from the Unified Field Machine to power the Palladium.'

Hinze cleared his throat and tapped a pencil against his desk.

'Charlie, did Penny tell you anything about the syneghasts before she died?'

I looked at Odysseus and then at Hinze. Hinze leant towards me, his eyes hungry, hands on his hips. In the corners of his mouth, a small fleck of spittle was forming. Could I trust him? Odysseus had already saved my life once, but I knew even less about Hinze.

Perfectly centred in his desk sat a pad of paper. Parallel to it were two sharpened lead pencils.

Tell them that the key to the syneghasts lies with Kepplar. My grandmother's final words as she lay dying in my arms. The Sinistrum had to be the 'them' she was referring to. I paused, like a kid on the seven-metre diving board at the local pool. Should I flee back down the ladder or dive in? Sometimes, you had to take a risk as Penny often reminded me.

'Grandma Penny said *that the key to the syneghasts lies with Kepplar.*'

'Ahh, James Kepplar, the modern equivalent of Newton and Einstein, and the inventor of the Unified Field Machine. He thought he was the first to invent such a powerful generator, but Julius Specter never published his earlier design. If Penny believed Kepplar might have a solution to the syneghasts, then we really need to explore this angle. I'm going to task our researchers with this straight away.'

For someone who administered an office and kept the books,

Penny had had unusual reading tastes. Besides the collected writings of James Kepplar, there had been several binders full of research papers on physics and manuals for watch repairs and horology guides. Mum had always said that Penny was the smartest person she knew, and that the war had denied her the chance to go to Cambridge and study physics. Had she always been looking for a solution to the syneghast problem?

'Good,' said Odysseus. 'Richard, what should we do with Charlie?'

'Why don't you let her watch some training videos about the Sinistrum?' said Hinze, with a smirk.

«·✕·»

For four hours, I sat in a small office with the steampunk version of a laptop—a typewriter-like mechanical keyboard attached to a high-resolution monitor screen. Video after video of standard operating procedures, from how to clean your Tempus Imperium to what the annual budget was for celebrating staff birthdays. I had never envisioned that a time-travelling agency like the Temporal Sinistrum could be just as mundane as working in the local council office at Currency Creek. Part of me understood the need for paperwork and procedure, because even at NASA there was someone whose job wasn't flying, designing or monitoring space flights, but using a ledger or spreadsheet to account for the number of nuts and bolts in a given project. However, I wanted to learn more about my grandmother and the Sinistrum's missions. Instead, I got instructions on how to pre-requisition a stapler and the correct sizing for paperclips.

What was the point of this? Did Odysseus and Hinze not trust me?

Gradually, my eyesight began to blur and I put my head down on the desk. *Five minutes*, I told myself, *a five-minute power nap*. I had been awake for what was probably close to nineteen hours straight now. No wonder I was so exhausted. I rested my forehead on my arms and closed my eyes. *Five minutes only,* I told myself, *just a five-minute power nap…*

≪·✕·≫

'Charlie?'

A round structure, burrowing into the desert. People dressed in white chanting 'We are the thread that follows the needle'. A pile of handwritten papers from a yellow legal pad waiting for cataloguing and restoration.

'Charlie?'

I woke with a start. I was back in that windowless bedroom lying on the bed.

'Charlie, time to get up.'

In the doorway stood Odysseus.

'Hinze wants to see us. I suggest you freshen up. I'll meet you at his office in twenty minutes.'

In the ensuite, I splashed water on my face and brushed my teeth with a brand-new toothbrush. The bristles were so stiff they made my gums bleed. It took four mouthfuls of tap water to wash the blood away.

≪·✕·≫

'She's too young, Odysseus.'

I had my fist raised, ready to knock against Hinze's door

when I heard them arguing.

'But there are only three other adjudicators left, and two are on incursions and Natsuko is in the infirmary recovering from smallpox. If Charlie is anything like Penny, she'll be a valuable addition to the Sinistrum,' said Odysseus.

'But she's still a teenager!'

'She's eighteen, Richard, which makes her legally an adult in her Chrono-sphere.'

I cleared my throat and knocked at the door.

'Ahh, Charlie, come in,' boomed Hinze.

I took a seat alongside Odysseus again.

'Charlie, I wanted to speak to you again, to see if you had remembered anything more that Penny might have said about Kepplar,' said Hinze.

I shook my head, 'No, nothing more.'

Hinze blinked. 'Well, the Sinistrum's known for some years now that Kepplar's Unified Field Machine is quite similar to Specter's. Our researchers think the answers to the syneghasts might be in Kepplar's research notes.'

'How do you plan to get those?'

'By sending Odysseus to the future. The post-Fulcrum world of 2120.'

'The Fulcrum? Wouldn't that be dangerous? Why not just go back in time and ask Kepplar?'

'The risk of a Continuity Error is too high. Getting the research notes after Kepplar's dead is safer, even it means a trip to the Fulcrum era.'

'But where will his notes be?'

'In the Needle, a complex run by his disciples situated somewhere outside of Los Angeles.'

I swallowed; my mouth still tasted like metal.

A round structure, burrowing into the desert. People dressed in white chanting 'We are the thread that follows the needle.' A pile of handwritten papers from a yellow legal pad waiting for cataloguing and restoration.

'When I arrived at the Sinistrum, I saw something,' I said. 'A concrete needle burrowing into the desert, and a pile of papers with mathematical formulae and algebra scrawled across them.'

'Where in the desert?' said Hinze. 'We've had some trouble locating this Needle. Kepplar's disciples hid their silo's location in the years before the Fulcrum.'

My teeth ground against each other. The vision sat fractured in my head, and now I needed to pick up each piece and stick it back together.

'Think,' said Odysseus, squeezing my arm. 'What details do you remember, Charlie?'

I circled above the Needle in my mind. A black buzzard high in the sky, resting on thermals. To the left, less than five kilometres away, the remnants of an interstate highway; and a burnt-out truck stop; nearby, a sign pockmarked with bullet holes.

'*Ma's Diner—The Best Cornbread in Petersville!*'

'What did you say?'

'There's a sign. *Ma's Diner—The Best Cornbread in Petersville!*'

'It must be near here,' said Hinze. His index finger was pointing at a map of the west coast of the United States. 'Just off the I-15 near Petersville. Good job.'

'Are you sure?'

'You're right, Odysseus, she's just like Penny.'

'Richard, I'd like Charlie to come with me,' said Odysseus.

'But she's not a trained adjudicator and barely knows how to use a Tempus Imperium.'

'We need her help to find the Needle's precise location and Kepplar's notes. Our researchers have struggled to pinpoint it for years, and now Charlie's taken us closer than that in less than half an hour.'

My palms began to sweat, and I wiped them on my skirt where they left two dark marks. I looked from Hinze to Odysseus and then back again, my heart pummelling against my chest.

Hinze tapped his fingers against his desk like he was playing a piano. They moved with dexterity, keeping to an up-tempo rhythm as he thought.

'Mm. We are down to our last four active adjudicators.'

Hinze tapped his fingers repeatedly like he was playing a resounding C-minor chord on the desk as the final crescendo before he turned to me.

'Charlie, would you do this for us? Help us recover Kepplar's notes?' His words were as sharp as his stare, fine-edged and bladed like a surgeon's scalpel.

My gaze darted from Hinze to Odysseus, then back again. I couldn't focus, the fear fluttering like a bird inside my chest.

'You would be taking an extraordinary risk by joining Odysseus on this incursion. The Fulcrum is a violent and dangerous time.'

I wanted to ask myself, what would Penny do? However, I knew this was a foolish question, because I already knew the answer. I'd seen the photos of my grandmother's incursions in the Sinistrum's museum.

Odysseus leant forward. 'Charlie, you've seen the Needle in the desert, and we're short on alternatives. Remember, I'll be with you. Consider it your first training mission.'

'Training mission? Really?' My stomach twitched.

'Charlie, we've lost so many adjudicators. Don't you want to stop the creatures that killed your grandmother?'

I nodded, despite feeling like I was caught in a rip pulling me out to sea.

«·✕·»

Two hours later, Odysseus and I stood in the centre of the Factoreum as Madam Zhao performed a last series of checks.

'Charlie,' Odysseus said. 'There's something Hinze didn't tell you about why your grandmother left. A syneghast attack disrupted our last mission together. She asked Hinze to mothball the Factoreum, but he refused.'

'Did you agree with him?'

'I thought at the time that your grandmother was being too cautious.'

'Too cautious? Honestly?' I said. *My grandmother's breath quietening in my arms.*

However, the hum of the Factoreum drowned out my question as a white star of light submerged us.

13

Los Angeles, March 2120

I woke with dirt in my eyes and throat.

'Get up, Charlie!' Odysseus tugged at my arm. 'We need to move now! A dust storm is coming!'

I pushed myself up and stumbled after Odysseus. We picked our way across smashed bricks, concrete slabs, tin sheets and broken glass. For a moment, I looked behind at the mustard-coloured cloud unfurling across the distant hills. Plastic bags and brown leaves flew in a frantic dance across the rubble while the roar made my ears hurt.

'In here!' said Odysseus as he dragged me down into a hole.

Odysseus flicked on his UV torch. We were in the remnants of an underground carpark. You could still see the line markings and symbols for pram and wheelchair parking. Burnt-out trolleys lay stacked at the base of a travelator that once led to a Safeway. Metal hit metal and the concrete pillars groaned, straining under the weight of the storm above.

124

'Charlie, pull up your scarf and put on your goggles. It'll keep the dust out.'

For two hours, the storm growled and pounded on the rubble above like a spoilt child. Odysseus and I sat huddled together in the twilight of the carpark. I fiddled with the Tempus Imperium on my wrist, adjusting the bezels and dials. *One—date, two—longitude, three—latitude.* Rehearsing again and again the same sequence of movements. Did Penny do this too when she had received her Tempus Imperium?

'It's over,' said Odysseus as he stood up and shook off a yellow coat of dust. 'Dust, silicosis. Potter's rot. Grinder's asthma. From what our researchers have been able to glean, many people died during the start of the Fulcrum from dust coating their lungs, leading to suffocation.'

'Aargh, that's awful,' I said, as I flicked the dirt from my pants and shirt.

'We're in what's left of LA, I think, near the outskirts. Madam Zhao thought it best to land us here, as we didn't have the exact coordinates for Petersville. It's going to be a long walk.'

A cockroach scuttled underneath my feet.

'Huh, it's true. It's the end of the world and cockroaches are the only survivors,' I said to myself.

'Shh!'

A trolley clunked, followed by the sound of running footsteps. Odysseus swung his torch around and caught a small child in its glare. She wore a faded pair of track pants patched with blue tarpaulin. Her mouth and nose were covered by a rag, smeared with an oily black substance.

I lowered myself to her level and crept forward. The child reared back, her bright eyes blinking in the spotlight of Odysseus's torch.

'It's okay. We won't hurt you,' I said, but then I looked down at myself. Despite the best efforts of the Anachronism Division, my jeans were too blue and my boots too intact. Even with our mad scramble across the rubble to this underground carpark, Odysseus and I still looked too clean. Even our lack of stench was a problem, as this child smelt of mould and rot.

Her big eyes watched me as I crept forward again. This time I offered her a protein bar that I had in a pocket. I broke a bit off and chewed it. She snatched the remaining two-thirds from my hand, gobbling it all up in three bites.

'Slow down, slow down. You'll choke,' I laughed.

'Are you one of 'em?'

'One of what?'

'A Needler.'

'No, no. We're not one of them.'

The child sat down, her back leaning against the carpark wall. She pushed a stray hair out of her eyes and looked at us again.

'Phew! Da says I mustn't speak to the Needlers without 'im, or they might take me away.'

'Where's your father now?' said Odysseus.

'Probably still down the bottom of Macy's.'

'Could you please take us to him?'

'What for?'

'A trade,' said Odysseus.

'We've got lots of wires and metals. I even found a car battery two darks ago,' said the girl with a gap-toothed smile. 'This way,' she gestured, leading us up an old emergency stairwell, 'Hurry. There's only a little light-time left.'

Outside, the wind whined, and the sun hung low, ready for a retreat. Across the rubble fell a gritty fog, making it hard to see

126

more than a few metres ahead. I pulled my scarf tighter and wiped clean my goggles. Yet it didn't slow the child. She strode from brick to concrete to scaffolding in a series of quick steps. Odysseus and I stumbled behind her. At one point, I fell and cut my hand on a piece of metal. Without my childhood tetanus shot, such a cut meant death in this place. Every now and again, the child paused, turning her head from side to side as she listened. Odysseus had said we were visiting the earth post-Fulcrum, but I had never envisioned this. Very few ruins existed above ground in this place. Most had been flattened by a series of rolling seismic waves that had swept through the city ninety years ago. Apart from the child and the cockroach, so far, I had seen nothing else alive.

Nevertheless, somewhere close to here was the Needle where Kepplar's followers lived.

'Da! Da!' The girl disappeared down a set of stairs hidden behind a green emergency door.

For a moment, I thought there had been a mistake. People crowded around me on every side. But when my eyes adjusted to the candlelight, I realised they were mannequins, some missing a leg, others a head. There were even child-sized ones stacked against a wall. In a corner, I made out a mattress covered in duvets and blankets and a pile of rusted cans and empty water bottles.

'Err–err–erghh… who are you?' rasped a voice from a mattress. A duvet fell back as a man pulled himself up to a sitting position, his rib bones visible under the tattered singlet he wore.

'Da, they gave me food,' said the child.

'You're not Needlers then?'

'No.'

'Good.'

'Allie, bring me that candle so I can see 'em better.'

127

In the threadbare light, he appraised us with one eye, the other covered by a cataract.

'Who are you?'

'Traders. We're looking for the Needle.'

Odysseus broke out two more protein bars and offered one to the man. He snatched at it and stuffed it into his mouth until he coughed, and bits of nut and chocolate flew into the air.

'Water! Water!' he gasped. The child passed him a half-filled bottle, and he gulped it down.

'Perhaps try to eat more slowly this time?' I said.

The man nodded. The child sat at the end of his bed watching him, a torn space blanket curled around her shoulders.

'What are your names?'

'Odysseus and Charlie.'

'This is Alice, my daughter. I'm Lewis. And these are our friends,' he gestured towards the store mannequins, with a grimace.

On the wall above his bed was a floor map of a Macy's Department Store. We were in a basement storeroom of some kind. On the opposite wall, someone had scratched out an alphabet chart. Beneath each letter were shakily scrawled words— *apple, bear, friend*—but I wondered, did this child even know what an *apple* was? Had she ever touched one? Or was it just a set of letters, a reliquary made from forgotten syllables?

'Da, can I show her our friends?' said the child, grabbing my hand and pulling me into the room behind.

Once the department store had used this room for a kitchen and a white goods display. There was a countertop, sink, fridge and a dishwasher on one side, while in the centre rested a family-sized dining table. Four mannequins sat around it— one male, one female and two children—eating a supper from empty plates. The man was clothed in a business shirt and tie, and the female in a silk nightie and a blonde wig. The bigger of the two child-sized mannequins had on a baseball cap, whereas the smallest wore the rags of a pink frock.

'Do you like 'em?' she said. 'I've made 'em just like this.' She handed me a faded page from a Macy's catalogue. On the front page was a photo of a family sitting around a similar table at Thanksgiving. The dining table piled high with a turkey, corn, carrots, potatoes and pumpkin pie.

'Is that food?' she asked.

'Yes.' I nodded, and pointed at each item. 'Turkey, corn, and this is pumpkin pie,' and so on.

'Tur-key, corn,' she repeated. Her tongue tasted each word, as if it was a lolly.

'Yes, tur-key, but my favourite is always the pumpkin pie with a dollop of whipped cream,' I said, lying. My knowledge of Thanksgiving was limited to the endless American sitcoms and films that overflowed from our Australian TV screens.

'What's a pu–mp–kin?' she said.

And I wondered, what words I could use? Supermarket? The colour orange? Wedges wrapped in plastic? Words with no scaffolding underneath, because that world lay in pieces outside.

'It's soft and its sweet. Sometimes you don't even have to chew it.'

'No chewing! But everything always needs chewing, says Da, 'specially dogs or cats.'

'Yes, but this is from before, when people had time to boil pumpkin in water to make it soft or bake it in the oven.'

'Cook food in water? Wow! They had 'nough water for that? Da and I try to store water when it rains, but sometimes it just doesn't come. Or when it does, it burns my skin,' said the child, her eyes growing wide.

'Come,' I said. 'Odysseus and your father must be finished talking by now.'

I tripped as a cat skidded away under my feet.

'Kitty!' said the child. She pulled a slingshot from her back pocket and took aim. The pebble hit the cat with a crack on the forehead, cutting off a growl as its head snapped back, and it fell with a thud to the ground.

The child picked it up the cat by its tail and beamed. 'Food!'

My stomach twitched at the cat's corpse covered in cuts and scratches, the pus-filled sore just below the tail and six tired-looking teats hanging from its belly. Unlike Telemachus, with his steel-grey fur, bright eyes and fondness for chin scratches, this cat had lived a life driven by the instincts of food, fight and survival. I shuddered as I pushed back against the wave of nausea that threatened to overwhelm me.

'Da, I caught a kitty,' said the child as we entered the room.

'Good, Allie. Tomorrow, you will take these people to the Needle,' explained her father.

'The Needle! But Papa, what about 'em? The Needlers?'

'Don't worry, Allie. You only need to show them from a distance. They'll stay with us for tonight's dark,' said the man, as another cough ripped through his body, and he collapsed back on the mattress.

The child butchered the cat with a dexterity that surprised me. A single cut down the belly, then the skin pulled inside out before she spitted the cat on an iron pole above a fire. I flinched, thinking of Tee in my arms and purring. Is that what we'd come too, because of the Fulcrum? When finished, she wiped the blood on her pants, where it mingled with the dust from outside.

'Don't forget to pull the door across, Allie,' said her father from the bed. 'Or the coyotes'll get in.'

She offered Odysseus and I several ribs from the cat, to which clung a few bits of cooked stringy flesh. But both of us refused, as even with a lifetime's worth of vaccinations, the risk of salmonella, toxoplasmosis or a stomach-churning parasite like trichinosis was too high. The Fulcrum was the last place where I wanted to be running a high fever and vomiting my guts up, even with the possibility of a medical evac. I watched the child eat every scrap of meat off the bone, then snap each rib in half and suck out the marrow.

'She'll take you at first light tomorrow,' said her father. 'Try to get some sleep first.'

Odysseus and I sat leaning against a wall. Both the child and her father had slipped into sleep quickly, the kind that I recognised, which came swiftly after a day spent running half-marathons or hunting feral cats.

'Try to get some sleep, Charlie,' said Odysseus. 'We've got a long walk out of the city tomorrow.'

Despite the concrete wall behind me, I dozed in fits, a sleep where dreams came in run-on-sentences that stopped abruptly when I slipped too far down the wall and woke up.

《·✕·》

Just before dawn, I heard a baby crying. I rubbed my eyes. Had I imagined it? Then it cried again, louder this time. Odysseus and the little girl both woke.

'Where's the baby?' I asked the girl.

'No baby. There's no baby,' she said.

131

Yet I could hear the infant's cries growing louder. Surely there was a parent somewhere who would comfort it? But it kept howling, a shriek sharp with pain and hunger.

'Charlie, stop!' said Odysseus, but I went up the stairs anyway and pushed the emergency door aside. In the dawn light stood a coyote holding a baby-shaped bundle in its mouth ten metres away, the screams growing louder. I picked up a rock and threw it hard at the coyote, which dropped the bundle and fled. The baby still cried, despite lying face down in the rubble. I turned it over, a cord with a ring on the end coming loose in my hands. For a minute, the stiff limbs made me think of rigor mortis. But how could it still be crying? It was then I realised that this wasn't an infant, but a baby doll created for little girls to nurse.

The child screamed.

Damn, Charlie! You've been tricked by a mutt and left the entrance open!

I ran down the stairs, inwardly kicking myself. I had been tricked by a coyote and a toy baby. Inside another four coyotes flanked the man on the bed. Streaks of morning twilight from the ceiling cracks and the open entrance lit up their red eyes and snapping fangs. On the other side of the room, Odysseus edged towards the kitchen display room, the child behind him. Two coyotes blocked their way to the stairs. What had I done? These weren't ordinary coyotes, the kind that dug in bins and compost heaps. They were larger and crossbred with dogs, and smart enough to control the centre of the room. Odysseus wielded a metal bar while the child held her loaded slingshot. I brandished the left leg of a male mannequin like a plastic version of a Neanderthal's club.

The coyotes growled and bared their teeth, circling the man on the bed. In contrast to the syneghasts, their bodies stank of heat. Their coats were ragged in places and stiffened with blood and muck. One coyote had a battered line of teats along her stomach, while another was missing an eye. Like lions, which separated the weakest zebra or giraffe from the herd, their focus was on the man on the bed and isolating him from us.

I banged the plastic leg against the wall, but the coyotes refused to move. Damn! One of the smaller ones, a mangy grey mutt, snapped at me and I backed off, moving towards the wall and closer to Odysseus and the girl on the near side of the room. My heart fluttered in spasms like a bird trapped in a box.

The man on the bed coughed, 'Take Allie. I'll distract them.'

'But Da—' said the little girl as Odysseus took her hand.

'Here,' the man sat up, and waved his arms. 'Here—'

The largest coyote jumped and landed on the man's chest.

'This way, Charlie!' said Odysseus as he pulled the child towards the kitchen display room.

I struck out with the plastic leg, sending the mangy grey mutt near me yelping into a corner as I dashed past.

Behind us the coyotes snarled and snapped as they ripped the man apart.

'In here,' said Odysseus as he pulled the child and me into an elevator. We forced the steel doors shut, leaving only a three-centimetre gap. A paw scratched at the space between the doors, and a yellow eye looked in at us.

'What should we do now?'

'We wait until sunrise. They should disperse by then.'

I sat down on the elevator's floor and leant against its wall. On the right side of the door were a series of numbered buttons and a small green sign that said *IN CASE OF EMERGENCY, PRESS THIS BUTTON FOR ASSISTANCE.* I wanted to laugh—what assistance? It would be only a hundred years too late.

The little girl sat in a corner by herself, hugging her knees and whimpering. Tears streaked through the dust and down her cheeks.

'This is my fault. I left the entrance open,' I said.

Odysseus touched me on the shoulder. 'Remember that in the Sinistrum, it's always the many over the few who must be saved.'

I turned away and started slowly hitting my head against the wall. *Thump!* I needed this pain—the dull-edged thud of my skull against the elevator's metal wall—as punishment for what I'd done. *Thump!* My stupid mistake had killed that man and orphaned the child. *Thump!* How could I live with myself?

'Charlie, you need to stop this now. We don't have time for it,' said Odysseus, shaking me.

'The girl's father is dead because of me! Because I made a mistake!' I cried, but Odysseus stopped me from thumping my head against the wall again.

'Charlie, we have a chance to stop this whole Fulcrum timeline from happening, so I need you to calm down.'

'But what about her?' I pointed to the child, who rocked in the corner and wept.

'We still need her to show us the way to the Needle.'

I went over and put my arm around the shaking child.

'He's gone. Da's gone,' she sobbed, her whole body shuddering with pain.

'He died saving you,' I explained.

'I know, I know,' she cried. 'But he's gone.'

'I'm so sorry,' I whispered over and over, while a nose caked in dried blood sniffed at the crack in the elevator doors.

14

For three hours, I watched the minute hand limp around the face of my Tempus Imperium. At 7 am, Odysseus took the metal bar and pried open the elevator doors. Sunlight pierced the gloom of the room in front of us, sprouting from the cracks in the ceiling. The family of mannequins still sat around the dining table, but only the boy had lost his cap.

'Where is it? Where's his hat?' said the little girl, as she scrambled around on all fours, looking for it.

'Here,' I said, picking it up from underneath the table and placing it on his head.

'You've got it wrong,' she said and corrected the cap's angle.

There wasn't much left of the man on the mattress in the next room, except for a few fragments of bone, hair and skin and a bloody stain. I flinched, but my tears had all been spent; instead, I tried to shield the child's eyes with my hand, but she pushed it aside.

'Da's gone now, like Mama,' she said, her bloodshot eyes staring up at me.

'Yes,' I said.

'Gone. Why does everyone eventually become gone?' she asked, but I didn't have an answer.

I grew up in a time where films and TV shows had ratings—G, PG, M, MA, and R—which protected children her age from decapitations, amputations and scenes where people sniffed cocaine. Yet in this post-Fulcrum world, survival required hunting and skinning your own game for food and hoping that you didn't step on a rusty nail and die of an infection.

'Should we bury him?'

'No, there's not time. It's at least a day's walk to the Needle.'

The child glanced for a final time at the bed and swallowed hard, before placing a water bottle filled with a brackish brown liquid and a filthy sleeping bag in a plastic shopping bag. She swung it over her shoulder like a beggar's sack and stormed out. I had the feeling that she had done this before, seen her world ripped into shreds, and then began again.

An overcast sky hovered above the ruined city. Once these buildings climbed towards the sky and office workers sent a babel out about 'KPIs', 'Benchmarks', and 'Putting on the back-burner', as pulses of light that lapped the world and came back in a matter of seconds. Now, there was nothing but rubble and exposed wires.

'Let's go,' said Odysseus as we followed the girl, who took step after step at the same pace. I was used to my friends back in Adelaide with their melodramas about parents, boys and grades: 'It's so unfair! Mum says we can't go to Bali this summer!'; 'I'd rather die than break-up!'; 'I'm such a failure, only getting a credit!'. Self-pitying monologues accompanied by tears, smudged mascara and online posts about it being 'SO UNFAIR!'; instead, this child kept a brittle silence as we trudged together.

She led us down onto a highway where a faded sign hung

from an overpass: 'I-15, Las Vegas 270 Miles'. We passed hundreds of cars huddled together on a five-lane road trapped in their last ever traffic jam. I peered inside a rusting SUV whose windows were still intact. In the back seat behind the driver's sat a toddler's child seat, a plastic teething ring and dangling toy bear attached to the headrest, and a grey husk still strapped inside.

'It's best not to look,' said Odysseus.

'But what happened?'

'The Fulcrum. The appearance of the syneghasts destabilised the time stream so much that it forked off and caused this Chrono-sphere. It began with rising oceans. The atmosphere became a greenhouse, trapping in the fog and pollution, turning water into acid rain. There were uncontrollable fires, earthquakes and pandemics. This is what the Temporal Sinistrum is trying to prevent, an extinction level event. Unlike the earlier potential Fulcrums I've told you about, this one isn't the result of one singular event like a nuclear war or a meltdown, rather it's a combination of factors that rapidly snowballs out of control.'

Both Odysseus and Hinze mentioned the Fulcrum, but I hadn't understood. On this highway, humanity were now the dinosaurs — the ones that survived the asteroid hitting the earth and the Ice Age — scrabbling through the ruins and hunting feral cats for food.

'How long have we got?'

'Another three hundred or so years before we become extinct. From what we've learnt from previous trips to this time period by our archaeologists, there are a range of survivors: the remnants of cults, doomsday preppers, survivalists, and militias. All willing to shoot first and ask questions later. Sometimes they trade with each other. Sometimes they just take through force. The group in the Needle is one of these cults. As you know, they worship Dr

James Kepplar, whose work on the "Unified Field Theory of Dark Matter" might provide us with answers about the syneghasts.'

'So we're posing as traders, then?' I said, 'Like we did with the girl and her father.'

'Yes, Lewis said that sometimes they traded with the Needlers for medicine and food. They require an endless supply of spare parts for their bunker.'

'But why was Alice afraid of them?'

'There're rumours that they abduct children.'

'Is it true?'

'I don't know, but a place like the Needle would need outsiders for genetic diversity. Be mindful of this, Charlie, in your interactions with them. You'd be seen as an ideal candidate, being young, of childbearing age, and relatively healthy compared to most outsiders.'

I swallowed and stared ahead at the child, past the tangle of the traffic jam and towards the hills. Around us the desert spread like a disease, its sands growing thicker and caking the suburban streets. Joshua trees sprung out of driveways and ripped holes in sidewalks. Tall and stark, their branches bent at unreal angles, they mocked the memory of a real tree. These Joshua trees lacked the green leaves and shade of other species of trees and instead spiked outwards with each branch. Nearby lizards sunned themselves and ignored us as we trudged past. Charred black oil-wells dotted this landscape, their remains whining in the wind.

Near a T-shaped intersection, I spotted a deer emerging out of the shadows of an old gas station followed by a fawn. In between the fuel pumps, a herd of bighorn sheep sheltered from the midday heat under the shade of the station's roof. I kept watch for rattlesnakes.

We headed down into a valley, past the remains of someone's last stand at a highway motel. Sheets of corrugated iron fenced in the motel, near a ten-foot lookout nest built on the base of a water tower. A spray of bullet holes scarred the fence panels. An abandoned humvee stood near the entrance, one door ripped off and another flapping loosely. *What had they fought over? Water? Tins of re-fried beans? Packets of mac-n-cheese? Or petrol?* The only ones who might know were two mummified corpses sitting with holes in their skulls in the back of the humvee, their wrist and ankle bones still bound with cable ties.

Soon we passed a burnt-out truck-stop, and a sign pockmarked with bullet holes: *Ma's Diner — the best Cornbread in Petersville!* The letters had faded to a pale blue, the frame cracked. One panel swung in the wind, a constant *whining* that followed us for miles. In the sky, two hawks hung on thermals, their black shadows following our footsteps like my guilt. *I'd orphaned this child.* My mistake had cost her the only person in this wasteland that cared for her. The guilt was now a noose, slowly tightening around my neck.

The child led us without complaining. I expected her to wail and scream after her father died; instead, there was only a void.

Eventually, the child stopped and pointed at a dirt road, above which hung the words painted in white, *The Eye of the Needle Ranch*.

'Is it down there? The Needle?'

The child gestured again.

'Thank you. Thank you for showing us the way,' I said, giving the child my last protein bars, which she stuffed into the plastic bag draped over the shoulder.

Part of me wanted to ask her to come with us. Not leave her alone amongst the coyotes, buzzards, and snakes, but I knew what Odysseus would say: the many ahead of the few.

As we walked away, I asked him what would happen to her?

'If she's lucky, she'll find another group to take her in. Otherwise, she'll probably die some awful death from an infected cut or starvation.'

When I looked over my shoulder, the girl stood below the ranch sign watching us.

15

In the desert, the Needle stuck out, a concrete irritant amongst the tumbleweeds and Joshua trees. We followed a well-maintained dirt road from the ranch sign to the structure. A metal blast door the size of four semi-trailers took up one side of the dome.

'Well, how are we going to get in?'

'Just knock?' said Odysseus.

To the left of the blast door was a normal-sized metal door, above which hung a security camera scanning the terrain. Odysseus pressed a buzzer on the door. A *crackle* of static, before a voice snapped, 'Who's there?' The security camera fixed its gaze upon us.

'We've come to trade,' said Odysseus, holding out some wires and circuit boards.

'Yes, we are interested in those,' said the voice. 'Proceed into the Eye.'

We emerged into a white-panelled room, where our footprints made a trail of dust. After the gritty twilight of the city, the fluorescent light and white tiles made my eyes hurt.

'Stand by for a health check,' barked the speaker on the wall.

A green-coloured laser started moving up my body. Beginning at my feet, it scanned me in segments like an MRI machine. After ten minutes, the same voice stated, 'Open your mouth and standby for an X-ray.' There were two quick flashes and then the voice spoke again: 'Now take off your clothes and head to the showers. We will clean your clothes and equipment and store them for when you leave. Put on the white robes when you're finished.'

'What about our UV torches and the Tempus Imperiums?' I whispered to Odysseus.

'We must leave the torches behind. It'll be too suspicious otherwise.'

'But what about the Tempus Imperiums?'

'I'm hoping we'll get away with some excuse for the watches. Maybe family heirlooms?'

I sighed. What did I know? Odysseus was the trained adjudicator, not me.

Inside the shower, the dirt came off me in estuaries of orange and red. I soaped shampoo through my hair twice and made certain to clean even the backs of my ears. When I stepped out of the shower, I noticed an absence. I smelt under my arms and at my wrists. The stench of the ruined city was gone, instead replaced by something familiar: lavender. I dried my hair on a towel and put on a linen smock with a v-neckline centring on three brown buttons.

Odysseus waited for me in the next room, dressed in a white smock like mine. Painted on the wall behind him was a proverb: *It is easier for a camel to go through the eye of a needle than for a rich man to enter the kingdom of God.*

'Charlie,' whispered Odysseus. 'Remember to be careful if we get separated. Places like this only survived the Fulcrum because they did things that you and I might consider unconscionable.'

'Like what?'

'Only sharing food and medicine if it suited them. Killing any perceived threats. Always the good of the many, over the few.'

'So just like the Sinistrum then?' I said, 'Abandoning a starving child?'

'Oh, Charlie—'

But before Odysseus could finish, a man entered the room. Unlike the child and her father, he had the luxury of a round belly.

'Those samples you provided were excellent. They're just what we need to keep the Needle running,' he said, his smile refusing to touch his eyes.

'I'm glad,' said Odysseus.

'What would you like in return?'

'Some medicine for my wife. She has the most awful cough that the dust storms make worse.'

'We will make the necessary arrangements. I am Jeremiah, one of the Elders. Both your health checks were excellent according to the scans. Most traders and their children we see suffer from conditions like rickets, scurvy or TB, but there was no sign of that in either of you,' he said, arching his eyebrows. 'In fact, based on the scans, I put your age at around sixty and the girl's at eighteen with well-developed and strong bones from her hips through to her spine.'

'I'm Clay and this is my daughter, Charlotte.'

As Odysseus spoke, Jeremiah appraised me like a farmer at a livestock sale. His eyes paused at the Tempus Imperium on my wrist, then darted to the one Odysseus wore.

'That's an interesting watch you have there. May I inspect it more closely?'

'Here,' said Odysseus, loosening the band on his Tempus Imperium and passing it to Jeremiah.

I almost gasped out loud. *What on earth was he doing?*

Jeremiah held the watch up to the light. 'So many complications and such fine workmanship. Would you consider parting with these devices? Perhaps for six months' supply of food and medicine? I'm sure our technicians would have a use for such a fine device.'

'No, I'm sorry,' said Odysseus. 'My daughter and I value these watches. Our family members passed them down from the time before the Fulcrum.'

'Oh,' said Jeremiah, his nose twitching. 'Oh, of course, I understand.' He passed Odysseus's Tempus Imperium back to him. 'Will you be staying with us tonight and share our evening meal? The dustlands can be dangerous at night, with cougars, coyotes and wild dogs. Sometimes even primitives who seem to have forgotten what it means to be human. We will give you the medicine tomorrow, before you leave.'

We followed Jeremiah down a spiral staircase that wound through several floors and took us deeper underground. Fluorescents lit up the staircase, and, in the centre, two glass elevators drifted up and down.

'We encourage our people to always use the stairs and save the elevator for the elderly and equipment,' said Jeremiah.

Each time an elevator passed me on the way up, I observed crates of supplies inside, but no people. Instead, there was a regular flow of people up and down the spiral staircase. Those going up travelled to the left on the outside, whereas those on the inside went downward. Several porters, marked by their backpacks and yellow fluorescent vests, carried smaller loads between levels.

By the time we reached the dining hall on Level 20, we were part of a large group. The dining hall consisted of multiple metal trestle tables and benches arranged in straight lines across the room.

Three were reserved for children, and adults sat at the rest. There were no clear family or friendship groups; instead, each person sat next to another in fifty-centimetre intervals. Placed at each seat in matching portions was a plate piled high with kidney beans, lentils and a tofu-made meat substitute. Jeremiah sat with other Elders at the front of the room on a raised platform. Above them hung a photo I recognised from the inner jacket of Kepplar's autobiography. The physicist sat at a computer with his fringe falling over his right eye.

A bell rang, and everyone in the room stood and chanted:

The thread follows the needle,
The minute follows the second,
The hour follows the minute,
The needle stitches us together.
We are the thread
That follows the needle.

After the last words, every man, woman and child touched their forehead and chest in a straight line and then sat down. I tried to catch Odysseus's eye, but he looked away. I wondered what the prayer meant. Why was a needle and thread so important to these people?

'You can start now,' said a voice to my left. A grey-haired woman sat next to me. As I watched, she scooped up the bean mix and started chewing.

'Thanks,' I mumbled.

'Your skills with a spoon and fork are much better than most of the other traders we let in,' she said. 'Most tear at the food with their hands like animals.'

For a second, I saw the child ripping the meat off the ribs of the cat in the gloom of the department store.

'My father taught me. He said that it stops germs from spreading.'

'A smart man.'

'I'm Charlotte.'

'Ruth,' she said. 'What did you trade for?'

'Medicine for my mother. When the dust storms come in, she can't stop coughing.'

'Poor thing. Many traders come to us for medicinal herbs. Some even choose to stay with us and become part of the Needle. After dinner, would you like to go on a tour?'

'I must check with my father,' I said, looking across at Odysseus, who nodded.

Ruth smiled and we began to eat. Though their food had the consistency of baby puree, these Needlers hadn't lost their culinary skills. I tasted elements of chilli and coriander. Around me, adults talked and joked, like they would in any Chronosphere over a shared meal. Thankfully, none of them knew that this community had only two hundred years left before it succumbed to the Fulcrum. Eventually, the Needlers would run out of spare parts for their air filters and Unified Field Machine, forcing them outside into the same world where we had left the child. Those fifteen-metre-thick concrete walls that were designed to withstand a nuclear attack would eventually crack and then crumble as the San Andreas Fault rumbled underneath.

The children ate without their parents; instead, three adults per table supervised them. Roughly aged between two and ten, the children wore the same plain white smocks as the others, but with red and yellow stains from the bean mix.

'Why aren't the children with their parents?'

'When a child is born, we send them to the Nursery, where those appointed by the Elders care for them,' said Ruth.

'Oh,' I said, 'I'd hate to be without my mother and father.'

'I understand that's how it was back prior to the Fulcrum, but in the Needle, we do things differently. Think of a piece of fabric being woven. Layer upon layer of thread, until something recognisable emerges. Each thread carefully placed to hold the fabric together. We raise our children to be these threads that the needle guides.'

I nodded and chewed my food.

After dinner, each table waited for a nod from Jeremiah to release them. The Needlers picked up their metal plates and cutlery and took them into an industrial-sized kitchen and stacked them on a steel bench ready for washing. Every single plate I saw was empty, apart from a few crumbs. Even the toddlers and older children had emptied their plates, unlike in my school boarding house, where so many girls took a plate loaded with noodles and pasta, ate two bites, then said they were full and watching their weight.

I followed Ruth back up the spiral staircase. We climbed up sixteen floors before she began the tour, making me thankful for all those endless runs at Currency Creek. Those extra kilometres had toughened my legs and lungs to the point, that I could even match Ruth and the porters stride for stride. Ruth reminded me of a real estate agent trying to sell a house as she explained the different levels. The top four flours were for greeting traders and decontamination. Next came three residential floors, each sleeping sixty Needlers. According to Ruth, there were several residential floors lower down as well. She showed me food preparation levels where beans, rice and vegetables grew hydroponically under large LEDs, and another two floors focused on raising medicinal herbs. On one floor were hundreds of tomato plants arranged in rows, where two figures in white smocks inspected the leaves of each plant.

'For pests,' said Ruth, pausing. 'Even with all our decontamination and other procedures, pests still sneak in. Five years ago we lost an entire crop of vegetables to locusts.'

I glanced across the lines of greenery again, but the only thing moving were the two white dots. 'Where are the animals?'

'We got rid of them. The disease risk from pigs and poultry was too great. Instead, we get all our vitamins and protein from what we grow here. We even make our clothing from the hemp plants down on levels thirty-five to forty. The plants also clean the air in the Needle.'

Next, I laid out my trap, using a set of carefully chosen words.

'How do you power this place?' I asked. 'My father said they used to have electricity when he was a boy, from solar panels. But his community ran out of spare parts and people capable of fixing them.'

'Ahh, that's next on the tour,' said Ruth. 'If you are interested?'

I nodded, her offer triggering the trap.

Ruth's smirk made me think of those TV shows my parents loved to watch—*Escape to the Country*, *Escape to the Continent*, *LA Escape* and *Selling NY*, shows where real estate agents with expensive dental work and designer suits showed couples around houses. The only thing Ruth lacked was a two-piece suit, a silk blouse and a pair of high heels.

I followed Ruth down two further floors and into the Needle's Engine Room. In between walls of black servers and panels of computer displays were five two-storey-high coils sealed within vacuum tubes.

'These floors house our Unified Field Machine, which Kepplar completed in 2000. It's the principal source of power for the Needle—a self-perpetuating spiral of electrical current.' As I watched, sparks of electricity travelled up and down the coils. 'Amazing, isn't it? We used to not show outsiders the Engine Room, but in the last twenty years we've become less worried. Some outsiders have even joined our community, based on seeing the Engine Room, as it's clear evidence of our long-term sustainability.'

'But how does it work?'

'Mm, you are an unusually inquisitive outsider,' said Ruth, turning towards me. 'You should consider remaining with us. I'm sure space could be found for your father as well.'

'I'm sorry, but I need to return to my mother with the medicine.'

Ruth sighed and glanced back to the Unified Field Machine.

'As I was saying, it works through a self-perpetuating kinetic current.' She pointed to a clear plastic pipe at the base of each of the coils.

'Wow,' I said.

'Yes—Kepplar wanted to test whether a full-size Unified Field Machine was sustainable. He built our refuge in a disused missile silo hidden away from the electricity grid and had the foresight to stock it with supplies. When the first earthquake smashed its way across California, people took refuge here. Kepplar himself didn't make it. His car was hit by a falling boulder on the Big Sur. We honour his memory daily here, because the Needle is the thread that binds us together.'

As she quoted the prayer line, Ruth touched her forehead and chest again with her left index finger, an action that reminded me of the nuns who used to teach religion in my Catholic high school, and who at the slightest surprise—a lightning strike, a redback spider in a classroom, or a bee swarm in the playground—said a Hail Mary and did the Sign of the Cross.

'Now where were we? Let's head downstairs to the museum.'

Ruth led me through a set of fire-resistant doors into a room lined with bookshelves and glass cases. Leather-bound compendiums of scientific journals and editions of Kepplar's books filled the shelves. In the centre of the room hung the same photo as the one in the dining room.

'Dr James Kepplar, our founder. I like to finish a tour of the Needle in the museum so that visitors can learn about our history. When you finish, we have beds prepared for you and your father on Level 5, Section B2.'

As Ruth left, the doors shut behind her with an inward suck of air.

Phew! Now, where were Kepplar's lab journals and research notes?

I started by looking through the leather-bound volumes on the bookshelf. There were several compendiums of scientific journals with titles such as *Modern Physics Review* and *Nature*, that all featured articles by Kepplar. I found three copies of his PhD thesis, and multiple copies of the textbooks he'd written in the 1990s, but still no research notes. I then checked the glass display cases: Kepplar's glasses and the fountain pen he'd received as a graduation present. Next to them was an iPhone plugged in and running his calendar, showing his daily schedule on the twenty-third of November 2011. There were several photos of Kepplar with another man, William Dupre, a Harvard-educated venture capitalist who'd supplied the funding to for his Unified Field Machine. Dupre stood in every photo in tight-fitting chinos and a pressed-collared shirt with a Ralph Lauren logo. The last photo depicted a grinning Kepplar in front of the Needle, dated '26 July 2025', with 'Three months before the Fulcrum' pencilled underneath. On the wall beside the case hung a hunting rifle labelled 'Dupre's favourite'. In another glass case sat a Bible opened to Matthew 19: 23, those same lines I'd seen earlier: 'It is easier for a camel to go through the eye of a needle than for a rich man to enter the kingdom of God.'

'Ahh, this is Dupre's Bible.'

I jumped. A young man with a smear of a black moustache stood behind me. His cheeks were pockmarked with red pimples.

'I'm sorry for surprising you. I'm the curator.'

I swallowed and tried not to retch, despite the flecks of white pus caught on his nasal hair.

'Why is Dupre so important?' I asked.

'When that earthquake happened, followed by a pandemic of haemorrhagic fever with a 45 per cent fatality rate, Dupre led the survivors to the Needle. He'd given Kepplar the funds to build it. Dupre supplied the guns and ammunition that helped protect us from the militias during the early days of the Fulcrum,' said the young man, pointing towards the rifle on the wall.

Alongside the Bible lay a scrapbook filled with newspaper clippings: 'Global Pandemic Death Count Hits 12 Million'; 'Island of Java Wiped Out by Major Tsunami'; 'Minute Men and Three-Percenters Militias occupy Ohio and Kansas State Capitals and Enforce Curfew'; and 'Four Hundred Dead Illegals Found Washed Up on the Shores of the Rio Grande'. Another glass case held a crumpled scrap of paper. On it, scrawled in capitals were the words:

> The thread follows the needle,
> The minute follows the second,
> The hour follows the minute,
> The needle stitches us together.
> We are the thread—
> That follows the needle.

'Is this the draft of the prayer your people said before dinner?' I turned to the young man.

'You read surprisingly well for a trader,' said the young man, raising his eyebrows, as the ripe pimple on his chin bobbed up and down. 'Dupre wrote it himself. He wanted the people of the Needle to become the fabric of a new world.'

I swallowed hard and shifted from foot to foot. Had I given myself away?

'My father always insisted that I learn how to read. He said it would help keep me safe.'

'A sensible decision. The dustlands are so dangerous—toxic waste dumps, nuclear reactors still in meltdown, old army firing ranges,' he paused, his eyes scanning me. 'My birth name is Isaiah.'

'Mine's Charlotte,' I said. Again, I felt measured—a thoroughbred mare at a racehorse sale—by this young man with acne spots and tofu flecks caught in his moustache.

'Ahh, Charlotte,' said Isaiah. 'Jeremiah mentioned you to me.'

'Why?'

'He said that you and your father seemed more educated than most traders and might be interested in this museum.'

'True,' I said, trying to look pleased.

'So where does your interest in physics stem from?'

'My father told me about physics and how gravity is the reason we don't spin off the earth into the sun.'

'I'm glad to see that not all knowledge is lost out in the dustlands. Here, let me show you something.'

Isaiah led me into a small room behind the bookshelves. Inside was a bed and a desk with a magnifying glass on an adjustable arm clipped to it.

'I'm restoring Kepplar's research notes and lab journals here.' Isaiah pointed to his desk, on which sat a yellow legal pad and a binder filled with archive-quality plastic slips.

I recognised the blue script looping across pages of the yellow legal pad. The same pages featured on the photographic plates in Kepplar's autobiography. The fountain-pen ink was smudged in places and the ring of a coffee mug stained the top right-hand corner. Part of me wanted to sit down and start flicking through the pages straight away, searching for references to anomalies and the by-products of dark matter. Yet I held back, as Odysseus had said we were traders and an interest in mathematical formulas might prove dangerous.

'At the moment, I'm placing them in this binder to protect them. They'll soon be on display with the other documents written by Kepplar's holy hand.'

Isaiah began reading out loud the headings for each set of notes and formulae: '*Thermodynamics Systems, Wormhole Creation, Computational Particles,* and so on. Here, sit down and have a look.'

I took his place with Kepplar's notes in front of me. I put on a set of white gloves and flipped over a page of the legal pad.

'Careful,' warned Isaiah.

I placed the loose page down on the table and then I felt it: the momentary twinge of electricity at my fingertips, the taste of acid in my mouth, a bright flash in my brain and pain searing backwards from my eyes.

I peered through the glass panel of an office door. Above the door, in gold lettering, were the words UC Berkeley Physics Department. *Inside, James Kepplar sat at a computer with a box-like monitor. Nearby was a metal coil, vacuum sealed in glass, connected to pressure valves and measuring dials where arrows flickered. He wrote on the same yellow legal pad. In one corner, a TV showed a basketball game: Michael Jordan mid-air, No. 32 for Utah rising to meet him, as the ball was slam-dunked for two. A commentator's voice: 'Chicago takes an 82-80 lead with less than a minute to go in the sixth game of the play-offs. Can the Bulls win three titles straight again?'*

Isaiah put his hand on my shoulder and I rubbed my eyes. I felt the back of the desk chair and the scrape of the smock against my skin.

'Are you okay?' he asked. 'You seemed to black out for a second there?'

'No, I'm fine,' I said, getting up from the chair. 'Just tired, that's all. Thank you. I should return to my father.'

'You're welcome to stay here and recover,' said Isaiah, brushing against my arm. It was then I noticed how he positioned himself between me and the doorway.

'No, it's okay,' I said and pushed past him.

I ran up the stairs, taking two at a time. In Level 5, Section B2, I found Odysseus lying awake on his bed. There was one alongside for me. We were the only two in a four-bed dormitory. The rest of the Needlers slept in eight-bed dorms in shifts.

I told him about Kepplar's notes and what I saw.

'Good,' he said. 'That gives us more to go on.'

I also told him about Isaiah and the way he looked at me.

'That doesn't surprise me,' said Odysseus. 'How do you think they maintain the genetic integrity of this place? By taking in outsiders or forcing those who come to trade to stay. That's why those health checks were so important—not just to make sure we weren't carrying any diseases, but to assess our suitability. I'm too old, but you're the perfect age for bearing children.'

'But what about Kepplar's notes?'

'We need to wait until most of the Needlers are asleep and then steal them. The Needlers won't move on you until tomorrow morning when they think we'll try to leave. Remember, whatever happens, be careful, Charlie. You don't want to be stuck in this

Chrono-sphere for the rest of your life. This place is a cult, and they'll see our theft as a form of sacrilege. I'd hate to think what they would do to us if they found out our true purpose.'

16

Despite the situation, I fell asleep quickly, comforted by the dormitory bed and its white sheets. The last time I'd slept had been against the concrete wall until the crying of that wind-up doll woke me. Suddenly, I felt cold and pulled the sheet and blanket over me, but I didn't warm up. There was a presence standing above me, breathing ice onto my face, two paws holding down my shoulders.

'Charlie! Charlie!' Odysseus shook my shoulders.

I sat up and rubbed my eyes.

'You're freezing,' he said.

'I know,' I said, pulling the blanket over my shoulders. 'I dreamt of a syneghast.'

'Hopefully, we can pull this off before a syneghast appears.'

The Tempus Imperium's face glowed 12:34 am.

'Most of the Needlers are asleep. We should be okay as long as we keep quiet,' whispered Odysseus.

Odysseus and I crept past several rooms of sleeping Needlers, the only light coming from the Tempus Imperiums on our wrists. Every dormitory was arranged like a military encampment, with each bed two metres from the next. On the left side of each bed sat a bedside table and a pair of slippers. In the beds, people lay snoring, stretching out their limbs, or curled into foetal positions.

I knew how to be quiet, as I had spent my teenage years in a school boarding house creeping between midnight feasts and using Fire Exits to sneak out to parties. Silence came not from standing on your toes, but from patience.

We soon made it to the spiral staircase, thirteen floors above the museum. We crept down the stairs, keeping to the shadows, the fluorescents from earlier now dimmed for the night. Part of me wanted to run down these stairs, taking two or more at a time, but I knew the danger. One misstep and I'd have a sprained or fractured ankle, putting us both in jeopardy.

Behind me, a gear clanked and shifted. I sucked in my breath and held it. Up ahead, Odysseus froze. I crouched low, hidden by the stair rail. Inside, my blood pressure rose, a flash flood of panic threatening. A metallic hum grew louder as the steel cables in the centre of the Needle moved upwards. A glass elevator emerged from behind the stair rail. Inside were pallets of food and other supplies, and a white-bearded man scribbling away in a notebook. He didn't look up once as the elevator passed our hiding place.

'Phew!' I slumped against the wall once the steel cable stopped moving and waited for my heart rate to slow down.

'Up, Charlie!' hissed Odysseus. 'Only five more floors to go.'

<< · ✕ · >>

Odysseus held open the museum's heavy doors as I crept past him.

Where were Kepplar's research notes? We checked the bookshelves and the display cabinets. Please, I prayed to myself, let

157

them be out on display now. Yet they were nowhere to be found.

'Damn!' I said. 'The papers must still be in Isaiah's room at the back.'

Odysseus sighed and clenched his fists. 'Tell me where they are, and I'll get them.'

'No, I'm the only one who's been in Isaiah's room before. I'll do it.'

'Are you certain, Charlie?'

'Yes,' I said, 'I can do this.'

'Penny would be proud. I'll keep watch on the staircase outside.'

I gulped and turned towards Isaiah's door.

Isaiah kept the door to his bedroom and study ajar. He slept on a bed arranged like the ones in the upstairs dormitories, with slippers to the left and a bedside cabinet upon which sat a half-finished glass of water. He snored. Drool dribbled down his chin.

Using the light from my Tempus Imperium, I searched his desk as quietly as possible. I soon found the binder containing Kepplar's research notes amongst a pile of books on Isaiah's desk.

'Charlotte? What are you doing here?' Isaiah sat up in bed and switched on the light.

I gasped, clutching the binder close to my chest.

'What are you doing with Kepplar's notes?'

'I need them. You wouldn't understand.'

'Put them down,' said Isaiah, standing up and snatching a pocketknife from his desk. 'Those belong to the Needle.'

'I can't,' I said and backed towards the door, but Isaiah was too quick and blocked my exit.

'Stop!' Isaiah demanded, as he nicked my left cheek and pushed me against the wall. I dropped the binder. The knife's blade glinted beneath drops of my blood. Isaiah's left hand touched my right hip, and pushed, like a shopper testing fruit for ripeness.

'I'm disappointed—so disappointed. Stealing Kepplar's notes? But it doesn't matter, you'll make a good breeding partner.'

'What the—'

'When Jeremiah told me about a female outsider, aged roughly eighteen, I knew my prayers to Kepplar and Dupre had been answered. The thought of being alone, of not being assigned a breeding partner, scared me, but then you came along. Wide child-bearing hips, clear of disease, no major disfigurements—perfect.'

'No,' I said, recoiling from Isaiah's hot breath on my neck as the tip of his tongue tasted my ear. 'I'm warning you. I'll call my father.'

'No, you won't!' hissed Isaiah, pressing the blade again to my chin. 'When Jeremiah and the other Elders find out...'

'Isaiah, I can't. You don't under—' I said, as the light in the room went out, snuffed out by shadows.

'A power blackout,' said Isaiah. 'Don't worry, they'll soon have the system back up.'

I shuddered at the coldness spreading up from the floor. Our UV torches were in storage with the rest of our clothes. Isaiah shivered and released me.

'Don't you dare move or make a sound,' he said. 'I've still got my knife.'

Isaiah took a match and lit a candle on his desk.

'This is strange. It's never this cold in the Needle.'

'Isaiah, be careful. It's a syneghast.'

'A what?'

'A by-product of dark matter. It's why we need Kepplar's research notes.'

'So you're not traders then?'

Isaiah's hand touched my hip again. The adrenaline flared

through my body like a flint being struck, and I brought my left knee up and into Isaiah's groin.

'You bitch! You bitch!' moaned Isaiah, falling to the ground.

I grabbed Kepplar's notes and left, taking Isaiah's candle with me.

'Odysseus! Odysseus!'

'Out here, Charlie.'

A *crack* echoed through the room. For a second, Odysseus stood holding the door open, then he crumpled to the ground. Behind me stood Isaiah, holding Dupre's hunting rifle.

'Look,' Isaiah giggled, 'It still works. I've been meaning to catalogue this properly for ages.' He pointed Dupre's hunting rifle at me.

Even with the light from the candle, the darkness grew. The chill solidified around us as the floor began to rumble.

'What's that!' said Isaiah, moving the rifle again. Three sets of yellow eyes came into focus. A low, deep growl echoed through the room as their paws scratched against the concrete floor. Two syneghasts circled Isaiah, but the last one focused only on me.

'Keep back! I mean it, keep back!' said Isaiah, but the syneghasts came closer.

'Stay back!' he screamed before firing off a volley of shots. *Plop! Plop!* Like water drops hitting a kitchen sponge, the syneghast absorbed the bullets.

'Charlie! Charlie!' a voice screamed. 'You need fire!'

I tried to move, but the chill bound me to the ground. I looked at the notes in my hand. Please don't let this be the one we need, I prayed, as I scrunched the first page into a ball. Despite the weight of the cold around me, I nicked the edge of the scrunched paper on the candle's flame and then flicked it towards the syneghast. As it shot from my hand, it flared bright yellow like a comet in the night sky until *whoosh!* Red flame shot upwards and the syneghast howled and burned in front of me.

'Charlie, you need to make the incursion now,' Odysseus said, a red stain spreading from his right shoulder.

'But what about you?'

'I'll hold the other ones off.'

'But Odysseus!'

'No Charlie, you need to go.'

'Odysseus!'

I set the coordinates for the Temporal Sinistrum on my Tempus Imperium.

Odysseus leant up against the glass display that held Kepplar's fountain pen. 'Here! Over here!' he called. Two of the syneghasts circled him. Isaiah's blank-eyed body lay stiff on the ground nearby as I disappeared into the white light.

17

And some in dreams assurèd were
Of the Spirit that plagued us so;
Nine fathom deep he had followed us
From the land of mist and snow.
Samuel Taylor Coleridge

France, September 1916

John closed his copy of the *Lyrical Ballads*, making sure none of the pages fell out. He had already lost several pages of Wordsworth's 'Preludes' and didn't want to lose any by Coleridge as well. He wrapped the book in an oilskin cloth and placed it inside his pack. *Thud! Thud!* Dirt trickled from the ceiling and the lamps rattled as another shell landed nearby.

John slapped his hand down on the back of his left forearm, catching a louse. It wriggled between his fingertips before he flicked it into the fire. He heard it *sizzle*, then *pop*. Before John had come to France, life had been a progression from grammar school to Cambridge. He tackled it with the rhythm of his rowing eight. *Stroke... stroke... stroke...* He'd intended to earn his law degree and practice in London. *Stroke... stroke... stroke...* Then he would marry his fiancée Emma, and have two children—a blond-haired boy like his mother and a little girl with his blue eyes. *Stroke... stroke... stroke...* In ten years' time, he saw himself standing by a fireplace and enjoying his pipe, a spaniel by his feet and the children playing around him. But then they'd declared war, and he'd caught a 'crab'—missed a stroke—and almost capsized. *Stroke...* Two weeks ago, Emma had written to him saying that she wished to break off their engagement. John hadn't replied yet, but he knew the delay could be blamed on the war-time post. Now his only satisfaction came from receiving socks from the Red Cross, and an extra ration of bully beef. At least where he sat, perched against a wall of turf, he was dry. Spread across the dugout's floor were several planks of wood that kept the officers' feet dry, unlike the enlisted men outside.

Yesterday morning, John had found a soldier dead. Though his brains decorated the sandbags behind him, the man was still gripping his rifle. However, the Captain had made it clear they must treat it as a death by sniper rather than suicide. The dead man's wife, mother and father were not to know; instead, the soldier would be blessed with an honourable death. The other soldiers weren't fools, as they knew what a trench suicide looked like. In the last year, one man hanged himself from a roof beam in a dugout, while another had stripped off all his clothes and run out into No-Man's Land, to be finished off by a German sniper.

Since the start of the July offensive, John's unit had been bogged down in this trench near the River Somme. An enemy machine gun that took down ten men at a time had ended their approach.

For days afterwards, John had heard the voices of those still trapped in No-Man's Land, a hoarse choir that cried, 'Water!', 'Help!', and 'Please!' throughout the day and night. Several times, he'd kicked at the sandbags and bruised his toes. Two stretcher teams went out under the cover of darkness, but sniper bullets chased them back to their trenches. By the fifth day, only one voice still called for water.

Some nights, in between the shells landing nearby and the quick *crack* of a sniper's gun, he dreamed of his childhood copper tub and his nursemaid Dorie filling it with steaming water in front of the kitchen fireplace and washing the grime off his knees with a rag, then soaping up his hair and running a comb through it.

John hated being so close to the River Somme. When the men dug down, they hit water, filling the trenches with mud. Mud that sucked off boots, rotted feet, and occasionally even drowned the rats that ran through the trenches. A week ago, the men had pulled out several bones while excavating a trench. Much too big for a man or horse, they became a favourite topic of conversation. One bone measured two yards and reminded Tom Williams, a farmer's son, of an oversized cow's thigh bone. They'd even found a skull with jaws big enough to fit a man's head inside, the teeth pointed and sharp.

'Sir, what kind of beasts are these?' the men asked.

'Dinosaurs. Prehistoric beasts from the dawn of time. They died out before mankind existed,' John explained, relying on his childhood memories of a trip to the Natural History Museum in London. Would they die out too? Thousands of men killed by machine guns and armour-plated tanks the size of the dinosaurs?

John stood up and pulled on his pack. Today, his unit needed to move further down the lines. Their orders directed them to move to another trench closer to Amiens. He pulled his father's silver watch from his pocket, a gift on his enlistment that required winding by four o'clock every day. On the back were the words 'Be strong, saith my heart; I am a soldier,' from Homer's *Odyssey*. Despite being a village rector, his father was a classicist at heart. Even John's middle name, Odysseus, had come from Homer's text. Homer's *Iliad*, *The Odyssey*, the poetry of Virgil, the plays of Aeschylus and Sophocles and the *Histories of Herodotus* filled his father's study. Sometimes as a child his father had let him touch one of the Roman coins with its picture of a dead emperor, or pottery fragments that he kept in a small glass-fronted curio cabinet on a bookshelf. The last remnants of a civilisation that had ended fifteen hundred years ago after being ransacked by barbarians.

'Are the men all present, Sergeant Hayes?' asked John.

'Yes, sir.'

'Well, let's go then.'

Since the start of the war, Hayes had been with John. He wore a moustache like Kitchener's that flourished in spite of the conditions. It sprouted out from beneath his nose and looped around his cheeks and finished in two pointed tips. When Hayes talked, he liked to twist one of these points. Before the war, Hayes had worked as a factory foreman in Birmingham, but had found his true calling in the trenches. If a soldier needed new boots, Hayes found them. If the men needed fresh socks, Hayes sweet-talked the Red Cross. Last Christmas, Hayes had surprised John and his fellow officers with a still-squawking goose under one arm. Earlier that week, he had even managed to heat some water and find John a shaving mirror. For the first time in weeks, John had seen himself: eyes dark-ringed, chin covered by a ragged beard, only his bent nose still recognisable. He had broken it in a boxing match in his first year at Cambridge.

As they left the trench line, John surveyed his unit. The

men—or should he call them boys?—could barely hold an orderly march. Some looked just out of the nursery, with high-pitched, warbling voices that belonged in a cathedral choir. Only a few remained from when John had taken command of this unit. Somehow, despite their attempts to cross No-Man's Land and the artillery bombardments, these men had survived. John wondered what made them different? James MacDonald had been a shop assistant in a haberdashery, whereas Tom Williams had worked on the family farm and didn't know his letters. In his first week on the Somme, John's commanding officer had blown a whistle and ordered them to attack, and a bullet had hit his forehead. The man had fallen to the ground with the whistle still stuck between his teeth. It didn't seem to matter whether you went to Cambridge or Oxford, or whether you signed your enlistment papers with an 'x': machine guns didn't discriminate.

Alongside John, a private hobbled, his boots too big and loose. John winced, well aware of the pain shredded blisters and wet feet caused.

'Private, those boots look too big for you.'

'Yes, sir. It's all the depot had.'

'What's your name, Private.'

'Private George Wallace, sir.'

'Well, Private Wallace. I'll see if Sergeant Hayes can find you another set once we get to our post.'

'Thank you, sir.'

The private smiled, a few stray hairs clinging to his chin beneath the grime. He must be barely eighteen, and that was if he hadn't lied about his age. His blue eyes and ready smile reminded John of Timmy, his younger brother. He could make anyone laugh with his tales of dumping Sally Piggott's plaits in

166

an inkwell or stealing extra buns from the shelf in the pantry. Gosh, he even drove their Sunday School teacher to distraction, despite being the rector's son. However, no one ever stayed mad at Timmy for long. John had always known that Timmy was his mother's favourite, but he didn't care. Everyone loved Timmy: from the village girls to Mrs Davies, the elderly widow whose arm he took before the Sunday services and guided to a pew. John sighed to himself, thinking about Timmy as though he were back home and still teasing Mother. Yet Timmy lay somewhere in France. He knew from his mother's letters that grief had silenced the family home again. His father in his study pored over his texts in Ancient Greek and Latin, while his mother knitted sock after sock by herself in front of the fire. Now only John carried the Clay name. His little sister Evelyn already had her own gravestone in the churchyard. A bright inquisitive baby, who'd laughed when John played peekaboo with her, she'd woken up one day with a fever and red spots. Dead within two days, they buried her in the grave next to Edward, John's eldest brother, who had drowned swimming in the local river aged twelve.

After two hours, John and his unit reached the remnants of a forest. Only a few faded orange and yellow leaves remained on the trees. It's autumn, thought John, and I hadn't even realised. Despite the overcast sky, there was a glimmer of gold that trickled through the forest like honey. John muttered Keats to himself: *Seasons of mists and mellow fruitfulness / Close bosom-friend of the maturing sun.* He wanted to stop for a moment and savour this colour, let his eyes taste it before the grey of the battlefield overwhelmed it, but he knew he couldn't. The men panted around him, bent over and using their rifle butts as walking sticks, awaiting his orders.

'Gas! Gas! Quick!'

John pulled on his gas mask. Once, on a summer holiday at Brighton, he'd seen a diver emerge from the sea. His eyes were encased in glass goggles, his head entombed inside an urn-shaped helmet. Now his men dove through their own green sea. Their eyes were wide behind their masks as waves of gas buffeted them, rolling through the forest and trapping them inside a green twilight.

A hand pulled at John's arm, and he stumbled against a tree. Beside him Wallace was on his knees, hands clawing at his throat. He kept opening his mouth wider and wider, gulping in the gas like water. A gas mask lay at his feet with a broken rubber strap. John sat the boy against a tree and waited for the gas to dissipate. His hands balled into fists by his sides.

Soon he and his men found a truck carrying the wounded and added Wallace to the dismembered and blinded in the back. John left him propped up and unseeing, his red eyes unfocused and flailing in his pale face.

In his head, John began the letter to Wallace's family: *Dear Mr and Mrs Wallace, I am writing to inform you*, his words in time with his plodding steps. By now he had written twenty such letters: messages of condolence and an acknowledgement of their loved one's service. And now yet another soldier whose life story had been limited to two paragraphs, some fountain-pen ink and a sheet of paper. John knew the shape a woman's body makes when she learns of her child's death. He remembered his own mother when they'd told her that his brother, Edward, had drowned at the local swimming hole. The village constable had held his hat while standing on their front doorstep, while his mother swayed backwards and his father stiffened into stone. The curse of her sobs had echoed throughout the house for days. Would Wallace's mother react this way? Or would she swoon and faint?

Soon John and his men turned away from the truck's path, as their route lay closer to the Front. John led the men in single file back down into the labyrinth built from sandbags, mud, and wooden planks. Part of him wanted to grab a ball of string and unravel it behind him so he could find his way out again. He'd always liked the story of Thescus and the Minotaur. The Devil-like Minotaur, with his ox head and horns, who consumed the best of Athens's youth like this war.

They passed men warming themselves over fires in steel drums, three playing cards, and others trying to sleep. They even passed a hand emerging from a wall, with only a few shreds of leathery skin still attached. The soldiers liked to give these corpses names—'Right-turn Joe' or 'Left-hand Pete'—and shake their hands for luck. Rats scurried past, their fat bellies making them easy targets. John kicked four out of the way, sending them into the trench wall with a *plop*. Finally, around the twenty-third corner, John found the East Lancashire Fusiliers and their next posting.

'So, you've made it,' said Lieutenant Holstead.

'Lieutenant Clay, sir. Johnathan Odysseus Clay. We lost a man to a gas attack.'

'Only one. That's a relief. We've been under-manned for days and they want us to launch another offensive against the Jerry-line over that ridge soon.'

'Yes, sir.'

'Tell your men to bunk where they can. They must be exhausted. I'll get my batman Mitchell to fix us some supper.'

Despite the meal comprising only stale bread with drippings, John gulped it down. Holstead poured John a measure of whiskey that soon made him nod with tiredness.

'You look spent, Clay. We'll talk tomorrow. Jerry's barrage

usually starts around six o'clock.'

John found himself a dry corner and pulled his blanket up to his chin. He was soon asleep.

<< · ✕ · >>

John awoke when a trickle of dirt hit his face. He coughed and flicked it off his nose. No one else was awake, so he put on his helmet and headed outside. Two men were on watch, their faces framed by the glow of their cigarettes. The dawn, bandaged by a gauze of mist, hid the ruptured skin of No-Man's Land beneath. John rubbed his hands together and cracked his knuckles as his breath crystallised into a cloud of steam. One soldier offered him a cigarette.

'When do you think the attack will be, Lieutenant?' said the soldier.

'Maybe today or tomorrow? Depends on what the generals have to say.'

'You know it wasn't your fault, sir. They gave Wallace a shoddy mask, and the straps broke.'

John scrutinised the man who spoke. He'd thought he knew most of the old-timers, those that had been with him since 1914. There were only about five left. But this man with his receding hairline appeared at least forty years old, and John didn't recognise him. Perhaps he was one of Holstead's men?

John looked for the second soldier.

'Oh, don't worry, sir. Fitz has gone off to find some tea for breakfast,' said the man.

John nodded.

'Do you ever think there's a bigger purpose at work here, sir?'

John paused. Just what he needed: a conversation with a

God-botherer to start the morning. He might have grown up the son of a village rector who'd based his sermons on the Gospels, where Christ told parables about a good Samaritan and a Prodigal Son and didn't punish people with plagues and pestilence, but the trenches were full of these one-note-preachers with their Bibles and prayer books, who saw the fires of hell in the enemy flares at night and damnation in every soldier's death. They seemed to have forgotten about eternal life and instead awaited for the Four Horseman of the Apocalypse and the Last Judgement. John believed such men needed to be court-martialled and sent to gaol. They upset the ordinary troops, who needed to believe that there was something better than seeing their best mate blown to bits or being so hungry that even a rat looked appetising.

'Don't worry, sir,' the soldier smiled. 'I'm not a preacher. Just a thinker. Hinze, Richard,' he said in what John realised was a Yankee accent.

18

My grandmother's last words as she slipped away in my arms. Odysseus calling the two syneghasts towards him as I made my incursion. The blood stain on the mattress where the girl's father once laid. Now I stood crying inside a sparking geodesic dome.

'Are you okay, dear?' said Madam Zhao. 'You look positively transparent. Why don't you rest for a minute?' Her eyes were wide as she helped me to a nearby chair.

'Where's Odysseus?'

'I don't think he made it.' Sobs fractured my words.

'Oh,' Madam Zhao's face stiffened for a moment. 'Here, drink this. It's Longling tea and it'll warm you up.'

My body shuddered in a series of seismic waves that nearly toppled me.

'You're in shock.'

Someone placed a blanket across my shoulders. In my left hand, I still clutched the yellow pages of Kepplar's research notes.

The tea tasted strong and bitter, quelling my quakes. On the wall, the clock flickered in red streaks, but still the time remained the same at '14:03 27/04/2025'.

'I have Kepplar's notes.'

'I can see that, dear. Why don't you leave them here? I'll make sure they get to Hinze. You should rest and have something to eat before the debrief.'

'But I'm fine!' I protested, despite knowing it was a lie.

'Charlie, you haven't stopped crying since you arrived. You need medical attention and rest.'

My cheek still bled from Isaiah's knife, while tears left grey and crimson smudges on my linen smock. Madam Zhao was right, I needed to recalibrate. A place to rip this smock off me and scrub away all traces of the ruined city and the Needle. She helped me to the same room as before, where the SOAP Manual still lay open.

'Charlie, you'll find soap and a towel in the ensuite. Your clothes are where you left them on the bed.'

'Okay.'

'Once you've showered, there's a small first aid kit in the vanity cabinet. In it you'll find some antiseptic cream and steri-strips for your cheek.'

I nodded, because I couldn't say anymore without weeping again.

'I'll check on you later,' said Madam Zhao as she shut the bedroom door.

Inside the shower, I screamed and sobbed, the pounding water and steam cocooning me. I wanted to punch the tiles but didn't. Instead, I balled my hands into fists, where the nails drew specks of blood.

Afterwards, I lay again on the single bed—counting to five

and taking deep breaths. My hands touched the bedspread, then my forehead and chest. This felt genuine enough, cotton and skin.

I thought I couldn't sleep, but it came for me instead. A black mass crashing into me, mid-thought, leaving me splayed across the bed.

«·X·»

I slept for over twelve hours, only waking when my bladder hurt so much that I dreamt of Isaiah's knife disembowelling me. Beside me on the bedside table sat a fresh glass of water and a sandwich wrapped in plastic. I tore into my food like the child from the ruined city eating a protein bar. However, the chicken in the sandwich tasted flat and rubbery, making my stomach feel queasy.

Madam Zhao knocked and then opened my door. 'I'm so glad you're up, Charlie. Hinze wants to debrief you now. He's already had our best physicists, engineers and technicians pouring over what you brought back.'

As we walked towards Hinze's office, Madam Zhao squeezed my arm. 'I'm so sorry about Odysseus. He's been part of the Sinistrum longer than I have.'

I nodded, despite my tears.

'You should know why your grandmother left us. She thought that the Sinistrum had become too powerful, and she'd had enough. Penny wanted an ordinary life, filled with family and children, where she didn't know what was to come.'

For a moment I remembered Penny, and me, age five, wandering through the public gardens at Mount Lofty, as the sun hung low in the west, the trees, the plants, even the birds, sparkling in the late afternoon sunlight. I'd picked up a dandelion and my grandmother had said, 'Blow Charlie! Make a wish!' I blew as hard as my lungs allowed, and the dandelion's seeds danced away on the wind.

'Look, Grandma! They're like tiny fairies.'

'You're right, Charlie,' she said. 'Remember Charlie, remember this moment. Take the time to delight in everything around you.'

Penny told me this when such thoughts were too big to fit inside my five-year-old head. I had run off, chasing the dandelion seeds. Thirteen years later, I finally understood what she meant. I saw the Needle, the rubble of a city crumbled into dust, a child skinning a cat for food, and I hated it. Ignorance was the comfort food that you wallowed in—a tub of chocolate ice cream, that packet of Tim Tams in the cupboard, hot chips with chicken salt—despite the extra flabbiness around the waist. But I couldn't do this anymore, as I knew what would come if we didn't stop the syneghasts. Would these notes make a difference? Stop that future I saw, and set another in motion?

'It's all right, Charlie,' said Madam Zhao, embracing me as I cried.

I pulled away from Madam Zhao and swallowed hard. She passed me a silk handkerchief embroidered with a beautiful bird. I wiped my eyes and then looked at the image again: a phoenix rising with wings outstretched, beak pointing upwards, and a plumage of flames in orange, red, and purple.

'A phoenix?'

'Yes, the ancient Greeks believed that when a phoenix died, it would be reborn. Odysseus gave it to me. He found it in a Tabriz bazaar in Tehran, just before the fall of the Shah.'

'I'm sorry,' I said. 'For staining something so beautiful,' as I passed it back.

'No, that's fine—what else are handkerchiefs useful for? Come on, we best get a move on. Hinze doesn't like to be kept waiting.'

«·✕·»

Hinze sat behind his desk, his foot tapping the floor at an aggressive pace. When I entered the room, he stood up and shook my hand, his eyes fixed on mine.

'I'm so sorry, Charlie. Odysseus was one of our best.'

I gulped.

'Why don't you take a seat? Madam Zhao's already explained some of what's happened,' Hinze nodded at Madam Zhao, who still stood in the doorway.

'I'll check in on you later, Charlie,' she said before departing.

'We've looked at those research notes you brought back,' said Hinze. 'But it's not enough. We need more details about Kepplar's Unified Field Machine and its connection to the syneghasts.'

There were no words for how I felt—did Odysseus die for nothing? These notes were as worthless as the ash that blew in the ruined city.

'I don't understand. I did what you asked and brought them back. Odysseus sacrificed himself for these papers.'

Hinze's gaze sharpened as he looked at me. There was an edge to him I recognised. Despite the civilities of handshakes and gin and tonics, he kept something hidden. When I was seven, Dad and I drove to Adelaide down through the hills, tailgated by another car. At the first set of lights after the freeway exit, the other driver got out of his car and approached us. Despite the camouflage of a BMW convertible and a designer polo shirt, this man stood on the same precipice as Hinze. The one where rage sat bubbling under the surface, waiting for a crack to vent. *Tread carefully*, I told myself.

'Are you certain you've told me everything?'

The words hung in the air. *Were they an executioner's blade at the start of its swing? Or were they a lifebuoy thrown towards me as I trod water?* Odysseus and Madam Zhao trusted Hinze. *Maybe I was wrong?* Maybe this edge was more to do with a man who could see his Sinistrum crumbling into dust? Foundations of stone and concrete liquefied into silt. I had already lost my grandmother, then Odysseus. The Fulcrum appeared as inevitable as the earth spinning and the sun rising. I decided to tell Hinze about my vision when I first touched Kepplar's research notes; the one where I saw him working in his lab in Berkeley in the 1990s.

'Ahh, I forgot you have the same gift as Penny. Thank you for sharing that with me,' said Hinze. His shoulders relaxed as he eased back in his seat and put his hands behind his head.

'Mmm, based on what you've told me, we need to send an adjudicator to Berkeley, but what date? It's clear it's the mid-1990s, but we need more details to construct a proper set of coordinates.'

Fragments flickered before me, like a match, hissing and fluttering, before erupting in flame. *Kepplar writing on his yellow legal pad; a small TV set in the background, showing an NBA game between the Chicago Bulls and Utah Jazz.* I forced my brain to zoom in on this TV set. *Michael Jordan mid-air, No. 32 for Utah rising to meet him, but he slam-dunks the ball for two points. A commentator's voice: 'Chicago takes an 82-80 lead with less than a minute to go in the sixth game of the play-offs. Can the Bulls win three titles straight and six in total in the Jordan era?'*

'The Chicago Bulls versus the Utah Jazz in the sixth game of the play-offs? That's excellent, Charlie.'

I exhaled and dropped my shoulders.

'But, we still have the problem of whom to send on this incursion? With Odysseus dead and the decimation of our ranks by the syneghasts, we are almost out of adjudicators.'

Hinze looked at me again, but this time I sensed calculations taking place.

'We have two currently on an incursion, and Natsuko is still recovering in the infirmary.' Hinze counted to three on his fingers and paused, before looking me over again. His gaze was abrasive, designed to scrape away my defences and assess me for who I truly was. I fidgeted with my Tempus Imperium, clicking the crown around several stops.

'You have the same talent as your grandmother and you know what is at stake with the Fulcrum now. Normally, I wouldn't even consider sending someone so inexperienced into the field by themselves. Would you consider doing this incursion for us?'

Part of me wanted to say no, walk out of Hinze's office, head down to the landing area, and set the coordinates for 2016 on the Tempus Imperium. I would be home in time to feed Telemachus and do my law homework. I felt I had seen enough: Odysseus's death, the orphaned child and her mannequin family, the rusted ruins of Los Angeles, and Isaiah's knife glinting with drops of my blood. Yet the thought of Penny held me back; she had left me this watch for a reason.

《·✕·》

Within twenty-four hours, I stood under the geodesic dome next to the Memoria Factoreum, where the cross-bars vibrated and sparked at the vertices. In the background, the coils of the Unified

Field Machine hummed in the single syllable of monotone. Madam Zhao scurried around the dome with her clipboard, double-checking the dials and computer monitors.

'Mmm,' she said, furrowing her brow. 'Pradeep, can you adjust the secondary exhaust fan?'

The Factoreum let out a low groan before it started whistling. A cloud of steam filled the room, making the dome spark and sizzle even more.

'What's going on?'

'Be patient, Charlie. I need to ensure that the Factoreum is stable before I let you make the incursion.'

My legs felt jittery and tangled with nerves. By repeatedly shifting my weight from foot to foot, I kept most of the tension under control.

Madam Zhao sighed and put the clipboard down.

'I think we've settled the overheating issue for now,' she said, passing me the coordinates on a piece of paper, along with a UV torch, small enough to fit in my back pocket.

'Hinze himself checked them,' she said.

'Thanks,' I said, as I twisted the bezel's rim and wound the complication and the date of the Tempus Imperium into the correct position.

'Ready?'

'Yes.'

'I'm sure Penny would have been proud. You'll make the pre-incursion on one.'

'Five, four, three, two…'

I pressed down on the Tempus Imperium's pin, just as steam filled the Factoreum's room and an earth-shattering rumble made the walls and ceiling shake, as dozens of alarms went off.

'Charlie!' I heard Madam Zhao calling, 'You need to abort now. She's over–!'

Her words cut off mid-sentence by the white light that consumed me.

19

San Diego, May 1978

I landed—crashed, might be a better way to describe it—in the back alleyway behind a Safeway supermarket. At least I didn't vomit this time. I sat with my head cradled between my knees, my back against a graffitied wall. What had just happened? My ears still rung with the sound of the Factoreum shaking, a rolling rumble that seemed to crescendo as I disappeared. Had it overheated? Damn, where was I? I stared at my Tempus Imperium—5:43 am on 21 May 1978—and blinked.

'Turn out the lights! It's too bright!' grumbled a voice behind me.

I whipped around to where a man lay crumpled in a doorway. 'Turn out the lights!' he said again before he pulled a piece of cardboard over his head and began snoring, two empty bottles of Wild Turkey by his side. A cat threaded through my feet, nearly tripping me. Sheets of newspapers fluttered in the wind: 'Welcome Home to the USS Midway, San Diego's Missed You!'

San Diego? I looked closer at the date under the newspaper's headline—*San Diego Tribune*, 5th May 1978. What? My heart thumped against my chest: nineteen years too early and seven hundred and fifty kilometres from Berkeley. Why? Did the Factoreum overheating throw me this far off course? *How was I meant to find Kepplar now?*

≪·✕·≫

As the sun rose, I came across a baseball field. On each side of the diamond were three rows of wooden seats covered in cracked red paint. I took a seat and tried to think. Should I return to the Temporal Sinistrum? Or should I continue with my mission? The question made me panic, and for a second, I saw Odysseus calling the two syneghasts towards him. What would he or Penny do?

Families trickled into the baseball ground for a Little League match. I felt self-conscious in my jeans and purple top. Most of the men had crew-cuts and the biceps that came from outdoor work. My history teacher, Mr Mortimer, had once said that after Pearl Harbour, what remained of the United States' Pacific Fleet had retreated to San Diego. Perhaps I could pass for someone's big sister home for the weekend from college?

Most of the Little League players appeared around eleven years old. The better kids were pitching balls at a batter, whereas the others ran after their own dropped catches and overthrows. Only one boy stood to the side, his glove hanging by his waist as he stared at the ground.

'Catch, Jim! Catch!' called a teammate, but the boy didn't hear. A fly ball arced high in the sky and dropped, but only now did Jim see it. He held up his glove like a shield, flat above his head. The ball

182

tipped the top of his glove and hit the ground. The batter dropped his bat and stormed over. He was a head taller than the other boy and had already hit six home runs during the warm-up.

'Jim! Why do you bother turning up if you can't even catch an easy fly ball!'

Jim blinked back at him; his eyes huge behind his glasses.

'You're useless,' said the boy, giving Jim a shove.

'Boys! Boys! That's enough! The game's about to start, and we're batting first,' said the coach.

Jim didn't go to the dugout; instead, he sat in the bleachers near me, crying. His fringe flopped over his eyes.

'I hate it! I hate it!' he sobbed to himself.

Where were this kid's parents? All the other boys appeared to have a parent cheering them on, but this boy cried alone.

'Where's your parents?' I asked, hoping that my Australian accent wasn't too obvious. My fingers twisted at the ends of my hair.

'At work,' said Jim. 'Mum's a nurse and Dad's got a research paper to finish. They make me come by myself! I hate it! Billy's always pushing and shoving me.'

'I'm sorry.'

'I can't wait until I leave this place. I'm going to be a physicist and study at UC Berkeley. Dad reckons it's one of the best schools,' Jim snivelled.

What could I do? I had bigger problems, like being twenty years too early and seven hundred and fifty kilometres from Berkeley and Kepplar's lab. Yet something inside me stirred. The same thing that kept me on the phone for hours when friends complained about cheating boyfriends or the parental pressure to study medicine.

Comforting Jim seemed so much easier than dealing with my own problems. He even looked like my ten-year-old cousin,

Nate, with legs and arms that grew so fast that his brain struggled to coordinate them.

'Often the best way to deal with bullies is to get them to see you differently,' I said.

'How?'

'Just look for a chance.'

Jim nodded.

'Jim! Jim! Get down here now, right field!' yelled the coach from the sideline.

'Here, don't forget this,' I said as I passed him his baseball mitt. Printed in blue ink at the base of the glove was the name *Kepplar*.

'Kepplar?'

'Yes, my name's Jim, I mean James, Kepplar,' the boy said before heading out to right field.

My head whirled around and around on a show ride that never seemed to stop. An eleven-year-old Kepplar here? But how?

Inhale... one... two... three... four... five...

What had I done?

Exhale... one... two... three... four... five...

Focus on the game, Charlie, distract yourself. I shielded my eyes with my hand and stared hard again at the players on the field, despite the sun.

《·×·》

By the fifth innings, the Pacific Beach Dolphins were up 3-2 against the La Jolla Sharks. Billy pitched fast ball after fast ball, hard and flat, smacking into the catcher's glove with a *thwack*. Kepplar stood, nudging a dandelion with his foot, his eyes downcast. Sometimes when the coach reminded him, he pulled himself upright, cocked

184

his glove and followed the pitch into the catcher's glove, although he seemed more interested in the trail of ants making its way across the first base mound than the actual game being played.

The next batter was La Jolla's star. Like Billy, he seemed twice the size of the other kids on the team. His La Jolla Sharks shirt was too tight around his stocky frame. Yet Billy soon had him down for the count—two strikes and three fouls. He needed to hit the next one. Billy pitched another fast ball, but this time he curved it. The batter swatted at the ball, sending it speeding into Billy's glove, where it tipped the top and spun up into his jaw with a *pop*. Billy clutched his face and collapsed, howling. No one moved. The coach's mouth was still open from telling the short-stop to move left. Only Kepplar moved, dropping his mitt and running towards Billy. He put his hand on Billy's shoulder and helped him up.

'Here, use your glove to support your jaw,' he said. Billy leant into the smaller boy, but Kepplar braced himself and avoided staggering. He helped Billy into the dugout. Only then did the umpire call a time-out, and the coach started screaming for an ambulance for the Dupre boy.

The Dupre boy? Billy Dupre? Wasn't Billy a nickname for William, making his full name William Dupre? William Dupre was the venture capitalist who'd provided the funds for Kepplar's Unified Field Machine. The one I'd first heard about at the Needle. What had I done when I told an eleven-year-old Kepplar to take a chance and get Billy, his tormentor, to see him differently? Had my actions determined the Needle? Time was a spider's web spun on silken threads, where if one branch vibrated, the rest did. *Thrum... thrum... thrum...*

I felt dizzy and clutched the wooden seat underneath me with my hands. I closed my eyes and tried to focus. *Breathe Charlie, breathe.* I opened my eyes and found myself almost alone in the stands. The ambulance and families had departed, leaving only the coach behind to clean up the dugout.

Kepplar had found his moment, but now I needed to find mine. How would I work out the coordinates for Berkeley in 1997? I couldn't just grab my phone and open Google Maps. I had to do this the old-fashioned way and find a library to work out the exact coordinates for Berkeley, or my next incursion wouldn't work. The Little League field backed on to a junior high campus; surely there would be a library in there. But breaking and entering? This wasn't the Needle, or a ruined city, but a suburb filled with kids on skateboards and people carrying surfboards on their way to the beach.

I scouted the school grounds. On one side, a group of kids played basketball. I looked in the windows: science labs, classrooms, the gym, and an art room. In the canteen, a janitor mopped the floor. Finally, I found the library—row after row of shelves stacked with books. Library books? Actual physical books from when students like me knew how to navigate a catalogue and use a call number to locate a text, rather than just Googling it?

First, I needed to find the door that the janitor used. *Think, Charlie, it's the only place that will be unlocked—somewhere with bins and privacy for a cigarette break.* I worked my way around, back behind the canteen to where a milk crate propped open a door. A still-smoking cigarette stub sat in a chipped coffee mug on the ground nearby. I crept inside.

From the kitchen doorway I spotted the janitor, who whistled as he wiped down tables. On one of the kitchen benches sat an order form and pencil. I flicked on the stove and set the paper alight before placing it in a large pot. I added paper to it until the smoke billowed out of the kitchen and hid myself behind the door as the janitor rushed in, swearing, 'Those darn kids! When I get my hands on them!'

I darted past and ran down a corridor stacked with lockers on either side and signs celebrating the school's football team.

The library sat at the end of the second corridor. Books, more books, hundreds of them, stacked on shelves and on carousels. Books about the First World War and dissecting frogs, copies of *Moby Dick*, *To Kill A Mockingbird* and *The Catcher in the Rye*.

I had to think—what did Mum once say about libraries? I knew what a call number was, but how did I find the one I wanted? There wasn't a computer terminal for typing in a search query. *Concentrate, Charlie.* Mum had described how libraries used to contain drawers and drawers of index cards, each card labelled with a book's bibliographic details and a call number. Near the front service desk, I spotted a wooden unit, with four-by-four rows of drawers, each one labelled alphabetically. Now I required some search terms, but without Google there to pre-order and refine my results, I needed to rely on myself. 'North American Geography'? 'West Coast Latitude and Longitude' or 'California Roads'? *Would this be enough?* I wouldn't know until I pulled the book off the shelf. The hours ticked by on my Tempus Imperium. My brain, trained on the quick hit of an internet search, struggled as I pulled book after book off the shelves and flicked through them.

The shadows grew longer between the library shelves, but I couldn't risk switching on a light. The janitor might have gone home, but anyone walking past might see it. I had to give up soon. Tomorrow, I'd find another library and keep searching. Yet the return chute caught my eye as I was leaving. Perhaps the book I required was in there? As I pulled out the trolley, an *Atlas of California* glinted at me, the book's jacket catching the last embers of spring twilight.

187

'What are you doing?'

I jumped. A middle-aged man with spectacles and a pot belly stood in the library's entrance. His collared shirt and slacks told me enough: here was the principal.

'Who are you? You look too old to be a student.'

I sucked in a breath and told myself, *You can do this, Charlie.* I had two choices—snip the green wire and defuse the bomb by talking to the principal, or run and hope that the explosion didn't kill me.

'Oh, I'm so sorry, sir,' I said, and fluttered my eyelids.

'Principal Hamilton.'

'You see, Mr Hamilton, I wanted to help my cousin with his homework, sir.' Each word stress-tested before being spoken. 'Jim desperately needed this library book.' Please, please make my Australian accent not so obvious. 'The janitor left the back door open, and I thought I'd sneak in and borrow the book. I'm sure my cousin will return it on Monday, sir.'

'Cousin?'

'Jim Kepplar,' I said.

'You mean James Kepplar?'

'Yes. I'm Charlotte Kepplar.'

'And what book?'

I placed the *Atlas of California* on the front service desk.

'Jim wants to research the latitude and longitude of Berkeley for Geography.'

'Sneaking in to borrow a library book? Now, I've seen it all. Usually if I catch kids here on a weekend, it's because they wish to toilet paper the hallways and spray shaving cream everywhere. You're the first one who's ever wanted to borrow a library book,' the principal chuckled.

Suddenly, the floor felt firmer beneath my feet.

'Your accent is Australian, isn't it?'

Even my best attempts hadn't been able to rub away all traces of it.

'Yes, I'm from Sydney,' I said, choosing the Australian city famous for its Harbour Bridge, Opera House and beaches.

'Sydney. I love Sydney. My wife and I went there for our honeymoon.'

I smiled. Good, I had snipped the green wire, and the bomb hadn't exploded.

'Oh yes, we are just over visiting my cousin and his parents for a holiday.'

'You said Berkeley?'

'Oh, Jim wants to go to UC Berkeley when he gets older. His teacher asked him as part of a geography project to research its latitude and longitude. I'm hoping this atlas will help him.'

'Here, let me see,' said the principal, pulling the book towards himself. He flicked through several pages before settling on a map of the Bay Area. San Francisco jutted out on the left and Berkeley, Oakland and Fremont to the right.

'Ahh, here it is Berkeley: longitude -122.27247, latitude 37.8715962. Tell your cousin that Mr Hamilton says to look at page twenty-five and to be more organised next time. We can't have strangers wandering the school.'

'Thanks so much,' I said, as he walked me to the door at the back of the canteen.

'I hope you enjoy your stay in San Diego, Charlotte. Make sure you spend some time down at our beaches. You'll find the ones in Southern California are the equal of anything in Australia.'

I thanked the principal and waved goodbye. Once the heavy door shut behind me, I looked again at page twenty-five

189

to confirm the coordinates: longitude -122.27247, latitude 37.8715962. I twisted the outer bezel for longitude then the inner dial for latitude before adjusting the date. Then I placed the *Atlas of California* up against the school's glass front door. The first staff member to arrive on Monday would find it and return it to the library, hopefully meaning that the young Jim Kepplar wouldn't get into any trouble.

In the alley behind the school, I pressed down the pin on the Tempus Imperium and waited for the white light.

20

Berkeley, May 1997

I landed in a hall near a spiral staircase. I swallowed hard and waited for the nausea to pass. The first beams of morning sunlight shone through the glass entrance doors. Arranged throughout the hall were several dinosaur skeletons: a T-Rex, a hadrosaur, and relics still encased in stone, while above me a Pteranodon flew on wings made from fossilised bone. Two triceratops skeletons caught my eye, a mother and a child. Her three horns were each as thick as my arms and had once been sharp enough to gouge a hole in a station wagon. Yet that meant nothing now: size, sharpness or maternal instinct. Time ensnared this mother and child, dead on a riverbank where the sand solidified around them. Millions of years later, a palaeontologist had discovered them in Utah, while excavating near a dam. Is this what would happen to Currency Creek, the Needle, even my social media feed?

I found a campus map near a fire exit five buildings over, headed north, and there was the Physics Department.

Outside, the eucalyptus trees surprised me, their scent marking the air and making me think of home—my parents and the farm. Back in my past—or was it the future?—stood our house with a red gum tree in the backyard.

I wiped a tear from my face. Would I ever see them again—Mum, Dad, and all my friends?

College students bustled around me in their UC Berkeley Bears sweaters and hoodies, schlepping textbooks and backpacks. On the steps to my left, three young men practised skateboarding stunts. The stories they told their friends were the only record of their leaps and flips. I'm the Australian exchange student, I reminded myself, that's my cover story. What if Kepplar remembered me? I needed to alter my appearance, but how?

To my left sat what looked like a college dormitory. I went in the door and headed to the basement, searching for a pile of clothing in size medium. The laundry room smelled of powdered bleach and lavender fabric softener. A dryer buzzed, and I opened the door and emptied the contents into a laundry basket. A pale blue Cal Bears sweatshirt landed on top, size medium—perfect.

'Are you finished with that drier?'

A boy in nothing but boxers, a Chicago Bulls jersey and acne stood behind me.

'Yeah, I'll just get my clothes out of your way.'

'Where are you from?'

'Sydney, Australia. I'm here doing an exchange.'

'What faculty?'

'Physics. I'm taking some of Professor Kepplar's classes.'

'I heard he's a hard marker.'

'I know.' I pretended to grimace.

'What's your name?'

'Charlie.'

'Well, Charlie, there's a party happening here tomorrow night. Why don't you come? They'll be a keg and plenty of tequila shots.'

'Sounds great, but I'm late for class.' I grabbed the sweater and dashed up the stairs.

'Hey, you forgot the rest of your washing!' the boy's voice echoed behind me.

≪ · ✕ · ≫

The campus looked out over the bay towards San Francisco with Alcatraz in the middle. Like most Australians, I'd planned to visit San Francisco one day, in between a stop in LA to see Disneyland and a trip to New York. In my time, San Francisco sat as the epicentre of the tech world: Twitter, Facebook and Apple were all located nearby in Silicon Valley. In 1997, one year before my birth, Nokia phones had been considered sophisticated, and most desktops came installed with Windows 95. iOS, iPhones, iPads, Amazon, tweets and online status updates didn't exist yet. The internet came down telephone cables that screeched as you connected, and wireless still meant the radio that Penny grew up listening to.

At Le Conte Hall, the home of UC Berkeley's Physics Department, I turned the brass handle on the oak door and entered, heading for Kepplar's lab on the second floor.

'No, no! You can't cut the funding now. We're so close. My Unified Field Machine will revolutionise the supply of energy!'

I stood outside Kepplar's door, listening to someone on the phone.

'If you don't, I'll take the design to MIT. I've already had

193

overtures.' The speaker sighed. 'Ok. Fine! Three months then,' he said and slammed the receiver down.

I pulled my hair back into a ponytail and put on the Cal Bears sweater. Would it be enough? I counted to ten, then knocked on the door.

'Come in!'

'Professor Kepplar, I'm so sorry to disturb you, but I have a question about class.'

Through my legs, a brown tabby cat darted, nearly tripping me.

'Please excuse Schrödinger,' said Kepplar, scratching the cat under the chin before it curled up into a basket by the side of his desk.

'That's cool. I love cats,' I said as I bent down to pat Schrödinger, who shut his eyes and purred.

Here he was—the man who built the Needle and invented a Unified Field Machine—sitting at a wooden desk surrounded by bookshelves. The eleven-year-old grown into a thirty-year-old man with black-rimmed bifocal glasses, a fringe that kept flopping over his eyes and a Nirvana *In Utero* t-shirt. His desk was a mess of motherboards, loose wires, precision screwdrivers, legal pads full of equations and fountain-pen cartridges. On his wrist glinted an Omega Sportsmaster, just like the one Penny owned.

'Wow, that's a nice watch!'

'Yes—a real classic. My father was a collector,' said Kepplar, his eyes flicking to the Tempus Imperium. 'I've never seen one like that before.'

'Oh, I inherited it from my grandmother. It's a Tempus Imperium, a type of chronometer.'

'What a lovely heirloom,' said Kepplar. 'I imagine it's

extraordinarily precise. If time travel ever becomes possible as Specter and Einstein proposed, then we will need such devices.'

I ransacked my memories, trying to drag up the rust-covered relics of Year 12 Physics, until I spotted a Newton's Cradle amongst the papers on Kepplar's desk.

'Doesn't a Newton's Cradle work almost the same way as that Unified Field Machine you mentioned in class the other day?' I said, as my fingers twisted the end of my ponytail into a thin rope of split ends. Would he take what I offered? The apple in the possum trap. The promise of chocolate if you gave the correct answer or completed a chore on time.

'How perceptive! Yes—you are right,' said Kepplar as he set the cradle in motion. The outside ball hit the three in the middle, until the end one on the other side swung out and hit the three in the middle again, reversing the process. *Tick... tick... tick... tick...* The silver metal balls swung like a metronome. *Tick... tick... tick... tick...* The speed gradually reducing, like my heartbeat as I realised he believed me.

'A Newton's Cradle creates a compression wave—a form of energy that travels from the first ball to the end one and then reverts. My Unified Field Machine does the same thing, but it's perpetual. The kinetic energy it creates is harnessable.'

'Wow,' I said. 'Could I please see it?'

'Oh, well,' Kepplar paused. 'Given that I barely have funding for another month, I might as well show it to you. Remember, it's only a prototype at the moment.'

Kepplar led me through glass doors into his lab, followed by Schrödinger. Around the room ran an external bench occupied by two sinks, a fume cupboard and a microscope. A blackboard coated in chalk equations occupied one wall, while in the centre of the room was another bench surrounded by several stools.

'Here, take a seat,' said Kepplar, offering me a stool. 'What was your name again?'

'Charlie. I mean Charlotte Lamp,' I said, my fingers fiddling with my hair again.

Kepplar blinked behind his glasses, the same blue eyes as the eleven-year-old boy from San Diego watching me. Under the bright lights of the lab, I felt like a specimen wriggling in a petri dish.

'Do I know you from somewhere?'

'Oh no, just from lectures,' I said, as my hand pulled the UC Berkeley sweater down further to cover the corners of my purple t-shirt.

'The prototype is here.'

In front of us was a rectangular prism approximately seventy-five centimetres long and forty centimetres wide, and half a metre high. On the outside were several meters, knobs, buttons, and gauges. The only one I recognised was the one for voltage. Like the electricity meter in the fuse box outside our family home, this one measured in watts per hour.

'Inside here, I have a mini-Newton's Cradle. By pressing this button, I set this process in motion. Unlike the one you saw in my office, my machine taps into the wave of kinetic energy and converts it into electricity.'

Kepplar flicked on one button and adjusted a knob, making the wattage needle flicker.

'Wow,' I said as the globes wired into the prism lit up.

I reached out and brushed the corner of the machine with my hand as the odour of chlorine flushed through my sinuses. *Specter in a laboratory at midnight, adjusting the dials on a similar looking machine. The stripping-out of Cold War mainframes and their replacement with decontamination rooms, hydroponic set-ups and a museum, inside a missile silo in the Californian desert.* This must be what powered the Sinistrum's Factoreum, but what about the syneghasts? Where did they come from?

'Are there any unintended consequences of such a machine?'

Kepplar pointed to the upper right corner of the rectangular prism. A small vortex of black smoke rumbled in the corner.

'Inevitably, such sizeable amounts of energy create waste. A kind of stochastic resonance that condenses into a black cloud.'

As I watched, the cloud twisted and spun in the corner, tapping against each of the three glass walls. It reminded me of a fox Dad had trapped once that had been killing our chickens. He'd put her inside a metal cage on the tray of his ute. The fox tested every corner for a weakness: a loose bar, a bent wire, the opening hatch and finally the padlock. This cloud was like that fox testing the sides of the rectangular prison.

'It's fascinating, isn't it? You could almost believe the smoke's alive. The way it moves.'

'What happens when you open the prototype up?'

'Most of the time, it just dissolves into dust. A machine of this size doesn't create enough waste for its particles to bond permanently together.'

'What if you built a bigger version?'

Kepplar laughed. 'A bigger version? In my dreams. I just took a phone call from the Dean's office. They're pulling my funding in August.'

'Don't give up,' I said, thinking of those in the Needle a hundred and twenty-three years from now.

Without warning, Schrödinger hissed and arched his back, his fur standing on end. The LED light on the ceiling fizzed and a dark coldness swamped the room. Beneath me, the ground convulsed in short, staccato bursts. *Syneghasts*, I thought, *just when I was so close to finding out what I needed.*

'Shoot! It must be an earthquake-caused blackout. Where's that torch of mine?' said Kepplar as he searched through an open drawer.

I took out my UV torch and tried to turn it on. Nothing! I shook it and pressed the button. ON/OFF! ON/OFF! ON/OFF! I unscrewed the cap and checked the lithium batteries, but still nothing.

'Damn! It's broken!'

'Huh?'

'My UV torch.'

'I don't follow.'

Paws scratched against the linoleum in the hallway outside as Schrödinger growled louder. I dropped to my knees behind the bench and pulled a protesting Kepplar down behind me. The fear made the hairs on my arms stand on end.

'Shhh. Be quiet or it'll hear,' I hissed.

'Who?'

'The syneghast. Be quiet or it'll kill us.'

Keeping low, I crept with Kepplar to a door next to the fume cupboard.

'What's in here?'

'Mostly lab and cleaning supplies.'

I pushed Kepplar inside the storeroom and followed, while keeping the door open a crack. The only light in the lab came in shards that stuck out like razor blades between the slats of the vertical blind. Kepplar shivered, and my skin prickled with goosebumps as the syneghast approached a hissing Schrödinger. Without warning, the cat jumped at the syneghast, but the creature swiped it aside with a paw, throwing it against a wall with a thump.

'Schro—!'

I elbowed Kepplar in the ribs, winding him.

'Shh!'

The syneghast stuck to the shadows and avoided the blades of light that hit the floor at regular intervals. It circled the central bench, its nose in the air, sniffing. Eventually it fixed on the Unified Field Machine, where the black smoke stretched out and tapped at the glass in front of the syneghast. The syneghast sniffed again and howled, arching its back. Unlike a dog's moan, this cry was discordant with pain. The black smoke responded with a tiny high-pitched whine of its own.

'They're communicating?' whispered Kepplar. 'What is it?'

'A syneghast. A by-product of another Unified Field Machine.'

'There's another?'

'Yes, Specter's.'

'Where is this machine? What is it used for?'

I swallowed. Do I stop here? Leave him with just the syneghasts and a forewarning that there was another machine like his in existence? But how to explain the creature in front of me, skin slick like oil and prowling Kepplar's lab?

'Time travel. It powers a device known as the Factoreum.'

'Time travel?' whispered Kepplar in my ear.

'Look, I'll explain later. First we need to deal with this thing. If I can get that blind open, we'll be safe. Or if you just have a working UV torch lying about, that'd also be useful.'

'The blind cord is on the left-hand side. Be warned, it's a little stiff. Also on the other side of the fume cupboard are two handheld UV lights which we use for substance detection.'

Three metres to the curtained window? Maybe four metres

to the other side of the fume cupboard? Would I make it? Both involved confronting the syneghast.

Kepplar nudged me in the back.

'What about fire?'

'Yes, that should work,' I said, thinking of the flames in 2120. 'What do you have in mind?'

'Well, we have a store of matches in here that we use for lighting Bunsen burners and lots of aerosol cans. We could make our own flamethrower.'

'Could you use that to distract the syneghast while I go for the window?'

Kepplar nodded.

I opened the door five centimetres more. The syneghast nudged against the Unified Field Machine, fascinated by its cousin trapped inside.

In one hand, Kepplar held a spray can of aerosol disinfectant and in the other a match.

'On my mark. Go!' I kicked the door open.

Kepplar shot a flash of fire towards the syneghast and I ran at the vertical blind. Behind me, the burning creature howled and jumped towards Kepplar.

I grabbed the blind cord and tugged, but the slats didn't open. The cord was tangled into a big knot and stuck. I glanced behind me. Kepplar lay on the ground, a burning syneghast's jaw clamped around his arm. With all my might, I pulled again, and this time the blind came down, crushing three glass beakers before hitting the ground. Late morning light flooded inside and smashed the syneghast into dust. I fell backwards onto the floor, my left wrist hitting the corner of a bench and shattering my Tempus Imperium.

21

I lay stunned, trapped between a sob and a scream—Berkeley, May 1997. The Tempus Imperium's face was cracked, and the hands bent into a cruel smirk. Behind me, Kepplar groaned and sat up, clutching his right arm, his shirt sleeve burnt and the skin black underneath. I wanted to pull my knees up to my chest and rock. *Trapped!* The word wailed like an ambulance siren inside my head. *Trapped!* However, Kepplar's moans soon woke me from my despair, and I got to my feet.

'Where's the First Aid kit?'

'Under the sink.'

I helped him to stand up and placed his arm under cold running water in a sink.

'I need to call you an ambulance,' I told him.

'What was that thing?'

'They call them syneghasts. Creatures of dark matter.'

'Mm, its coat did seem to soak up the light and warmth in the room, like a black hole. You referred to a them?'

'Err, umm, the organisation I'm sort of working for—the

Temporal Sinistrum.'

'A temporal what? Ouch!' winced Kepplar as he shifted his arm under the water.

'The Temporal Sinistrum. An organisation of time travellers.'

For a second, I thought Kepplar was going to faint. His face was grey and tense, as though it was costing an ounce of flesh for every thought.

'Here,' I said, 'sit down on one of the stools.'

'Thanks,' Kepplar grimaced, again adjusting the position of his arm under the water.

'We've met before, you and I, in 1978, at a Little League match.'

'Little League? I hated baseball growing up and dropped it after two years. The only good thing to come out of it was my friendship with Bill Dupre.'

'Do you remember that day when your relationship with Dupre changed?' I asked. 'When you helped him up after he got hit in the face?'

For a second Kepplar stared at me, making a series of calculations, then blinked and rubbed his forehead. 'It can't be,' he murmured under his breath. He looked at me again. 'It's you, isn't it? You're the girl who spoke to me at the baseball match when I was eleven.'

'Yes.'

'I recognised the way you fiddled with your hair.'

I grimaced, my attempt at a smile twisted by the knowledge of what the destroyed Tempus Imperium meant.

'You were right. By helping Bill that day, I changed my life. He stopped bullying me, and I began helping him with his homework.'

'Where's Dupre now?'

'He went to UCLA on a football scholarship but blew out his knee. He now works for a hedge fund on Wall Street and is always looking for investment opportunities. I still see him for drinks once or twice a year.'

I plucked a thread in this spider's web in 1978 and found the reverberations of that *thrum* in 1997 in Kepplar's lab in Berkeley.

'Well, it looks like I'll be staying here for good now,' I said, showing him the damage to my Tempus Imperium.

'Is that how you did it? Travelled here?'

'Yes, the Tempus Imperium helps people like me move around the timeline. It signals the Sinistrum's time machine.'

Kepplar staggered and grabbed at a lab bench for support, his face pale with perspiration.

'Help me to my desk,' he wheezed.

Once Kepplar sat down, I picked up the phone receiver and started to dial 9-1-1.

'Wait,' he said between gritted teeth. 'If we call now, they will cart me off to a hospital and you'll be stuck here.'

I nodded in between my sniffles.

'There's more of those syneghast-things, aren't there?'

'Yes, we're trying to work out where they come from. We thought your work on the Unified Field energy might help us find what's causing them. Their time machine relies on a similar device.'

'Let me think,' said Kepplar. For a second it seemed like a screen came down over his eyes and blocked out everything, even the pain in his burnt arm, as he thought about what I said.

'All right, Charlie,' he said, his words spat out in spasms. 'I want you… to go… into the next office… and open the top drawer of the desk… you should find some OxyContin.'

'But what about the people in there?'

'Oh, don't worry… my grad students are at a conference in Honolulu…' Kepplar breathed in deeply. 'Simon has a prescription drug problem. He doesn't think I know… The OxyContin will numb the pain so I can help you.'

Kepplar swallowed two tablets with a swig of coffee from a mug on his desk and leant back in his chair, willing the painkillers to work. I didn't wrap his arm in any dressings; instead I filled a small plastic tub with cold water and made him rest his burnt forearm in it. In spite of my efforts, the skin bubbled and blistered, making me feel sick. To distract Kepplar, I filled him in about my grandmother, Odysseus, the Temporal Sinistrum, the few details I knew about waypoints, and the syneghasts. I hinted at the Fulcrum and avoided the Needle, as the risk of creating a Continuity Error was too high given its connection to him.

When Kepplar stopped clenching his teeth, I knew the painkillers had worked.

'Before we work on fixing that fancy watch of yours, I need to use the lab blackboard to work something out,' said Kepplar. Amongst the broken glass, blind slats, and scorch marks, he found a stick of chalk and started writing on the blackboard. 'This equation describes the process behind my Unified Field Machine. You say that this Sinistrum has a version of one, created by Julius Specter, a former student of Einstein's at the University of Berlin? From what I've read, he was quite brilliant, but disappeared during the 1940s. Many scholars thought he might have been murdered by the Nazis. His only two published papers on particle movement and energy distribution were part of my inspiration for this machine.

'These waypoints—where are they located again?'

'The few I know about—Mt Fuji, Stonehenge, Lapland, Monument Valley, Delphi and Miyajima.'

'All areas known for their seismic activity and sunsets. Let me think. This Factoreum uses its Unified Field Machine to push people through time. Hmm…' Kepplar paused for a moment, concentrating, before wiping out his original equation and starting again. 'If we think of time as a form of energy, a progressive, inevitable forward momentum, then we have two different forms of energy being brought together—one kinetic and the other chronological. Two equations and their variables which require combining.'

While he worked, I paced from one side of the room to the other. In less than a year, I'd be born to Helen and Oliver Lamp of Currency Creek, but I would already exist in California if I remained here. I could never return to Australia; the risk of a particle paradox would be too high according to the Temporal Sinistrum.

'Now this is the equation an astrophysicist from NASA recently published in *Nature* to explain the existence of black holes, and the way light is trapped.' Kepplar wiped his brow. He was breathing heavily, but wrote again on the blackboard. 'If I bring the two equations together, then we have this result.'

Kepplar then wrote an equal sign and paused. Perspiration dripped from his forehead and fogged his glasses.

'That makes little sense,' he muttered to himself, and then checked the equations again. Using a yellow pad on one of the benches, Kepplar wrote the equations out again and double-checked at each stage, nodding to himself. Finally, he came to the answer and underlined it, before letting out a sigh and sitting down again.

'Charlie, the problem is your Factoreum and the power it draws from the Unified Field Machine. Every time you travel through time, the process produces a syneghast from the residual dark matter. The culmination of so many syneghasts spread throughout the timeline would be this Fulcrum you described.'

The doubts that I had originally hidden—swept under the couch when I'd read the Sinistrum's history—were exposed now.

No wonder Penny had left the organisation. They were causing the very problem they claimed to be solving. I swallowed, but who could I tell? I was trapped in 1997 with a Tempus Imperium that sat in pieces on a lab bench.

Kepplar took in a heavy breath and stood up again.

'Now we need to fix that watch of yours, but first I will need the precision screwdriver set on my desk. Could you please bring it in here?'

'Hold that thought for a second,' I said, and took Kepplar's glasses from his nose and wiped them clean of ash and sweat before returning them.

'Thanks,' he said.

In Kepplar's office, I hunted for the screwdriver set until a tap on the door's glass pane interrupted me.

'Professor Kepplar, are you in there? A janitor heard glass breaking.'

A campus security officer filled the doorway. I froze like a kangaroo trapped in the headlights of an oncoming car.

'Where's the professor?'

'It's okay, Elias. I'm in my lab,' called out Kepplar. 'Charlie's just looking for something to help clean up the mess. We knocked over a few glass beakers and test tubes.'

The guard looked me over. 'Just as long as you're all right?'

'Yeah, all good, Elias.'

'Okay, Professor, I'll leave you to it,' said the guard as he departed.

On one bench, Kepplar arranged his precision screwdriver set alongside a soldering iron. Next to it, he placed a magnifying glass and a lamp. I deposited my Tempus Imperium in the middle with its broken face and bent hands.

'Could you make me a coffee? This OxyContin is going to

my head and making it hard to think.'

Kepplar held his burnt arm against his side as he worked. From time to time, he directed me to hold the watch at an angle or flip it over as he examined it under the magnifying glass. Sometimes he flinched from the pain, but he kept working even as sweat dripped from his forehead.

'I might be able to fix this,' he said. 'I've always been good at tinkering. When I was a child, I got in trouble for taking apart every clock in the house.'

I made us both black coffees using the lab's percolator.

Kepplar unscrewed the back plate of the Tempus Imperium and peered inside with a magnifying glass. An array of cogs and gears lay in front of him, but two gears were askew, their teeth misaligned. A circular piece of silver-while metal sat to one side, the size of a five-cent piece.

'Ahh, here it is—the battery and antenna. The thing that signals your Factoreum and powers this device. I don't think it's damaged, but let's check it under the microscope.' Using a pair of tweezers, Kepplar picked up the battery and placed it under an electron microscope. 'Ahh, as I thought, it's made from a rhodium alloy with traces of lithium and platinum.'

'Why rhodium?'

'Rhodium is a great catalyst. Surely, you've heard of catalytic converters? Car manufacturers use them to clean an automobile's emissions by removing nitrogen oxide from exhaust fumes. Here, the rhodium alloy battery acts as a catalyst by transforming the power from the Factoreum into a force that can move a person through the time stream via this fancy wristwatch.'

'Is it damaged?'

'I don't think so. Rhodium is pretty tough and resistant to

corrosion.' Kepplar beamed, despite the throbbing from his burnt arm. He returned the battery to the Tempus Imperium and realigned the gears. Next, he turned the watch over and loosened the pin that held the hour and minute hand in place. Using tweezers and a small mallet, he straightened the bent hour hand. Last, he fixed the loose pin on the outside by screwing it back into place.

'I'm sorry. I don't have any glass to replace the front casing. I could cut some Perspex and install it as a temporary replacement. Would that be suitable?'

Without its glass housing, the Tempus Imperium looked naked.

'Yes—go ahead.'

Kepplar measured the Tempus Imperium's diameter and cut some Perspex to size. He placed it over the watch face and tightened the outer rim.

'Here,' he said, passing me the watch.

I put it on and smiled, comforted by its weight. The same comfort I felt as a small child when Grandma Penny had held my hand as we waited to cross the road. I clicked the bezel two stops and adjusted the crowns in a series of stiff movements, but it held.

Kepplar slumped on his lab stool, the adrenaline evaporating as the pain overwhelmed him.

'Here, let me help you into your desk chair. It'll be more comfortable.'

Kepplar leant on me as I helped him to his office. His face turned grey as he collapsed back into his chair and closed his eyes for a moment. 'Charlie,' he said, gripping my wrist tightly and handing me the page of equations from the yellow legal pad. 'Take this. It's proof that your Temporal Sinistrum is causing the syneghasts.'

I looked at his scrawled pages of notes. Here it was: the proof that the Sinistrum was at the centre of everything. Would Hinze and Madam Zhao believe me? Without Odysseus to verify this information, would they shut down the Factoreum and possibly the whole Sinistrum on the word of a novice?

'Thank you,' I said. 'I'm going to leave in a minute, but first I will call for an ambulance. Its 9-1-1 in the States, isn't it?'

Kepplar nodded, before speaking. 'You only hinted at the Fulcrum before? What is it?'

'A gradual extinction of humanity because of the instability caused by the syneghasts. An instability at the very base level of atoms. Death, diseases, earthquakes and fires. Some of humanity will survive the initial catastrophe, like some dinosaurs did after the asteroid hit, but only for a few hundred years.'

Did I explain too much? Was I the cause of the Needle? These paradoxes were a sore that my mind kept picking at, in spite of knowing better.

'Oh,' said Kepplar. 'The end of everything?'

'Yeah, it's horrendous,' I said, frowning, as scenes from a horror movie flashed through my mind: the child scrambling through the rubble, the bloodstained mattress, and the Humvee with two husks in the back. 'That's why I need to get back to the Temporal Sinistrum's headquarters.'

'I'm glad you found me again, after all these years,' said Kepplar. 'Hopefully these equations will make a difference.'

I rang 9-1-1 and waited until I heard two paramedics and a stretcher cluttering up the stairs. I then stepped into Kepplar's lab, closed the door behind me and set the coordinates on the Tempus Imperium for 9 pm, February 20th, 2016, and Penny's place.

22

Pripyat, April 1986

Penny rubbed at a small scar behind her right ear from an incision where the medical team had inserted a new Lingua-Franca microchip for speaking the Russian dialect preferred in southern Ukraine. At the moment, she stood in an almost empty cafeteria, cracked linoleum under her feet, wearing a white skirt, shirt and hat like all the other women in this facility. Her name today was Sveltlana Petrosky. It was 11 pm, according to the clock that hung over the counter.

'Have you finished refilling the urns yet?'

'Almost,' replied Penny.

'Well, make sure that you only use two tablespoons of that instant coffee. It is our last tin, and it has to get us through to the end of the week,' said Oxana. Age fifty-four, mother to four children, and a widower according to her file at the Sinistrum.

Penny poured water into the last urn and set it down on a table near the cafeteria's wall. On the outside of the coffee tin, a woman in a red headscarf brandished a mug under the heading:

The Worker's Favourite—Red Army Coffee. Inside, a thin layer of instant coffee coated the bottom of the tin. No wonder people were tired of Communist rule, mused Penny. Between daily queues for bread and other essentials, as wells of the tens of millions who died in the gulags, the people were exhausted. She emptied in two tablespoons and sloshed the urn around to mix it, until the water took on a brackish, light brown colour.

Oxana sighed behind her. 'I don't understand how they can supply our best engineers and technicians with this instead of real coffee.'

'I've heard that Sofia in administration can get the real thing. Her husband's on the local Executive Committee,' Penny said as she put the lid back on the urn.

'I bet Sofia cooks meat twice a week, then?'

'Yes, I wouldn't be surprised. Being married to the Deputy Assistant Secretary has its advantages.'

Oxana coughed and cleared her throat before looking up at the cafeteria clock. 'Ahh, 11:15 pm. Let's have a cigarette break before the night-shift comes down.'

The cafeteria was on the ground floor of the administration building near Reactor Two. Outside, the spring night felt warm against Penny's skin and smelt of pine trees and grass. Although the plant was well lit, Penny could make out several constellations in the sky above her: Ursa Major, the bear; Hydra, the sea serpent; and her favourite Leo, the lion. To the left of her loomed the cooling towers of the four Chernobyl reactors, a trail of steam coming from each of their tops.

Penny tapped out two cigarettes and offered one to Oxana.

'Thank you, Comrade,' said the older woman. 'What will you do with your leave next week?'

'Probably return home to Opishyna to visit my parents,' said Penny.

'Opishyna? My husband brought me back a lovely water jug from there several years ago.'

'Yes, they're famed for their pottery.'

'Is there a young man waiting for you in Opishyna?'

'No.'

'You're the right age for marriage, Svetlana, and those hips are wide enough to bear several babies for Mother Russia.'

'No, there's no one at the moment.'

'What about one of the technicians or engineers? I've seen the way Comrade Volkov looks at you.'

Penny blushed.

'What's there not to like? A talented junior engineer with a degree from Moscow University. I heard from Natasha that he's got family connections to the Party.'

'He does have such a pleasant smile.'

'Look, I'll speak to Natasha. Her husband, Comrade Akimov, works the night shift with Volkov. We'll see if we can arrange something this weekend. Maybe a picnic in the woods? I so wish that the new amusement park was open. Every day my children come home from school asking about it.'

'Well, all right then,' nodded Penny.

'Oh, is that the time?' said Oxana, looking at her watch. 'We better head back inside. The first group from the night shift will be down in a minute for their coffee.'

Penny stubbed out her cigarette in a rusty ashtray near the door. *Would the amusement park open?* For once, she didn't know, as it hadn't been covered in the mission brief.

《·✕·》

Two weeks ago

Penny looked again at the photos in her briefing folder: the concrete towers of Pripyat, families picnicking in the woods and children eating ice cream. Only one week until she and Odysseus departed.

'So the control rods in Reactor Four will become temporarily stuck, causing a limited meltdown,' Hinze pointed at the blueprint of the RPMK reactor in Chernobyl.

'A partial nuclear meltdown?' questioned Odysseus, who stood to Hinze's left. 'Isn't that too dangerous, even for us?' Behind them, the clock on the wall said '11:17 29/12/1990'.

Odysseus's left arm brushed against Penny's waist, out of Hinze's sight.

'Yes, but containable, like the Three Mile Island accident in Pennsylvania in 1979. There'll be just enough chaos and international pressure to lead Gorbachev down the path of Perestroika and Glasnost and avoid the projected Fulcrum of 1990.'

'But isn't it risky?' queried Penny. 'For us and the Chrono-temps?'

Penny glanced at the inside of her right elbow, where a purple-coloured bruise hid the pinprick from an injection. Last week, she and Odysseus had received their iodine-based vaccinations that inoculated them against the effects of radiation. Tomorrow morning, the medical team was scheduled to implant a Lingua-Franca microchip optimised for speaking Russian with a Ukrainian accent behind their right ears.

'Of course, we are all aware of the risks, but the consequences of not ensuring that this accident happens are enormous. We'd

213

have a major Continuity Error on our hands. Rather than the fall of the Berlin Wall in 1987 and the collapse of the Eastern Bloc, the world would end again because of nuclear war. A coup of Stalinites, KGB officials and military generals would topple Gorbachev, turning the Cold War into a nuclear-powered hot one with 1990 the time of humanity's demise, according to the latest Fulcrum report by our archaeologists.'

'Look, if our researchers are certain about this,' said Odysseus, 'I'm sure Penny and I can handle it.'

Despite Odysseus's assurances, Penny had flinched. When she touched Hinze's blueprint of the RPMK reactors at Chernobyl, she saw it. For a microsecond, she left the room with Odysseus and Hinze and found herself inside Reactor Four at Chernobyl. The roof was blown off, and the walls buckled inwards, while men screamed as radiation flayed off their skin and a syneghast padded up and down the corridors of the Control Centre.

After two hours, Penny and Odysseus left Hinze's office.

'John, it's one thing to prod a Chrono-target in the right direction,' said Penny. 'But playing with nuclear reactors?'

'You saw something, didn't you?'

'Yes, when I touched the blueprint. Utter destruction. A catastrophe. Far worse than Hinze would have us believe.'

'Why didn't you tell him?'

'You know Hinze—he believes most visions are exaggerations. He's all about modernisation, utilising scientific processes. Hinze has said himself that it's time to move beyond visions and use an empirical approach to assessing the likelihood of Continuity Errors.'

'Why don't I talk with him about it? We've worked together for many years, and he trusts me.'

'But the last time you raised one of my visions with him, he ignored you. The Watergate mission went ahead and was a success. He's mothballing the other visionaries like Holt and Nostradamus and instead relies on the Timeline Exchange Centre to monitor the time stream.'

'Well, what do you want me to do about it?'

'Nothing. If we don't go, he'll send someone less experienced. At least if it's you and me, we might limit the damage.'

Odysseus glanced up and down the corridor before he put his arm around Penny's waist and pulled her close to him. He wanted to smell the Chanel No. 5 that she dabbed each morning on her neck and wrists. He flicked one of the loose strands of hair that fell across her face out of the way and looked into her blue eyes.

'Not here, John,' she hissed, but didn't push him away.

'It's been a long time since you and I completed a mission together.'

'Yes, but I'm tired of this. I've been part of this organisation for eight years, and I don't think I can last much longer. I want a life: marriage, children, and the opportunity to not know for once.'

Odysseus kissed Penny before she pulled away.

'John—I love you, but you'll never leave the Sinistrum. You're like Hinze and Madam Zhao—a lifer.'

'Penny, I promise that once this assignment is over, we'll talk.'

Penny shrugged and headed down the corridor as Odysseus watched her.

<< · X · >>

Dyatlov tapped his fingers against the control panel in front of him. 12:30 am, almost time to start the test. The test that those incompetents on the dayshift had already delayed by ten hours, and that now he, as the night supervisor, must complete. A test designed to simulate an electrical power outage and ensure that the backup generators kicked in quickly enough so that the reactor didn't overheat.

Odysseus looked at the control panel in front of him—a sea of blue and green lights, levers, gauges and dials. He had spent hours studying the function of every button and lever before he arrived. These new Lingua-Franca devices made reading the Cyrillic Russian alphabet so much easier. Several years ago, he had spent many months preparing for a Cold War mission by learning to read and write Russian. Now they just inserted a small microchip on the bone behind the ear, which interfaced with his brain.

'Vasily, what time do you think we should take our meal break tonight?' said Akimov.

'Oh, after the test. Maybe around 3 am?' replied Odysseus.

'If you are lucky, Svetlana might be on cafeteria duty again?' winked Akimov. 'I've seen the way she looks at you.'

Odysseus chuckled. He liked Akimov, a young graduate from the Leningrad Institute for Nuclear Studies. Tall and long-limbed with fair hair, he enjoyed teasing Odysseus and the other engineers about their love lives.

'Totitinov, I hear your wife's pregnant again. At this rate, you'll be able to start your own ice hockey team soon.'

Older than both Akimov and Odysseus, Totitinov wore a black moustache and state-issued thick-rimmed glasses. In his wallet, he kept photos of his wife and three children, with whom he shared a two-bedroom apartment in one of the many concrete housing towers that dotted Pripyat.

'Vasily, you shouldn't wait too long. Svetlana will marry soon if you are not careful. You should ask her out.'

'Well, I might do it if she's in the cafeteria during our next break,' said Odysseus, despite knowing that there would be no meal break at 3 am. In less than an hour a partial meltdown would occur, causing radiation to spill out, dosing the workers and the surrounding area with an amount akin to five hundred x-rays at once before the control rods dropped into place and stabilised the reactor's core. Those generals, KGB directors and Stalinites who sought to overthrow Gorbachev would be undermined as Soviet Russia focused all its energies on cleaning up the Chernobyl mess.

'Comrades,' snapped Dyatlov. 'There is no time for such idle conversation. We start the test in less than five minutes.'

'Someone's expecting a promotion out of this,' whispered Akimov in Odysseus's ear.

Unlike Akimov and Totitinov, who both went home each morning to an apartment with children's drawings pinned on the refrigerator, Dyatlov's only company was a bottle of vodka: three shots and then sleep. The Temporal Sinistrum's case file described him as 'irascible,' 'difficult to work with' and a 'worsening alcoholic.'

'Two minutes until the test begins,' said Dyatlov. 'Please take your positions, Comrades.'

Without warning, the electric lights died around them, plunging the control room into darkness.

'What! That's a minute too early,' said Dyatlov. 'Comrade Totitinov, report!'

Odysseus turned; something was panting behind him, each breath spreading a glacier of coldness across the room.

'Why is it so cold in here?' said Akimov.

A growl.

'What on earth?' said Dyatlov. He took one of the emergency

torches with the lithium batteries from the wall and shone it at the beast. The size of a pony, its features resembled those of a dog. A long thin nose, pointy ears and saw-like teeth that dripped chains of silver saliva onto the ground. Its coat, the colour of an oil slick, glistened in the flashlight.

Around them, the windows of the control room rattled louder and louder.

'Totitinov, the control rods! You need to drop them now! Or the reactor will overheat!' yelled Akimov.

The beast howled and crouched, its eyes fixed on Dyatlov.

A syneghast, thought Odysseus, *my first one.* He knew what a syneghast was from the field reports of the few adjudicators who had survived an attack, yet he still found the chill hypnotic. The cold froze his limbs and made it hard for him to think. Totitinov struggled to respond to Dyatlov's commands, his hands moving too slowly as he pushed down the lever to drop the control rods.

'They're stuck halfway! They won't move!' said Totitinov.

Boom! An explosion rocked the control room, flinging the men to the ground and cracking the walls and glass window in front of them, while the syneghast dissolved into ash. The emergency lighting flickered back on as hundreds of fire alarms shrieked around the building.

'What was that?' snapped Dyatlov.

'I don't know,' said Akimov.

'Comrades Vasily and Akimov, you need to check the state of the reactor now.'

'Yes, Comrade Dyatlov.'

Odysseus opened the control room door and headed down the corridor towards the reactor with Akimov. On one side, the walls buckled inwards, as though punched. Something was wrong, Odysseus knew. They should have been able to drop the control rods and let water cool the reactor.

Chrono-temps ran around Odysseus and Akimov, their white uniforms stained with blood and dust. Two workers pulled another man along, while a fourth man stood bent over, vomiting against the wall.

'What do you think has happened?' said Akimov, white-faced, his hands shaking as they pulled open the steel door that led to the reactor core.

The fire raged inside the reactor core, an angry supernova. Metal and concrete lay twisted across the ground like severed limbs. Despite the rising clouds of smoke, the moon glowed in the sky above them. Two birds lay beside them: one already dead, and another twitching for a few seconds, before stiffening.

'Oh, my God!' said Akimov. 'It's gone! The entire roof of the reactor!'

For the first time, Odysseus noticed the black chunks of graphite that dotted the debris. 'The control rods, they've shattered, Akimov!' *This can't be happening*, Odysseus thought, because the reactor needed those control rods to operate.

'That's not possible!' replied Akimov.

'The reactor's in meltdown,' said Odysseus. A syneghast had done this, turning a partially controlled meltdown into a supernova.

Odysseus realised he needed to get Akimov out of this place, otherwise he would die from radiation poisoning. He pulled at Akimov's arm. 'We've got to leave now and tell Dyatlov.'

Back in the control room, Dyatlov paced up and down the floor. 'The control rods, you say? That's not possible.'

'I saw it with my own eyes, Comrade Dyatlov,' said Odysseus.

'You agree with Volkov, Comrade Akimov?'

Akimov looked from Odysseus to Dyatlov and then vomited across the floor.

«·✕·»

Penny heard the mugs and saucers rattling first, then the chairs and tables. She glanced at the Tempus Imperium on her wrist: 1:23 am, which was two minutes too early. According to the Research Division, the explosion occurred at 1:25 am. Penny stumbled as a shock wave from the blast rolled through the cafeteria, upending the urn and spilling steaming water across the floor.

'Svetlana! Look!'

The older woman stood in front of the cafeteria window. Where there had once been four reactors, now there were only three. A blade of blue light sliced up through the sky above where the top of Reactor Four should have been. A cigarette sat trembling on Oxana's bottom lip, while a chorus of sirens and alarms shrieked around them, accompanied by running footsteps.

'It's on fire!' said Oxana.

Waves of flames billowed from what had been Reactor Four. The blue light scared Penny, as it meant that radiation was ionising the atmosphere. This wasn't the small, controlled accident that Hinze had assigned her and Odysseus to oversee. The blue light and fire meant that the reactor had overheated so much that the steam had blown off the roof, causing a full meltdown. What had gone wrong? She and Odysseus had done everything right—he'd replaced an engineer on the night-shift team, and she had taken a job in the cafeteria.

From the window, Penny watched fire engines crowding around the base of Reactor Four. No fireman wore a breathing mask or protective gear; instead, they stood there in heavy jackets, knee-high boots and helmets, not realising that the worst danger was the one they couldn't see—the radiation attacking their cells and DNA. The first sign was vomiting; then your skin reddened as your cells scalded you from the inside. Temporary treatment might help, but in most cases, within two months, they would suffer a full vascular collapse and death.

'They must have called in every firefighter in Pripyat,' said Oxana.

'Stand away from the window,' said Penny. She might be safe from radiation poisoning with her iodine-based inoculation, but Oxana wasn't. Radiation was such a patient assassin. Years after the atomic bomb at Hiroshima and Nagasaki, many who had survived without injury succumbed to cancer. The radiation corrupted a person's DNA by breaking down the bonds that held each cell together.

'What should we do?' asked Penny.

'We'll clean up,' said Oxana. 'Then we'll make sure we still have enough coffee for the workers. It's going to be a long night.'

≪·✕·≫

'There's not enough water to cool the reactor!' said Totitinov. His glasses were fogged with perspiration as he struggled to adjust the water levels with a lever on the control panel that refused to move.

'Quiet!' said Dyatlov. 'I need to think.' Dyatlov paced the floor in the control room, despite the obstacle of Akimov's vomit. Five minutes ago, two technicians had dragged the almost-unconscious Akimov to an ambulance.

'The reactor can't have exploded. This is not possible! It can't be possible! Akimov and Volkov are wrong,' muttered Dyatlov to himself.

'What does the dosimeter say, Comrade Volkov?'

Odysseus searched through the paperwork on his control panel. Where was it? He found the dosimeter on the floor where its red needle hovered at the furthest point of 3.7 roentgens.

'3.7 roentgens, Comrade Dyatlov.'

3.7 roentgens? This has to be wrong! Odysseus looked at the dosimeter again.

'3.7? That's not as bad as I expected.'

'Comrade Dyatlov, the dosimeter only goes to 3.7,' said Odysseus. His words drowned out by another explosion. He tried to speak again, but Dyatlov ignored him.

'I need to speak to the Pripyat Executive Committee and assure them that everything is under control. You and Comrade Totitinov must remain here until the dayshift arrives. I'll get administration to call them in on my way out,' said Dyatlov as he left the room.

'Totitinov, he's wrong. I saw it with my own eyes. Graphite on the ground. The roof blown off the reactor. We must do this without him.'

'But Vasily, the water release's stuck! I can't move it.'

Odysseus looked at where Totitinov pointed on the control panel. *Damn that syneghast!* Hinze's plan for a partial meltdown had spun off the road and crashed. If Odysseus didn't help Totitinov cool the reactor, the whole of the northern Europe could be uninhabitable within weeks from the radiation fall-out. The buttons flashed red under the emergency lighting. Odysseus punched the button down again and again, but the water gauge refused to move.

'We can't do it from here. We need to release the water manually.'

Totitinov gulped, 'You mean we must go down there?' He pointed out the control room's window to a building close to the bonfire of Reactor Four.

'Yes,' said Odysseus. 'We need to leave now. There's no time.'

As they passed Reactor Four, Odysseus and Totitinov spotted three firemen hunched over and retching. Ambulances loaded stretcher after stretcher of men dressed like them in white cotton clothes. Dozens of dead birds and insects littered the ground, their wings still spread from flight.

Soon, the two men found themselves at the top of the stairs that led to the basement and the water pumps. Waist-height water flooded the room, yet the large circular handle for the release remained visible under the green emergency lighting. Odysseus winced, remembering another day under an emerald twilight, where a boy gasped for air during a gas attack. *Private Wallace—wasn't that his name?*

'Vasily?' said Totitinov, pulling at his arm.

'All right—let's do this,' Odysseus said and went down the steps first, followed by Totitinov. The water's warmth surprised him as he waded across the flooded basement towards the handle. *It must be radioactive, Totitinov will be lucky to survive this.* Together, the two men started turning the handle around to release water into the remnants of Reactor Four's core.

'Vasily, if I don't make it, you need to ensure that they take care of my family,' gasped Totitinov.

Odysseus nodded as Totitinov's skin reddened in front of him. This wasn't some sunburn from a family trip to the Black Sea, rather a sign of radiation poisoning. Two more minutes and there'll be enough water, just two more minutes. Totitinov lent up against him and closed his eyes, Odysseus felt the man gag and swallow as he tried to hold back the nausea racking his body.

'Totitinov, it's okay. I think we've done it. We can leave now.'

Totitinov moaned, his hand still gripping the handle.

'Comrade, you need to let go now. I'll help.'

Totitinov put one of his arms across Odysseus's shoulders and leant into him as they limped up the stairs. Once outside, Totitinov fell to his knees and spewed up his dinner.

'Borscht and potatoes, my wife will be so disappointed,' Totitinov croaked, flecks of potato caught in the hairs of his moustache.

'I'm certain that'll be the least of her worries, Comrade,' said Odysseus as he helped Totitinov to stand. 'Let's get you to an ambulance.'

≪ · ✕ · ≫

Penny waited, sitting on a park bench. Families walked past her, pushing prams, children beside them despite it being 4 am. The sirens had forced them from their beds and now they were heading to the railway bridge to watch the plant fire. This park bench was her and Odysseus's rendezvous point if things went awry, as per SOAP Manual Rule 50.2.3—*Always have a pre-arranged rendezvous and extraction point for every mission*—but Odysseus was three hours late.

'Svetlana, why don't you come with us? We're going to watch the fire. No one can sleep because of all the sirens,' said her neighbour, Olga, who occupied the apartment next to her own with her husband, Dymtrus. Their six-month-old son Peytor stared bright-eyed out of the pram at Penny, who now wore a brown cardigan, blouse and skirt, like most of the women here.

'It's all right, Olga. I think I'll just sit here, if you don't mind.'

224

'Okay,' said Olga. 'Remember that you promised to come to dinner on Sunday.'

'Yes, that sounds wonderful,' said Penny. 'Is there anything I can bring?'

'No, don't worry about it. See you soon,' said Olga as she and Dymtrus continued walking towards the bridge.

Usually lying to Chrono-temps came easily to Penny, the words sliding off her tongue like eggs from a frypan. Yet the blade of blue light that towered over them and the people on the bridge made it different. The locals treating it like a late-night fireworks display, despite the grasshoppers and birds falling dead from the sky. It wasn't meant to happen like this; Hinze had told them it would be a 'small, partial meltdown'. An 'easily containable' accident, like what had occurred at Three Mile Island in 1979. This was worse, much worse.

Even the people on the railway bridge were in danger. Unlike Penny, these people were vulnerable to the invisible waves of radiation that were rippling outwards from the exploded reactor. Mothers with babies in prams, young men sharing shots of vodka, a little girl carrying a doll in one hand and leaning against her father's leg. A group of boys, aged ten or eleven, kicking a soccer ball against the bridge's railing. Some were her neighbours, and she knew their first names: elderly Viktor who helped her carry her shopping upstairs, Tatiana and her two children, and Mikhail throwing Peytor up into the air and catching him as the infant giggled. A warm wind blew, making the trees flex backwards, then snap upright. Ash encircled Penny and the people on the railway bridge, making a fine layer of dust through which the boys kicked their soccer balls, while toddlers sat down in it and ran the grains through their fingertips like it was sand.

'Svetlana?'

Penny looked up from her musing, Odysseus stood to her left, his white uniform stained with vomit and blood.

'You're bleeding?'

'Not me. Akimov. He got severe radiation burns when Dyatlov insisted we check the state of Reactor Four in person. That man! So stubborn! I'm sure his actions tonight caused more deaths than needed.'

'Shhh!' hissed Penny and gestured towards the steady stream of people still walking towards the bridge. Odysseus shrank back into the shadows. They fell silent, both counting the seconds until the last group of people passed them.

'What happened?'

'Just before the accident, a syneghast appeared. Maybe it distracted the operator just enough to cause the test to malfunction? I don't know.'

'But it wasn't meant to go like this? "Small and containable," Hinze said.'

'I know, I know,' said Odysseus, shaking his head. 'Your vision was right.'

≪ · ✕ · ≫

Three weeks later, Penny laid a small suitcase out on her bed and began packing. She didn't have much—some photos, a diary, a bottle of perfume, and her Tempus Imperium. She had already memorised her cover story for 1948. As far as Penny was concerned, the sooner she left, the better. She'd had enough of the Sinistrum and these so-called missions. The one at Chernobyl had been a disaster, and when she'd tried to discuss the syneghast in the Control Room with Hinze,

226

he had shut her down. To him, it was just bad luck, but no one could deny the increasing frequency of these creatures. *Could there be a link to the Temporal Sinistrum?* Penny had raised it with Madam Zhao over a cup of tea, but Madam Zhao had only reminded her that a coincidence and a correlation weren't the same thing.

Even five days later, these concerns still chafed at Penny, a rawness that was easily inflamed. She missed her parents and wanted a family of her own. The only problem was telling John.

《·✕·》

Odysseus sat at his desk, thinking. He leaned forward and cupped his forehead in his hands and massaged his temples, a kneading that aimed to flatten out the migraine sprouting behind his eyes. In front of him sat an open manila folder, from which spilled loose, freshly printed sheets of paper. In red ink stamped across them in big capital letters was the word *DECEASED*, the ink bleeding into the black text and photos underneath. Under one photo was the caption *Sergei Akimov*, and on the other the name *Mikhail Totitinov*. Both were dead within a month of Chernobyl, their bodies encased in lead coffins, concrete poured into their graves and the mourners limited to only their wives. The syneghast had changed the timeline, and this was the consequence.

Only Dyatlov still lived. His file contained several newspaper clippings from *Pravda* detailing his 'trial.' According to the Research Division, Dyatlov had spent several years in a Siberian gulag before being released under a General Amnesty in 1990. He'd died in 1995 at 7:32 am on a chilly autumn morning, one hand clutching his chest and the other holding a half-finished shot glass.

Normally, Odysseus had no trouble in reconciling himself to

the Temporal Sinistrum's mission, where the focus was on saving the many, not the few. History needed to keep flowing along a singular continuum, and a nuclear war between the United States and the Soviet Union had been avoided according to the latest report by the archaeology division, but at what cost? The red numerals of the clock that sat on his desk now said '14:03 27/04/2025,' but had it been worth it? Odysseus felt the tendrils of that migraine again, strangling his thoughts. Totitinov's children would grow up without a father, while Akimov's wife would never remarry. These were just the two names he recognised amongst the thousands of victims. He looked again at the press clippings and KGB reports that the Sinistrum had gathered. It would take the Russians many years to clean up Chernobyl. First, they would try dropping boron from helicopters to slow the meltdown inside the collapsed reactor, but most of the pilots would miss. Even with helicopter floors reinforced with lead, the pilots would soon become too nauseous to fly. Next, they would send soldiers out on the roof, crudely battered lead sheeting shoved down their underpants, while they shovelled fragments of graphite and boron back into the ruins of Reactor Four for ninety seconds. Only in 2010 would they cap the reactor, entomb it like they had those who died in the first few months under a mausoleum of concrete. Of the people standing on the railway bridge that night, only two would live for more than five years after the explosion. Near Pripyat, a plague of lymphatic cancers would stalk children and kill their parents.

'John.'

Odysseus hadn't heard Penny approach. Her eyes looked red, and loose strands of hair fell across her forehead. Since they had returned from Chernobyl, they had barely spoken. Penny always left the room when he arrived and refused to answer the notes he left on her desk and under her bedroom door.

'What's wrong?' he asked.

'It's time, John.'

'Time? Time for what?'

'I'm leaving. I've had enough. It's been eight years since you recruited me during the Blitz.'

'Penny?'

'No, John, it's done. I've had the Research Division construct me a cover story. I'll return to London in 1948.'

'Why?'

'These syneghasts. None of our engineers or scientists know why the attack at Chernobyl turned what should have been a straightforward incursion into a disaster.' Penny's eyes flicked to Odysseus's desk, and the scattered Chernobyl files.

'What about us?'

'I love you, John, but you'd have to give this place up.'

'You know I can't do that,' Odysseus said. 'Hinze and the Sinistrum need me. When I saw so many young men die amongst the mud and machine gun fire of the Somme, I swore that my life's purpose would to be prevent such events spiralling out of control again. The Temporal Sinistrum is meant to prevent the chaos of the Fulcrum.'

'I'm sorry, John, but nothing you say will change my mind. You and Hinze are determined to stop the Fulcrum, but all the Sinistrum ever manages to do is delay it, and now we've got this new problem of the syneghasts. At least if I return to 1948, I'll have some semblance of a normal life before the 2025 Fulcrum, or even longer if the Sinistrum manages to postpone it again.' Penny sighed, letting a tear escape. She pulled out a lace handkerchief and wiped it away, smudging her mascara.

'Goodbye John,' her voice trembled. 'I leave tomorrow morning.' Penny turned around and left Odysseus's office, shutting the door behind her.

Odysseus slumped back in his office chair.

PART 3

23

Adelaide, February 2016

9 pm. Two hours ago, I'd stood in Penny's living room and agreed to leave with Odysseus Clay. But nothing here had changed, only me. The cushions were still disembowelled and spilling their white stuffing across the floor. *1947, 2120, 1978, 1997, 2016.* One hundred and seventy-three years traversed in less than a week. I swayed and fell to my knees. What had happened to me? I wore clothes that weren't my own and a UC Berkeley sweater covered in grime. I still clutched the piece of paper with Kepplar's equations. All I wanted to do was curl up on Penny's couch and sleep for twelve hours.

I placed the equations on the coffee table, then lay down on Penny's living room carpet and stared at her ceiling. A ceiling that we had painted together over an exeat weekend when I was in Year 9. On one side the roller strokes were invisible, but the quarter I'd done was a little rougher and more uneven. My thoughts kept returning to what Kepplar had said. Each time an adjudicator moved through time, it created a syneghast. The existence of so many syneghasts would cause the Fulcrum in less than nine years. I remembered how the ground rumbled and groaned each time I saw a syneghast and imagined it on a tectonic scale. Images from high-school geography documentaries flashed through my mind: a collapsed freeway in San Francisco in 1989; the Shinkansen's tracks splitting apart near Kobe in 1995; a wave of water hitting the beaches of Bali, the Maldives and Thailand in 2004. Each grainy fragment of TV footage had been carefully chosen to avoid showing the dead; instead a class of fourteen-year-olds was just given the final death toll. In 1989 it was 63 dead, 1995 equalled 6000, and on Boxing Day in 2004 over 220,000 were killed. These numbers made my head hurt, and I knew from what I'd seen in 2120 that the Fulcrum was much worse. *Exitus Acta Probat*–'the end justifies the means' was the motto of the Temporal Sinistrum, but what if they were the problem in the end? Who would believe me? Who could I trust? Odysseus and Penny were gone, and that only left Madam Zhao and Hinze.

I lay on the floor waiting for the tide of black fatigue to drown me. I only moved when I heard Telemachus at the back door. *Miaow! Miaow!* I opened it and the cat sauntered inside, rubbing up against my body, unbothered by my change of clothes. I scratched behind his ears and whispered, 'Tee, I don't know if I can do this?'

Three missed phone calls, five texts and a couple of voicemail messages all left by Mum and Dan crowded the screen of my mobile phone: *Charlie, where are you?*, *Why haven't you replied to my messages?*, and *C—what's up? R U OK? D.*

My shoulders tightened as I looked at Dan's message and the heart emojis accompanying it. Here was another problem for me to solve, this relationship that now made me feel like an actor on stage. I loved Dan, but only as a best friend. The Needle, the ruined city, San Diego and Berkeley, had brought my feelings with all their sharp edges into focus. For too long I had acted my part and said my lines, especially over this last year where outings in Dan's ute had become a welcome escape. What should I do? Risk our friendship and break up? But part of me wondered why I was even worried about it. Boys and relationships all seemed so inconsequential now that I'd witnessed the Fulcrum.

Instead, I chose the easier option and called Mum back.

'Charlie? Is that you? What's going on? One of Penny's neighbours called and said the front door's open and all the lights are on, but no one's home?'

At the sound of her voice, I wanted to cry and tell her everything. Although even I knew that meant a trip to a doctor, followed by a referral to a psychiatrist.

'It's okay, Mum,' I said. 'I've been listening to music on my headphones and didn't hear the neighbour knocking on the front door.' The lie flung out like a fishing lure.

'Well, okay then, you know what these retirees are like. They've got too much spare time, so will complain about anything.'

'Yes, Mum,' I said, blinking back tears.

'Charlie, you sound so tired. You should go to bed, dear.'

'I will, Mum. Give my love to Dad. Good night.'

Despite my absence, the hours still turned in this Chronosphere. Mum had cooked a pork roast and left me several messages while Dad did the store accounts and fed the animals. On a Friday night, they watched shows about murders in British villages where houses had thatched roofs on the ABC.

I locked the front and back doors and pulled down the blinds, and then grabbed the ripped pillows and stuffed them in the garage bin. I put the drawers back in their holders. Telemachus padded behind me like a grey ghost while I swept and vacuumed. Next, I stripped off and showered. My skin turned red under the water as the mirror and bathroom window steamed up, and a trickle of grime ran into the drain. I left the jeans and UC Berkeley sweater in a pile on the bathroom floor. I put on my own pyjamas, pale pink with a Hello Kitty pattern, and brushed my teeth. Finally, I lay down on my bed and pulled up the sheets, sniffing for that hint of lavender that came from Penny's fabric softener. I turned off the lamp and waited for sleep, with Telemachus curled up by my feet. My body ached, flat and heavy, but it took nearly an hour before exhaustion's black tide overwhelmed my darting thoughts.

《·✖·》

Knock! Knock!

9:30 am: ten hours since I'd passed out on the bed and slept deeply. The exhaustion devouring me. No dreams, nothing, except a blackness that obliterated everything.

Knock!

I rolled over and swore to myself. Who on earth would it be at this time on a Saturday morning?

Miaow! Miaow!

Telemachus head-butted me under the chin, wanting to go outside.

'Charlie, are you there?'

Knock!

Nearby a leafblower howled, while two neighbours chatted over a back fence. Like pieces of glass catching the light, fragments came to me: Odysseus Clay, the child and her slingshot, the Needle, a Little League game in San Diego, meeting James Kepplar, and

235

finally the knowledge that it was the Temporal Sinistrum causing the syneghasts after all. Did these memories actually belong to me?

'Charlie?'

'Bugger! It's Dan,' I murmured to myself as I swung my feet out of bed.

'Coming!' I yelled, straightening my pyjama top and checking myself in the wardrobe mirror. My hair looked like I had just stuck my fingers in a power point. I patted it down as much as possible and rubbed away at the redness of my eyes. What was I going to tell him?

'Charlie, it's me, Dan!'

'I'm coming,' I yelled, almost tripping over my sneakers as I stumbled down the hallway.

Dan stood on the front step, smiling, brandishing two coffees and a couple of ham and cheese croissants.

'I thought I'd surprise you, given you weren't returning my messages.'

'Oh, I'm so sorry. I worked closing last night. Why don't I get a plate for these croissants?' I said as Dan followed me inside, passing my backpack in the hallway with Penny's papers still inside.

Dan placed the croissants and coffee on the table and turned to me. 'Closing at Happy Jacks?'

'Uh, umm… Mario called me in for a late shift.'

'I rang Happy Jacks at 9:30 pm last night looking for you.'

'Oh,' I said, looking down at the linoleum on Penny's kitchen floor.

'What's going on, Charlie? I thought you seemed so much better over the last couple of months. But now you're lying to me, and I don't understand why.'

I waited, letting the silence fossilise between us. For once in our relationship, I didn't know my lines. Instead, I sat down at Penny's kitchen table and let my head rest on my hands, tears streaming down my face.

'Charlie, please tell me what's wrong,' said Dan, bending over and putting his arm around me.

'It's hard to explain,' I mumbled.

All I wanted to do was lean back into that hug and tell Dan about the Temporal Sinistrum, syneghasts and the Fulcrum, but I knew I couldn't. I needed to make that choice, the one whose sharp edges hurt and would sever me from him.

'Dan, I think it would be best if we broke up.'

'B-b-but,' Dan stammered, for once lost for words. 'But, Charlie, I love you.'

I sucked in a deep breath. 'I know, but I don't love you in that way. Even though you're still my best friend.'

Dan stiffened. 'I guess that might explain a few things,' he said. On the way out, he slammed the front door, the vibrations shaking the two coffees on the table until they flooded over.

I closed my eyes and let out a sob, the sound ripping through me. For three minutes, I allowed myself this pain, letting it twist and scar inside as I wondered whether Dan would ever speak to me again. I needed the wound throbbing and raw, to remind me of why I was doing this. Dan, Mum and Dad these were the people I loved and had to save from the Fulcrum.

I tipped out the coffees and put the croissants in the trash and instead made a cup of tea, strong with a dab of milk like Penny taught me, and a bowl of porridge. Next, I washed my face, put on some moisturiser, and then dressed myself in my favourite 'Class of 2014' hoodie. Now I recognised myself in the bathroom mirror.

I made space on the kitchen table and opened my backpack.

I always sat with my back facing the window, as the other seat used to be Penny's. There was still a scorch mark from a cup of tea singed into the tabletop and the markings of a black sharpie from when five-year-old me had redecorated it with pictures of Mickey Mouse. *Clunk!* My Swiss Army knife tumbled out of my backpack and hit the floor. I picked it up and held it in my hand for a second, tracing the inscription. Memories of Mum, Dad and Penny singing me 'Happy Birthday' in this kitchen four years ago flashing through my mind. *Pink candle wax dripping onto the cake's icing, and the smell of ash. Dad handing me a box wrapped in blue paper with a silver bow that contained this pocketknife. 'Look, Charlie. It's got two types of screwdrivers, a saw, even scissors, and a wire stripper.' Dad grinned and flipped the knife over. 'We even got it engraved with your name—*To Charlie, Happy 14th, love Mum and Dad. *With this, you'll be ready for anything.'*

Ready for anything? My insides still felt raw from the look Dan gave me as he left. I gazed at the pocketknife and traced the inscription. Words that Dad had had professionally etched on one side of the knife in 2012. 2012? It was now 2016 and four years later. In 2025, the Fulcrum began, meaning I had only nine years left of a normal life at most. Am I really ready? Ready to leave Dan? Ready to return to the Sinistrum?

I put the pocketknife back in my back pocket and looked at the photos again. Penny with Odysseus sitting at a table in a cafe; Penny standing alongside the Factoreum's control panel with Madam Zhao; Odysseus standing in front of the Eiffel Tower. The last one looked like any normal tourist photo that a honeymooning couple in Paris might take. Odysseus and my grandmother? Although I understood now about her life with the Temporal Sinistrum, I struggled to comprehend that she'd had a lover before

Grandad. She'd always been honest about that 'SOE officer' who'd died in occupied France, but now the reality faced me in these photographs: the 'SOE officer' was just code for Odysseus.

I stood up from the table and started pacing, with each loop taking me through Penny's hallway to the living room and back to the kitchen again. The weight of the Tempus Imperium on my left wrist kept reminding me that I needed to go back to the Sinistrum and share Kepplar's findings. Soon I went outside and paced around Penny's backyard, thinking. Over the back fence, I saw women with takeaway coffees and strollers sitting on a park bench talking. Toddlers climbed and slid through a playground while their siblings swung on the swings. A father kicked a football to his sons, who wrestled for the mark. Inside my backpack sat my new Student Union diary with the timetable already completed: Monday morning, Introduction to Law 101, while on Tuesday at 2 pm was a tutorial for Comparative Politics. I had two choices: one, I could stay here and hide, attend classes, make pizzas for Happy Jack's Pizza Shack and deal with what I had done to Dan, while pretending I didn't know what was coming; or two, I could return to the Temporal Sinistrum. According to Odysseus, the Fulcrum began in 2025, only nine years from now. In the Needle, I saw the newspaper headlines from when it started: 'Global Pandemic Death Count Hits 12 Million,' 'Island of Java wiped out by major tsunami' and 'Minute Men and Three-Percenters Militias occupy Ohio and Kansas State Capitals and enforce curfew.' Even I knew that the island of Java was part of Indonesia, one of Australia's closest neighbours. I wanted to retreat to this suburb where I knew the way from the bus stop to Penny's place, where kids wrestled for marks, toddlers climbed in playgrounds and my parents were only a phone call away. Yet I couldn't give up; both Penny and Odysseus had believed in me.

I went back inside where the clocks on the wall ticked in time with my footsteps. Telemachus sat at one end, licking his hind legs and giving me a bemused look. Only the cuckoo clock remained stuck. I'd tried winding it at 4 pm like Penny had taught me, but it refused to work. The night Penny died; it had shrieked 'Cuckoo!' in one last gasp before becoming stuck. I'd wound and wound it, but all I did was cage the bird inside those two tiny doors.

Don't forget to wind the cuckoo clock at 11 am once a week and feed Telemachus—the postscript from Penny's final letter. I looked at the other clocks on the wall: only one minute to eleven. But as a child she'd told me to wind it daily at 4 pm. Oh well; I sighed and adjusted the weights that dangled from the bottom of the clock to tell the correct time. When I let go, the weights rose automatically, one after the other, the first for time, the second for the cuckoo and finally the third one for the music box. Had I done it? Had I fixed it? I reconnected the ticking hand. *Tick-tock... tick-tock...* The hands clicked over to 11 am and the cuckoo burst out of the Swiss chalet's doors and shrieked. A startled Telemachus put his ears back and hissed at the clock. The bird sung cuckoo ten times, but on the eleventh note it stopped. Damn! Had I done something wrong? Broken it? There was a *thunk*, followed by the sound of something whirring inside as a tiny door opened at the base and a piece of paper dropped out.

What the—? I picked it up. It was tightly folded and yellowing, and I had to be careful not to tear it. The paper came from one of the cheap legal pads that Penny had preferred.

Colley Reserve, Glenelg.

11 am Australia Day, 1966.

I recognised her flowing cursive, but what did this message mean? 1966? I took a look at myself in the hallway mirror—

jeans and sneakers, hopefully not too anachronistic for the time period. On Penny's desk sat an old jar of pound notes, shillings and pence from before Australia had decimal currency. I stuffed a handful of notes and coins in my front pocket, despite having no real understanding of their value. Next I grabbed my phone and searched for the GPS coordinates for Colley Reserve, a process so much quicker than hunting through library books in 1978. -34.97858 and 138.5113. What did I have to lose? I knew what I was about to do probably went against every Sinistrum rule, but so what? I no longer cared, now that I knew their Factoreum was the cause of the syneghasts. I pulled Telemachus out from under my bed, ruffled his ears and whispered 'Sorry Tee,' and shoved him out the back door. Lastly, I stuffed Kepplar's equations into my back pocket along with the pocketknife, clicked in the coordinates on the Tempus Imperium, and pressed down the button.

24

Glenelg, Australia Day 1966

I landed behind the row of tin sheds that ran alongside Colley Reserve; on the other side was Glenelg beach. A tattered sideshow alley was full of tired-looking stallholders with cigarettes hanging from their bottom lips while their transistor radios crackled with the news and static in the heat.

'PM Harold Holt and his cabinet to be sworn in today.'

'Less than a month to the new decimal currency. Don't forget to trade in your pounds and shillings!'

'Benaud's Australians need to win the Fourth Test to tie the Ashes.'

10:15 am; only forty-five minutes until 11 am. Already the sweat was beginning to clamber down my back and arms. Today was going to clear the old Fahrenheit mark of 100 degrees easily before lunchtime, and I was wearing jeans. Bugger! No one had warned me that chafing and time travel could be an issue. Above me, the sun was burning a hole in the sky. The few clouds appeared puckered-up and desiccated out in the distance where the ocean rolled back and forwards in a ceaseless see-saw. I could already see the heat wafting off the sand in simmering waves; the flags were set up and two bored looking surf lifesavers sat watching the few morning swimmers. Where should I go? The last thing I needed was sand in my Converse sneakers, and I lacked a hat.

I turned down the sideshow alley, where chocolate wrappers and bakery paper bags drifted listlessly on the ground. Most of the games seemed familiar: throw a ring on a Coke bottle, post a ball down the clown's mouth, toss a dart at a board, shoot a moving duck with an air rifle. The prizes ranged from stuffed bears to china dolls in frilly dresses with glass eyes and crooked noses.

'Two shillings for three shots in this fine shooting gallery!'

'Pardon? Me?'

I looked at the man, red-faced and sweating, standing in front of the shooting gallery. Smoke curled from a rolled-up cigarette in the corner of his mouth.

'C'mon, lovey,' he said. Ash dropped from his cigarette and he stamped out the embers. 'Why don't you have a turn and be me first customer this morning?' He winked, 'Lovey, it's only two shillings? Or are you waiting for a boy? I could do a special for the two of you—four shillings for six shots.' The man chuckled, his teeth yellow, with the front two missing.

10:35 am: still twenty-five minutes to go. Why not? At least the roof of the shooting gallery cast a long shadow.

I counted out the unfamiliar coins from my pocket and the man handed me an air rifle. The stock was still greasy from his tobacco-stained fingers. In front of me, a row of ducks mechanically marched along in two rows. I held the air rifle to my shoulder and looked down the barrel at the ducks. The barrel's weight was off and dragged slightly to the left. The man rolled another cigarette and put it in his mouth, his eyes bemused by my seriousness.

Since I had been a child, I'd known how to shoot. At home in Currency Creek, we kept two guns in a safe—a hunting rifle and the shotgun. The hunting rifle was for rabbits, foxes and other vermin, whereas we only used the shotgun for putting down an injured farm animal. When I used to come home for exeats, I'd often meet Dan and some of the other local kids and we'd go out rabbit shooting at night. The oldest teenager would drive us in someone's ute, while the rest of us hung on for dear life in the back tray. Eventually, we'd stop and switch on the spotlights, letting them spear through the darkness until they hit a rabbit, their bright eyes blinking as I or someone else lined up the shot. I liked mine to hit between the eyes, rather than on the furry mass of its plump body, so that death was quick.

Thud... thud... thud... Three ducks down, and the man's cigarette hanging on his bottom lip, rapidly turning to ash.

'What in the name—?' he spluttered.

'Oh, I grew up in the bush,' I explained.

'You can choose from the top row,' he said, finally letting his cigarette drop to the ground.

I picked out a bear with a lopsided grin and loose stitching near his stomach.

'I would have chosen the doll with the gingham dress and blonde curls,' said a voice behind me.

I turned to find a small girl, her brown hair in a short bob, dressed in bathers, shorts and sandals. She looked about six, but had that precocious confidence that manifested in a willingness to talk to strangers and share opinions on everything.

'I've always preferred bears,' I said.

'That was an excellent shot. I didn't know girls could shoot that well,' she said.

'I grew up on a farm,' I said. 'Would you like this bear?'

'No thank you, but I think my brother Gavin might. He's only four.'

'Where's he? Is Gavin with your parents?'

'No, he's with my big sister, Julia. She's ten. They're playing by the sprinklers.'

10:45 am; only fifteen minutes left. I didn't have time for this, but the girl had grabbed my hand and was dragging me towards Colley Reserve. At least we were heading in the right direction.

'I'm Anna,' she said. 'Anna Devereux.'

Devereux? Why was that name so familiar?

'Where are your parents?'

'Mother's at home doing the washing, and Father is at work. Mother said we could go to Glenelg for a swim as long we listened to Julia and were home by midday.'

Three children, under the age of twelve, and no parental supervision? Things really were different in the 1960s. Why did the name Devereux seem so significant to me? My brain kept pulling at this thread, but I couldn't unravel it. I had too much else to think about it. According to Kepplar, even the incursion I just did from 2016 to 1966 might have released a syneghast. I should have returned to the Sinistrum, but I kept delaying as I didn't know who I could trust.

'There they are!' yelled Anna, letting go of my hand and running towards the sprinklers. Her brother was running through them, over and over again. The sprinkler's jets of water ticked around in a broad circle, like the hands of a clock. *Tick... tick... tick...* The little boy's skin was already turning red from the sun. Nearby, the older girl watched him from under a shady tree. Alongside the boy ran an older man with thin, pale and wispy blonde hair, who wore nothing but a pair of tightly fitting blue swimming trunks. The man looked roughly in his mid-twenties, and I already hated the way he kept grabbing the little boy and tickling him.

'Anna, don't forget the bear,' I said.

'Gavin! Julia! This nice girl's going to give us the bear she just won.'

Anna led her brother over to me, where Julia joined us. The blond-haired man held back, rolling out a towel under one of the trees and lying down. Yet he kept his eyes fixed on the three children in a way that made me feel like a mouse when a hawk spots it from the sky.

'Hello, I'm Charlie,' I said, offering my hand.

The little boy grabbed and shook it roughly.

'I'm Gavin. Isn't Charlie a boy's name?'

'Yeah, I guess so,' I said. 'It's actually short for Charlotte.'

'Who's that?' I asked, gesturing to the man who lay on his towel watching us.

'He's Nate,' said Gavin. 'He's our friend.'

'How long have you known him?'

'Oh, only since this morning. Gavin stubbed his toe on the way to the beach, and Nate picked him up and helped bandage it,' explained the older girl.

'When are you due home?'

'Mother said we should take the 11:10 bus home,' said Julia.

'But Nate said he'd give us a lift in his car,' whined Gavin. 'And it's so hot.'

From his towel in the shade, the man watched us. His gaze

246

was still and unmoving, like the way a hawk hovered above its prey waiting.

I glanced at the Tempus Imperium. 10:55 am. Penny's note had said 11:00 am at Colley Reserve. If I made sure that these children got on their bus, I would miss whatever rendezvous the note referred to. However, I didn't trust that man and the way he watched these children with the hungry look of a wolf from a fairy tale.

What was the story behind that Devereux name? *Damn you, Charlie, and your stupid conscience!*

'Why don't we go to the bus stop now? If we hurry, we might just get there in time,' I said, annoyed at myself.

'But Nate said we could for a ride in his car!' said Gavin, starting to sob.

'Now, Gavin, Mother is expecting us to come home on the bus,' said the older girl. 'She might be unhappy if we come home in Nate's car.'

'I want to go in Nate's car!' cried the boy again.

'Look,' I said, bending down, 'I won this beautiful big bear and thought he'd be perfect for you.'

The boy looked up at me, tears running down his cheeks. 'He is big.'

'Now, Mr Bear really wants to go on his first bus ride.'

'Yes, Charlie's right, Gavin,' said Anna. 'We have to take Mr Bear on his first bus ride.'

The boy took the bear out of my arms and hugged him. I took his hand and that of Julia and strode towards Jetty Road and the bus stop with Anna trailing behind us.

For a second, I looked towards the man lying on his beach towel and nodded. Already his pale skin had started to redden and peel from the sun. Not a nod of thank you, or acknowledgement, but rather recognition. Our stares met, and for a second he dropped that mask and I saw the predator inside—the flash of white teeth, and those cruel eyes. I smiled at him as I chatted to the children about their swim and what they would do when they got home.

«·✕·»

It was 11:15 am by the time I returned to Colley Reserve. Had I missed that 11 am rendezvous?

Tick... tick... tick... the sprinklers spun around on their axis, shooting giant arcs of water into the air and across the lawn.

The man was gone, and the Devereux children were safely on the bus. Anna had waved to me from the window as it disappeared down Jetty Road.

Tick... tick... tick...

'You did the right thing back there, making sure those children caught the bus.'

I turned to face an older woman in her mid-forties. I rubbed my eyes, blinded by sunlight.

'I was about to intervene myself when you did. There was something wrong with that man.'

I blinked again at that voice. It might be younger and with a stronger accent than I remembered, but I knew it.

'Penny?'

The last time I had seen her alive, I'd performed CPR as she died.

She looked at me again, with that stare I recognised. I expected my skin to tingle or my blood to boil. According to Sinistrum rules, crossing paths with yourself was extraordinarily dangerous, but a grandparent was nearly as bad. I wobbled on my feet and nearly fell over. Penny caught my arm and helped me to the shade next to the surf club, where the sprinklers still spun on their axis.

Tick… tick… tick…

'Here, have some water,' she said, her blue eyes boring into me, as I drank.

'You do look like Helen,' Penny said. 'Same eyes and hair colour, but Helen is only five.'

'I'm Charlie. I mean Charlotte. Her daughter.'

'Do you realise how dangerous this is? Your mother's only about ten miles away with Henry and Margaret. You've broken almost every Sinistrum rule I can think of by coming here.'

'How do you know that I'm here because of the Sinistrum?'

'Your Tempus Imperium, or should I say mine?'

I looked at Penny's left wrist, but she was only wearing the Cartier.

'Why are you here, Charlie?' she said, fixing me with those blue eyes that I'd always found so hard to lie too.

'Because you left me a note,' I said, handing her the one I found in the cuckoo clock.

'Well, that is my handwriting, but I still don't understand.'

I explained to her about Kepplar's belief that the syneghasts were being caused by the Factoreum and adjudicators moving through time.

'I just don't know what to do,' I said. 'Who can I trust? Madam Zhao or Hinze? Would they really mothball the Factoreum to prevent the Fulcrum and stop the syneghasts?'

'Have you told John?'

'You mean Odysseus?' I paused. 'He's dead.'

Penny flinched, before taking out a handkerchief and

dabbing her eyes.

'How? Was it a syneghast?'

I nodded.

'The end justifies the means,' quoted Penny. 'It was Hinze who made that phrase the Sinistrum's motto. For nearly eight years of my life I believed it, until the disaster at Chernobyl. I thought the Sinistrum had a divine purpose, but then the number of syneghasts started increasing.'

'You were at Chernobyl?'

'Yes—myself and John were there when Reactor 4 exploded.'

'But I thought the Temporal Sinistrum's role was the maintain the timeline?'

'So did I,' said Penny, squeezing my hand. 'So did I. I really thought what we were doing had purpose. Charlie, did John ever tell you why I joined the Sinistrum?'

'No.'

'Like John, I was recruited when I was at my most emotionally vulnerable. I'd just survived an air raid on London that had killed two of my colleagues at the Ministry of Health. John was recruited from the Western Front, Zhao from the Cultural Revolution and Hinze from Seattle during the Spanish Flu. When did they seek you out?'

I swallowed, a gulp of hot, dry air that almost made me retch. Surely, I'd create a paradox if I told Penny about how I witnessed her death?

'It's okay, Charlie,' Penny said, pulling me into an embrace. 'From the whiteness of your face, I can tell that it involves both of us. Don't tell me, or it'll have the potential to create a Continuity Error.'

I nodded, wiping away a tear.

'What am I going to do? Will Madam Zhao and Hinze

believe that it's actually the Factoreum creating the syneghasts?'

'I'd be surprised if Zhao didn't. She'll at the very least want to suspend its operations and test Kepplar's hypothesis herself. Hinze is a different matter. He was responsible for turning the Sinistrum from a small-scale operation into something much larger. He's always wanted to phase out the reliance on paragnostics and industrialise the process.'

'But what I should I do?' I asked. 'They're expecting me back any minute.'

'Return and see what happens. Sometimes that's all you can do, Charlie. Just remember to trust your instincts.'

There it was again, that note I had missed in her voice. A tone like the embrace of a warm bath, a sunrise, or a walk at twilight on a hot day. I looked at her, drinking in those features one last time. Sure, Penny was younger, but she was still the same person. The same eyes, nose, hair and that accent. Oh, how I'd missed that voice on the other end of the telephone! I wanted to put my arms around her and not let go. I wanted to bury my face in her shoulder, smell her perfume and sob about everything: my grief, Dan, Odysseus, the Sinistrum, and what I'd witnessed during the Fulcrum. But I stopped myself, by gulping down several lungfuls of air.

Tick… tick… tick… The sprinklers were still going, drenching Colley Reserve's lawn as we talked.

'Well, I b-b-best return then,' I said, standing up despite my trembling bottom lip.

'You've a good heart, Charlie,' said Penny. 'Helen has raised you well. I saw what you did for those children.'

'Devereux,' I said. 'Their names were Gavin, Anna and Julia Devereux.'

What had I done? The Devereux children were the reason

why parents in Adelaide refused to let their offspring walk home alone from school. The reason why people locked their doors at night. The Devereux children who had disappeared one hot summer's day in 1966. Had I changed their fate by ensuring they got on this bus? Kepplar in 1979 and now the Devereux children—was I the one responsible for destabilising the timeline?

'Charlie, what is it? You look faint again.'

'Those children. I might have changed their fate.'

'Oh Charlie, not every change an adjudicator makes creates a paradox or Continuity Error. I've had missions go wrong that haven't caused a Continuity Error. The Sinistrum likes to exaggerate the effects of un-vetted meddling in the timeline, to ensure no adjudicators go rogue.'

My shoulders dropped, the tension releasing itself in a long exhale. I knew I could trust Penny, as she never lied.

'Okay,' I said, giving her one final quick embrace. 'I'm off then. Goodbye, Grandma.'

I clicked the Sinistrum's coordinates into my Tempus Imperium and waved for the last time at my grandmother.

25

Los Angeles, August 2121

The child darts through a Safeway carpark in between burnt-out cars and melted trollies, a pack of dogs behind her, barking. She leaps through a broken window-front, but her hand catches on the metal frame. The child finds the cool room and slams the door behind her. She pulls down a wire shelf and pushes it against the door as the pack hurls itself against it. She knows she needs to wait until the pack exhausts itself and leaves. She wraps the gash on her hand in the rag she's worn for weeks as a mask to protect her from the dust storms. The child then takes a padded jacket in fluorescent yellow hanging off a hook by the door and makes a nest from the empty cardboard boxes. She pulls the jacket over herself to keep warm as she drifts off to sleep.

The next morning, the child wakes shivering. The cut on her hand is red and pus-filled, and she is so tired. She drinks the last of the water in her pack and curls up asleep again. For days, she shivers and sweats, unable to move or get more water. She dreams more and more of Papa, waiting for her with pumpkin pie and turkey at a dinner table set for four.

«·✕·»

Sinistrum HQ

'You're getting much better at this, Charlie,' said Madam Zhao, helping me up. In the background, Pradeep whistled to himself as he adjusted the dials on a control panel.

The image of the child lying in the cool room, her breathing slowing over days, sat trapped in my mind. The Fulcrum—could it be stopped? Or were there too many syneghasts? The dome above me sparked twice at a cross-point as a steam valve hissed and the fans of the Factoreum whirred.

I felt a flicker of nausea, but it passed. I patted my back pocket, checking again for my pocketknife and the paper containing Kepplar's handwritten equations.

'Here,' I said, passing the equations to Madam Zhao.

When Madam Zhao concentrated, she chewed her bottom lip. Her eyes ran across the paper over and over again. 'Mm, let me think.'

'Well, what does Kepplar have to say?' asked Hinze, peering over her shoulder.

'According to Kepplar, it has to be the Factoreum. Every time an adjudicator makes an incursion, a syneghast is produced, as shown by this variable. The more incursions, the more syneghasts, increasing exponentially until the Fulcrum.'

'He must be wrong,' said Hinze, snatching the paper from Madam Zhao.

'No, Richard, I think he's right; here, let me show you.' Madam Zhao picked up her clipboard from a control panel and began to demonstrate the basis for Kepplar's equations. Her movements were just as fluid as Kepplar's as she rewrote his numbers and added in some of her own calculations in a separate column.

'You see, Richard, it's this unexpected variant.' Her pencil tapping on the offending number. 'We've never actually considered how the quantity affects the concentration of energy during an incursion. The higher the concentration, the more syneghasts produced.'

'You're wrong,' snapped Hinze. He turned to me and jabbed his forefinger into my chest. 'Are these the only notes you brought back, Charlie? Did Kepplar say anything else?'

'Yes, these are what Kepplar gave me. He did show me his prototype for the Unified Field Machine. He'd trapped what looked like a tiny syneghast inside it.'

Hinze glared at me, threads of white spittle forming in the corner of his mouth. As we talked, Madam Zhao moved from control panel to control panel, flicking switches and pulling levers. The constant hum of the Factoreum's engine and fans began to slow.

'Madam, you need to stop that now,' said Hinze, the whites of his eyes visible.

'But Richard, we must shut down the Factoreum immediately, even if it risks a syneghast intrusion.' said Madam Zhao.

'Madam, I've warned you. Please stop,' said Hinze, his voice growing louder.

'Richard please! As Chief Engineer, the risk is too high. Kepplar's equations show that every time an incursion is made, a syneghast is produced. Once the Factoreum is safely off then we can figure out what to do. You know the process takes at least six hours for the machine to shut down. This will give a chance for the last two adjudicators to return to the Sinistrum,' Madam Zhao flicked another lever to the off position.

'Madam, I'm ordering you to stop,' said Hinze. 'Charlie isn't exactly an expert at physics. And I need more time to study these equations myself.'

My eyes jumped from Hinze to Madam Zhao. I didn't know what to do.

'It's too dangerous, Richard. We should switch the Factoreum off now and pause all incursions.'

Madam Zhao pressed another button.

'Madam, this is my last warning,' said Hinze.

'I'm sorry, Richard, but I need to do this,' said Madam Zhao.

'Guards!' said Hinze. 'Please escort Madam Zhao out of the Factoreum's control room and imprison her downstairs.'

Behind Hinze, two guards in uniforms emerged, blank-faced. They placed a set of metal handcuffs on Madam Zhao and dragged her out.

'Richard, for the sake of our friendship—please!'

'Guards! And make sure you confiscate her Tempus Imperium!'

I stared and gulped. What had just happened? My mouth was open, but there were no words. Instead, my brain swam in endless circles like a goldfish in a bowl.

'Pradeep, you are now the Chief Engineer,' announced Hinze.

Like me, Pradeep had watched the whole exchange, his brown eyes flicking between Hinze and Madam Zhao. Now he straightened himself up, and answered Hinze in a stammering voice, 'Yes, Controller.'

'And switch everything back on! Damn that woman!' said

Hinze, whose gaze finally returned to me. 'Well, Charlie, am I going to have any trouble from you?'

'Err, no,' I mumbled. What had I done? I felt pinned by Hinze's glare. This was my fault. Penny had advised me to see what happened, and now everything had gone wrong.

'I suggest, Charlie, that you return to your room and rest until you are wanted.'

I shrugged my shoulders and left the room.

<< · X · >>

I found myself back in the same windowless bedroom as before: four walls and a solid door, a bed, desk and chair. Alcatraz, Robben Island, even Yatala Prison back home had rooms just like this. Five minutes after I lay down, I heard a click in the door's handle as a key was turned, locking me in. On the desk sat a framed black-and-white photograph of Penny, Odysseus, Hinze and Madam Zhao sitting at a cafe table in 1920s Paris drinking coffee alongside a handwritten note.

Dear Charlie,

I thought you might like this picture. It's of myself, your grandmother, Odysseus and Hinze, celebrating our last incursions success.

Sometimes, after a success, members of the Temporal Sinistrum might celebrate with a visit to a famous time period. We chose this cafe on the Left Bank because writers frequented it. That night, I remember Hemingway and F. Scott Fitzgerald sat one table over from us, and

*were so drunk that the entire cafe could hear their
conversation about Gertrude Stein's latest Salon.*

*Kind regards,
Madam Zhao*

She'd used a thick-nib fountain pen, more suited to Chinese calligraphy than writing in English. Some strokes, like the 't' in 'F. Scott Fitzgerald' were far too thick. One of my tears dropped on the paper, smudging her signature. What had I done?

I lay down on the bed and pulled my knees up to my chest. Every time I closed my eyes, a tear escaped. Inside my turmoil tumbled down a steep slope of rocks and shingles, tearing in half, breaking apart and drawing blood. Madam Zhao was imprisoned because of me.

I rolled over and looked at the photograph on the desk again. Penny looked only slightly younger than the version I'd met in 1966, but in comparison I was a failure. Nothing I had done since returning to the Sinistrum had prevented the Fulcrum; instead, I'd made things worse. I twisted and turned the outer rim of my Tempus Imperium. I had the power to travel through time strapped to my wrist, but there was still nothing I could do. The risk of meeting myself was just too high. Both Odysseus and Penny had warned me about it. Aargh! I wanted to scream and punch the walls, but I stopped myself by focusing on my breathing.

Inhale... one... two... three... four... five...
Exhale... one... two... three... four... five...

I rolled back to face the wall, but a bulge in my back pocket stopped me—my pocketknife. Because I'd come to this room willingly, no one had bothered to search me. I lay back and began opening and closing each element: bottle opener, scissors, wire-cutters, tweezers, two knife blades, a Phillips head and flat head screwdriver, and finally that hook for removing stones from horse's hooves. I got up and examined the door handle. If I unscrewed the whole lock, I might just be able to force it open.

26

I waited until my Tempus Imperium told me it was midnight before I crept out of my room. Each night, the Sinistrum shut down so that Factoreum could cool and recalibrate. At the bottom of the stairs leading to the basement, I passed a sleeping guard, with a dob of spit vibrating on his chin.

<< · ✕ · >>

Madam Zhao sat chained to a water pipe in the corner of the basement, her lab coat filthy with one eye blackened and a fat top lip. *What had I done?* I had envisioned a prison cell no bigger than two-by-two metres, with a barred window and a slot in the door for receiving food. Anything was better than these grey concrete walls, a puddle in one corner and mould spreading across the ceiling. Madam Zhao coughed and spat out a wad of green phlegm, which clung to the wall for a second before slipping to the ground.

'I'm so sorry,' I leant down on one knee, keeping my voice low. Outside, the guard slept on—*Phlumm-um-um… Phlumm-um-*

um… Phlumm-um-um—his breathing punctuated intermittently by a guttural snore.

'It's all right, Charlie,' said Madam Zhao. 'You are here now. That's what matters.'

'What happened to your face?'

'One of the guards shoved me against a wall.'

'What a brute!'

'It's only a black eye. I'll live. But you need to help me escape,' said Madam Zhao, rattling the chains around her wrist.

'The key. Where can I get that from?'

'Hinze will have it. You're going to need to pick the lock.'

'Me?'

My doubts whirled in gusts of anxiety. I had visited 1947 and seen Bradman play, survived the Needle in 2120, watched a Little League match in 1978, and defeated a syneghast in 1997, but picking the lock on a set of handcuffs? It was one thing to dismantle a door handle with a screwdriver. However, handcuffs needed precision and knowledge, not just blind intuition and some familiarity with a screwdriver. *Phlumm-um-um… Phlumm-um-um…* Another bone rattling snore from the guard snapped me out of my panic.

'Yes, you Charlie. You'll need a tension wrench, which looks like a thinner version of an allen key and a piece of wire. Luckily, I've already got a bobby pin just above my left ear.'

'Will this help?' I said, pulling out the Swiss Army knife my parents had given me for my fourteenth birthday.

'Does it have a long piece of metal with a hook on it?'

'Yes,' I said, opening the knife and revealing a hook. 'I've never known what this is for.'

'Good, that'll do for the tension wrench, but you're still going to need a piece of wire.'

'Where will I find it?'

'Go down the corridor, past the stairs, and head down to the storage room at the end. They'll be boxes and boxes of case files, but there should be a wooden crate filled with odds and ends in the corner.'

'Okay,' I nodded, 'I'll try to be quick.'

《·✕·》

Access for Authorised Persons Only said the sign on the Storage Room door. I pushed it open and switched on the two LEDs. They flickered for a second, but only one came on, filling the right side of the room with watery light. The other side remained hidden by shadows, shrouding the rows of metal shelving filled with boxes, each one labelled with a date, name, and list of contents.

```
Mission: BATTLE OF HASTINGS
Date: 14 October 1066
Contents: Arrowhead still stained with King
Harold's blood
Agent(s): Odysseus Clay

Mission: ARTHUR TUDOR
Date: 2 April 1502
Contents: Blankets stained with sweat
NOTE: His brother became Henry VIII, and
married his widow, Catherine of Aragon.
Agent(s): Penelope Jones, Odysseus Clay
```

Four rows over, and another four hundred years.

Mission: *WOLF'S LAIR PLOT TO KILL HITLER*
Date: 20 July 1944
Contents: Von Stauffenberg's eye patch, several pieces of a wooden table leg
Agent(s): Richard Hinze

Mission: CHERNOBYL
WARNING – PLEASE WEAR APPROPIATE PROTECTIVE GEAR WHEN OPENING THIS BOX.
Date: 26 April 1986
Contents: Graphite fragments from Reactor Four, a fireman's helmet
Agent(s): Penelope Jones, Odysseus Clay

Chernobyl? So Penny really had been there when it exploded. But in 1986, she would have been working as an office manager at a shipping company, and preparing for Mum's wedding. Could Penny have been in two places at once? Chernobyl? Adelaide? The threads of time travel plaiting together, but never knotting. A young Penny in the Soviet Union, while a much older Penny drove a VW Beetle through the streets of Magill on her way home. A string bag filled with a milk carton, a box of Weetbix, bread, margarine, and some Pink Lady apples on the passenger seat.

I wanted to open the box and find out what had happened, but Madam Zhao still waited. The wooden crate of odds and ends sat at the very end of the last row between two sprung mouse traps. One was empty except for air, but the other held a still-breathing mouse whose two black eyes stared up at me. Despite the crossbar snapping its spine, the mouse's whiskers twitched.

I looked away and then stomped on its head. 'Quick', Dad had always said, 'It's best to be quick when an animal is so much pain.'

I pulled out the wooden crate and placed it under the only light globe that worked. My hands sifted through strips of metal, odd nails and screws, and pieces of wire as threadbare as the hair on Hinze's scalp. Eventually, I found two pieces of copper wire of different lengths and left.

≪ · ✕ · ≫

When I returned, Madam Zhao sat up and smiled, despite the purple swelling that closed her left eye.

'Here,' she said, brandishing her wrists. 'I need you to follow my instructions.'

I swallowed and took a deep breath. *How hard could it be?* I knew how to change a tyre under moonlight, repair a fence and assemble flat-pack furniture. My father had always insisted I learn how to use tools, as we lived in the country and help was never just a phone call away.

'First, we need to shape our tools. Could you please remove the bobby pin above my left ear? Next, bend the edge of the thinnest piece of wire, as that'll become your pick.'

I followed Madam Zhao's instructions and laid out the tools on the ground in front of her.

'Now, using your pocketknife as a tension wrench, feel out the position of the pins in the lock. Next, employ the bobby pin to rake the pins until you disengage the lock. You'll need to keep the pressure on the tension wrench constant, while you do this.'

I poked and twisted at the inside of the lock until I felt a click and a pop and the lock opened.

'Well done, Charlie!' said Madam Zhao as she dropped the handcuffs and rubbed her wrists. '*Exitus Acta Probat*—the end justifies the means. That's the problem with Hinze, he believes in absolutes. When his wife and child died of the Spanish Flu, he saw in the Sinistrum a way to prevent such mass tragedies in the future. Hinze just can't fathom how the organisation he has served for so long is the culprit.'

'Why do you believe me? You're just as invested in the Sinistrum as Hinze.'

'I've studied Kepplar's work for a long time, and he was one of the best physicists of the twenty-first century. That equation you handed me made sense, as it contained a variable that we hadn't considered before, related to the concentration of energy.'

'When did the syneghasts first appear?'

'Syneghasts have always existed. What's different now is their concentration. If Kepplar's equations are right, the Factoreum is responsible. The more incursions, the more syneghasts. It's simple. We need to switch the Factoreum and the Unified Field Machine off and stop the production of syneghasts for now.'

'But what about the ones already in existence?'

'If we limit their number, we might be able to hunt down the remaining creatures. But we'd need to re-work the Factoreum completely to make this possible.'

Next, she grabbed my wrist and looked at the Tempus Imperium still strapped to it.

'Good, it's 1am. The night shift has finished. Most people are in bed. You'll need to grab Kepplar's equations from Hinze's office while I start the shutdown process.'

'But what about Hinze?'

Phlumm-um-um... Another booming snore rattled the light

265

fixture on the ceiling.

'Hopefully, Hinze had a few too many wines and is asleep.'

«·×·»

In the hallway, the only light came from the emergency signs that offered an *EMERGENCY EXIT, FIRE ESCAPE*, or *ONLY BREAK GLASS IN CASE OF EMERGENCIES*. If I pushed open a Fire Door and went down the stairs, I could leave. Outside, another version of a city I loved existed—Adelaide in 1947. I would be the only me, another infant version not born until 1998 at Victor Harbor Hospital. By 1997, I'd be gone; fleeing across the oceans to Europe and as far away as possible from particle paradoxes. Yet Penny trusted me with her Tempus Imperium, and I couldn't let her down.

Throughout my life, I had always turned to Penny when things got to me. Particularly in the last couple of years, when Dad's business barely broke even thanks to the new Bunnings in Victor Harbor.

'Darling,' she would say in a mama bear growl. 'Don't worry.'

Even though I cried about not becoming a house captain, or only getting a B+ from a teacher who couldn't even remember my name, Penny told me I'd get my chance.

'Just be ready, Charlie, to take it when it comes,' she said.

Hinze's office was empty. On the drinks trolley sat a finished bottle of Renaissance claret. *Surely anyone who drank a bottle of that wine would be asleep by now?* I grabbed the slip of paper with Kepplar's equations from his desk and headed towards the Factoreum's control room.

Apart from the green emergency lighting above the fire escapes, the only other light came from Madam Zhao's hand torch, bobbing around the room.

'It's here!' she said, shining a torch on a Control Panel. 'My Tempus Imperium. Hinze confiscated it when they brought me down to the basement.'

Like mine, it contained the same complications and pins, but instead of a brown leather band, hers was made from silver metallic links. Madam Zhao strapped it to her wrist and took a screwdriver from an open toolbox nearby.

I gave her the slip of yellow paper with the equations, which she glanced at again.

'Proof—so incontrovertible. Yet Hinze's stubborn enough not to believe Kepplar.'

'Why?' I asked.

'It would undermine everything he believed in.'

'Really?'

'Yes, Hinze was one of the Sinistrum's first adjudicators. Recruited by Specter himself for his mathematical and technical prowess.'

'But if Hinze is so clever, how can he deny the reality of Kepplar's equations?'

'Richard has always been an absolutist who struggles with ambiguity,' said Madam Zhao. 'Now, Charlie, enough of that. I need you to keep watch. It's a six-hour shutdown process that must be done in a precise order or we risk destabilising both the Factoreum and Unified Field Machine.' She glanced at her Tempus Imperium. 'It's 1 am now and we need to finish before the morning shift starts at 7 am.'

'What'll happen to the Palladium? With the Factoreum shut down, a syneghast might get inside.'

'Don't worry Charlie. It'll be several hours before that's even a possibility. I'll pull the intrusion alarm at 6:45 am, so everyone evacuates in time.'

Tick-tock… Tick-tock… Tick-tock… went the clock above the Factoreum's dome. Three hundred and sixty minutes or twenty-one thousand and six hundred seconds to shut this machine down and stop the syneghasts from multiplying further.

《·✕·》

The hours passed, pooling into boredom, despite the sounds of Madam Zhao working. I fixed my eyes down the corridor towards the stairs. If anyone came, they would have to come through this doorway. I fiddled with my pocketknife, pulling out each element again—the blade, screwdriver, saw, scissors—one after the other, until I grew weary and put it back in my pocket. Tiredness nudged at me like an old friend. 'Trust me,' it said, 'Trust me. A small micro-sleep won't matter.' Like boys at parties who offered you that one beer or a pill, it hinted at something darker. Twice I slipped backwards, my head smacking against the wooden door frame and waking me from a second-long doze.

'Charlie, here, take this,' said Madam Zhao, passing me a cup of coffee. 'You look like you need it.'

The caffeine hit me like a right hook, snapping me awake.

'How's it going?'

'The shutdown's preceding. So far, we've managed to maintain the correct sequence.'

'How much longer do you think it will take?' I said, glancing at my Tempus Imperium, 4 am, only three hours until morning.

'Only two and half hours at the most. I'll need to check each of the cooling coils as the shutdown continues. They've been increasingly unreliable and I would hate for one to fail now. Just remember that at 6:45 am, I'm going to pull the intrusion alarm switch.'

'Thanks for the coffee,' I said as she disappeared back inside the room.

27

'Charlie! Charlie!'

There it was again, that same voice. Me not much higher than the middle row of shelves in a supermarket aisle, tears streaming down my face.

'Charlie!'

Sobs racking my body as faceless figures shuffled past, pushing trolleys and talking into phones. I'm alone, I told myself, I'm lost. Freezers filled with milk cartons down one end of the aisle, and a teenager with a nose ring scanning groceries at the other. I sniffed again and wiped the snot on my sleeve.

'Charlie!' said Penny, pulling me into a cuddle.

≪·✕·≫

Sinistrum HQ

I rubbed the sleep out of my eyes. Defeated by exhaustion, I had slipped into a doze and now something cold and heavy, the size of a twenty-cent piece, was pressed into the side of my forehead.

'Move!' hissed a voice in my ear.

I stood up and stepped away from the wall. Hinze manoeuvred himself behind me and then pushed me into the Factoreum's control room. He held a freshly oiled Luger in his right hand.

'Do you like it?' Hinze grinned. 'It's from my private collection. I believed it belonged to an SS guard stationed at Auschwitz.'

'No, I don't,' I said. 'Especially when it's pointed at me.'

The glint in his eye scared me. I preferred the bureaucrat Hinze who sat in his office chair and straightened his pens, not the one in front of me with his hair wild and the first two buttons of his shirt undone. Was Hinze's sanity slipping? Had it been pushed off a cliff edge by Kepplar's equations and the knowledge that his beloved Sinistrum was to blame?

'Madam! Madam, it's time to stop this! You need to bring the Factoreum back online immediately,' Hinze called out, his voice echoing through the control room.

Madam Zhao emerged from behind one of the control panels. 'Richard, put that gun down before you hurt someone.'

'No, not until you restart the Factoreum.'

'You know I can't do that. I've initiated a full shutdown of everything, including the Palladium. In less than an hour, the Sinistrum will be offline.'

'But that will leave us vulnerable to a syneghast attack!'

'Not if I pull the intrusion alarm at 6:45 am as planned. That way there will still be enough residual power left in the Factoreum to evacuate the building before any syneghasts arrive.'

'No!' Hinze yelled, showering me in spittle. 'This will ruin everything I've worked so hard for! That even you've worked so hard for.' He pointed the gun at Madam Zhao.

'Richard, I'm sure you've had time to look closely at Kepplar's equations now. They're incontrovertible proof that we're the problem. We need to finish the shutdown now, then work out what to do.'

'No! Reverse it!' Hinze said, waving the Luger in the air.

'Richard, you're wrong this time.'

'No—'

Hinze's sentence was cut off by a tremor rolling through the control room, throwing us all to the ground. I crawled under a desk and put my hands over my head. The building rattled around us, growing louder and louder as control panels and furniture toppled and cracks formed in the ceiling and walls. The Sinistrum's lights flickered on and off in short staccato flashes before going out completely, but it was that glacial coldness that told me the cause: a syneghast. Upstairs, a siren wailed, an automated scream that told the residents of the Temporal Sinistrum that it was time to evacuate. The Factoreum clicked and clicked as each person evacuated.

'Madam Zhao? Madam Zhao?' I called out, as I emerged from under the desk. In the dim twilight of green emergency lighting, I groped around for a UV torch but could find nothing amidst the rubble, bent metal panels and splintered furniture.

'Over here, Charlie,' she replied.

I found her to my left, trying to push aside a fallen control panel.

'Do you have a UV torch?'

'No. What about you?'

'Nothing. I've looked.'

'A syneghast is coming. Can't you feel the cold? We need to leave now.'

'First, I need your help. Hinze's trapped underneath.'

'But the syneghasts?'

272

'If we're quick, we might just all escape.'

'He just threatened to shoot us!'

'I know, but Richard used to be a friend of mine and I can't leave him behind.'

Damn! I knew Madam Zhao was right. 'Okay.'

'Good girl. Now, on three lift the panel. One… two… three… lift!'

With a groan, the control panel slipped off Hinze, revealing his crumpled form beneath. He was singing softly to himself, despite his legs and arms being twisted into unnatural angles. I couldn't see the Luger anywhere.

This is the way the gentlemen ride—
Gallop a-trot, gallop a-trot.
This is the way the farmers ride—
Hobbledy hoy, hobbledy hoy.

'Shhh! Save your strength,' I said and placed a hand on his shoulder. For a second I saw Hinze as a man in his early thirties with a small wriggling boy on his knee, who sang off-key: '*This is the way the gentleman ride—*'

'There, there,' I said.

'Veronica and Jack-Jack, that was their names. You can see him, can't you, Charlie?'

'Yes.'

'All I ever wanted was to stop another tragedy like what happened to my Veronica and Jack-Jack,' Hinze coughed, flecks of blood streaking his clothing. 'I thought that by working for the Sinistrum, I could do this.'

'Quiet, Richard,' said Madam Zhao, as Hinze exhaled a long foaming breath that caused the blood to froth from his mouth and nose. He took two more painful breaths before his chest stilled and his eyes emptied of life.

'He's gone,' said Madam Zhao. 'Now, it's time to—'

She didn't have time to finish her sentence because two sets of silver eyes had fixed upon us from the door to the control room. I shivered as the shadows in the room deepened. The syneghasts' gaze was like a snare, pulling tighter and tighter in a loop around my throat.

'Charlie! Charlie!'

Madam Zhao's voice an echo disappearing into the abyss.

'Charlie!' Madam Zhao shook my shoulders.

'What?'

'There's only enough energy left for a single-person incursion.'

Around us, the remnants of the Factoreum were starting to shake again, with more cracks appearing in the cooling coils and splintering the walls. Steam vented and rumbled, shaking the machine even more. The syneghasts circled us, their ears twitching as they toyed with us. I might have got this far, but I didn't have the knowledge that Madam Zhao did. She knew and understood the Factoreum and Kepplar's equations. If anyone was going to dispose of the syneghasts and stop the Fulcrum, it had to be her. I was nothing but an eighteen-year-old university student who missed her grandmother.

'Here,' I yelled, my arms waving at the syneghasts and drawing their gaze.

'Charlie?'

'You need to punch in the coordinates now,' I said, stepping away from her. 'Over here!' I yelled again to distract the syneghasts, even though all I wanted to do now was to sleep. To slip into the netherworld of an oxygen deprived, hyperthermic coma where a syneghast stood looming over me, dripping chains of silver saliva.

274

'Thank you, Charlie,' said Madam Zhao, as she punched coordinates into her Tempus Imperium. 'Penny would have been proud of you.'

'Just promise, you'll stop them,' I said.

'I have Kepplar's equations here,' Madam Zhao patted the top pocket of her lab coat. A bright light started to envelop her as the rumbling from the Factoreum grew louder and louder. However, just as Madam Zhao was about to step inside, the geodesic dome exploded and threw me across the room. The syneghasts evaporated in the flames. I lay there, slipping in and out of consciousness, my left arm clutching pointlessly at my side as a pool of blood grew around me. *This blood is going to be so difficult to wash out of my clothes*, I thought, as I drifted into blackness.

28

Currency Creek, February 2035

I stood, a rag covering my mouth, leaning on a spade. Two freshly dug graves were in front of me with wooden crosses made from fence posts. Scratched into the wood the names of my parents and the date. A hot wind blew, making me pull Dad's Akubra down to cover my ears. I coughed, my chest racked by spasms until I regained my breath. In the distance, a trail of smoke wafted up from the Fitzpatrick's farm. For three days now, it had burnt, as there was no one left to put it out.

Out the back of our house, I filled a steel drum with my parent's wedding album, my school certificates, old birthday cards, formal photos of me and Dan, and lastly Penny's folio with the photographs still inside. Next I poured in some petrol and set it alight. I watched the flames lick at the inside of the drum, consuming the papers. I'm too late, I told myself. I've always been too late. The Fulcrum happened, and I didn't stop it.

Towards evening, I drove Dad's ute along the main street of Currency Creek. Weeds sprouted from the gutters and potholes littered the road. The front window of Lamp's Agricultural Supplies was smashed, and the pub was boarded up. Someone had pulled down the iron soldier from his podium on top of the war memorial to make bullets. Dogs roamed the streets—kelpies, blue heelers, and mongrels—hunting for scraps. Red Xs in spray paint marked some houses, indicating infected inside.

I didn't stop.

«·✕·»

Sinistrum HQ

Blink... blink... blink... A long thin LED flickered above me. I was lying in a white hospital bed covered by a waffle blanket as a thread of cool, pure oxygen pumped in through my nose. I flexed my right wrist, and it stung where a drip was inserted. Above me, a saline solution dripped into a plastic bag and down through a tube into my vein.

'Ugh!' I tried to sit up, but the pain clawing at my left side was too much.

'Don't move.' A familiar voice, somewhere to the right. 'You need to rest, Charlie.'

'But the Fulcrum—' The words were barely out of my mouth before an intoxicating blankness began to dissolve the bed's outline.

«·✕·»

Next time I awoke the room was made from straight lines. Cream walls, fluorescent lighting, and a water jug on the table beside me. I blinked; the light was hurting my eyes, making it hard to focus. On the right, a machine measured my heart rate, blood pressure and oxygen levels, while a bag dripped a mix of morphine and saline into my bloodstream. Using my left hand, I touched the bandage covering my side, just below the rib cage. I winced: despite being sedated, the pain was a beast that even growled in its sleep.

'Where am I?' I croaked, the words scratching the back of my throat.

'Don't speak,' a voice said to my left. 'Here, take a sip of this.' A hand and a Tempus Imperium I recognised offered me a cup with a straw. I sipped the water down, where it moistened the rawness of my throat.

'They had to intubate you, Charlie. By the time I arrived, you were barely breathing. That's why your throat is so sore.'

There it was again, that tone I remembered.

'Odysseus?'

'I'm here,' he said, squeezing my hand. I blinked again, then let my eyes focus on his face, his crooked nose and greying stubble. The features of a man my grandmother had once loved. The last time I saw him, he'd been bleeding from a shoulder wound and calling a syneghast towards him in the Needle.

'How?' I asked.

'That's a story for another day, Charlie.'

'But the Temporal Sinistrum? Madam Zhao?' A high-pitched beeping accompanied my words. The green light on the heart rate monitor stuttered faster and faster. 'Kepplar's equations? The Fulcrum?'

A nurse bustled in, took one look at my monitors and whispered to Odysseus, who nodded. She began to inject a clear liquid into my drip.

'Charlie, we'll talk later, when you've recovered.'

'But—'

'Quiet now.'

I fixed my eyes on Odysseus, trying to hold on to him and consciousness. Yet the weight of the tranquillisers was too much, and I soon slipped back into that abyss.

《·✕·》

'Water?' I croaked, my throat burning again.

'Here, sit up,' said a nurse, holding a glass to my lips.

'Where's Odysseus?' I asked in a hoarse whisper.

'He'll be back soon. He left a book for you.'

I looked around again, trying to find signs of the explosion and the heat of the flames. No plastering, no patching, not even a crack in the wall. It all looked brand new under the antiseptic white light of this hospital room. '14:03 27/04/2025' said the clock in red numerals hanging above the door.

'Where am I?' I asked the nurse, as she bustled around the room taking my blood pressure and adjusting the monitors.

'I think I'll let the Controller explain.'

'Controller?'

'Yes, Controller Clay.'

Odysseus—the Controller? How? The answer to these questions lay somewhere in the ragged scraps of my memory: Kepplar's equations, Hinze's denial, freeing Madam Zhao, a syneghast attack, and finally the Factoreum explosion. Yet nothing had made a difference. The date of the Fulcrum remained the same. The future poised like a guillotine's blade, waiting for humankind to mount the stairs and kneel.

On the bedside table lay a copy of *The Odyssey*, the title in embossed gold lettering. The nurse helped me sit up, and I opened it,

279

flicking through the pages and admiring the illustrations: The Trojan Horse with the Greek warriors hidden inside, Odysseus tricking the Cyclops, Odysseus enduring the Sirens, Odysseus murdering his wife's suitors and then reuniting with Penelope and his son, Telemachus. On one page, the Goddess Athena spoke to Telemachus, Odysseus's son: 'You are no longer a child: you must put childish thoughts away'.

'I'm glad you like the book, Charlie,' said Odysseus.

'Odysseus!'

'It's good to see you sitting up. You had me worried for a while there,' he said, taking a seat next to me.

'Thanks,' I murmured. 'How did you escape the Needle?'

'Chance, I guess. After you made your return-incursion, I led the last syneghast up to the food level. The UV lamps they used for their hydroponic set-up were enough to kill it. Thankfully they ran on rechargeable lithium batteries.'

'But what about the people in the Needle? Isaiah? How did you explain it?'

'Jeremiah saw everything. He'd been monitoring the plants via video when the power went out and he saw the syneghast. I played on his fealty to Kepplar and Dupre. He had his medical people patch me up so I could return.'

'Where am I?'

'The backup Sinistrum headquarters. Every version of the Sinistrum has had a pair known as a Dyad, which acts as backup. A smaller facility, but with a fully operational Factoreum at its centre. We brought it online once the original was destroyed.'

'A Factoreum powered by a Unified Field Machine?'

Odysseus nodded, as proud as a newborn's father.

'But those cause syneghasts! You have to shut the Factoreum down now, or you'll never stop the Fulcrum.'

'Calm down, Charlie. As the new Controller with a much smaller Sinistrum, I've already imposed a limit on the number of incursions. We just don't have the staff. It'll be sometime before we return to normal operations.'

'But Kepplar's equations prove that every incursion produces a syneghast!'

'Where are they Charlie, these equations? We couldn't find them in the ruins of Hinze's office. And the notes you brought back from the Needle were useless. I can't just mothball the entire organisation without definitive proof of this so-called link between the syneghasts and incursions. We still need to prevent that Fulcrum.'

'I gave them to Madam Zhao, just before the explosion.'

'You did?' said Odysseus, his eyebrows raised.

'Where's Madam Zhao?' I asked, only realising now that I hadn't seen her at all.

'We don't know. We think she made an incursion, but that the explosion sent her off course. Our Research Division is scanning the historical records in the Timeline Exchange Centre as we speak. She's now a wanted fugitive.'

'Why?'

'Her shutdown caused the syneghast incursion and the explosion. And it was against every Sinistrum protocol.'

'You need to send an adjudicator back to ask Kepplar now.'

'We can't, Charlie. You've spoken to him twice now, significantly increasing the chance of a Continuity Error.'

'Kepplar will show you—'

'Charlie, you know the rules. I explained them to you myself.'

I slumped back in the bed. There it was again, an absolute, like the Sinistrum's motto, *Exitus Acta Probat:* the end justifies the means.

Suddenly I felt so tired. The realisation that I had failed hurt so much that it made my left side ache. In my mind, I kept seeing flashes of a steel drum in which moments of my life burned: school reports, my parents' wedding album and my baby photos. The photos curling up in the flames, the images bubbling as they blackened.

'You look pale, Charlie. We'll talk when you are recovered.'

<< · ✕ · >>

It took me two weeks to walk five metres. My left side still ached when I overdid it or bent over, but I stopped the morphine. I found the way it smoothed down the edges of my thoughts too dangerous, so instead I gritted my teeth and bore the pain. After three weeks, I felt well enough to meet with Odysseus.

Odysseus smiled when I entered his new office. 'Charlie, I'm so glad to see you are up and about. How's the pain?'

On his desk sat that same photo of him and Penny together in front of the Eiffel Tower.

'Manageable,' I said, wincing.

'Charlie, we need to talk about your future,'

What future, I thought? The Fulcrum was still going to happen, and no one believed me about Kepplar. Yet I kept my gaze steady and my breathing controlled.

'Over the last decade, the Sinistrum's ranks have been decimated by the syneghasts. We have very few adjudicators left, even fewer with real paragnostic ability.' I nodded at Odysseus to continue. 'The impending Fulcrum makes things even more dangerous, and we could use your help.'

Odysseus's words hung between us like a tightrope. I could choose to walk to the other side or remain safely on the clifftop.

'But I made so many mistakes. I got that girl's father killed.'

'I think you underestimate yourself, Charlie. One death, when you could save billions.'

There it was again, that absolute. I gritted my teeth, my face nothing more than a neutral mask as I twisted the ends of my hair around one of my fingers. I had once trusted this man with my life, but now my doubts were spreading like weeds. The officiousness and the zealotry that I so had disliked in Hinze now seemed to have infected Odysseus.

'I'm not certain. I need to think about it.'

'I thought you might say that. How about you take some time back in your Chrono-sphere?'

A Chrono-sphere with ten years at the most left before the Fulcrum started? Mum, Dad and Dan: could I save them? I chose my next words carefully, as they needed to camouflage my doubt.

'Yes, that would be great.'

I got up, but then Odysseus spoke, 'Charlie, before you go, I have something for you—your grandmother's Tempus Imperium and this inscribed pocketknife. I had the engineering department fix it up.'

The watch's new glass casing shone, scratch- and crack-free, with a matching black leather strap.

'Thank you,' I said, as I strapped it to my wrist again.

29

Adelaide, February 2016

Penny's spare key still sat under a garden gnome by the front door, the one who clutched a sign saying *Home Sweet Home*. Telemachus rubbed himself up against my legs as I went inside. Despite the throbbing in my side, I bent down and scratched him behind the ears.

Around me, Penny's street glistened in the early morning light. A neighbour walked past towed by a Jack Russell, while a rubbish truck rumbled as it moved along, emptying the bins. The house was as I'd left it three days ago: curtains drawn, beds made, with dishes washed up and drying on the side of the sink. *9:30 am on Tuesday 22 February 2016*, according to my Tempus Imperium. If I caught the next bus, I might still make my 11:30 lecture on Contract Law—a degree that would prove pointless if the Fulcrum happened in 2025. I picked up Telemachus and he purred. If only my life was simple as a cat's: eat, sleep, and play outside.

Next to the clocks in the hallway hung the photo that Mum

had used at Penny's funeral: a young Penny in black and white, taken during World War Two. She smiled in the photo, her hair curled and her neck framed by a set of white pearls. I took the photo off the wall and looked at it. Like me, she'd faced this choice—*Grandma Penny, please tell me what to do.* But nothing: no electric surge, no metallic taste in my mouth, no pain searing my sinus cavities. Maybe the explosion had damaged my paragnostic abilities? I replaced the photo on the wall and went into the kitchen to make a cup of tea.

My mobile phone still sat on the kitchen table where I'd left it. A clutter of messages filled the screen: Pizza Shack confirming my availability, Mum checking up on me, and two from Dan—*C can we talk? D* and *C I still love you. Call me please?!?* Dan had even updated his relationship status online to *It's complicated.* I swiped them away and opened the browser, searching for the Devereux children, Gavin, Anna and Julia, whom I'd met on Australia Day. Nothing. I scrolled through the search results, then went to the local paper's website and searched the obituaries. 'Gavin Devereux passed away March 26, 2010, after a long illness. Beloved husband of Mary-Anne, father of Michael. Brother of Julia and Anna.' By my maths, he'd been forty-eight when he died. Forty-eight? The horror of the Devereux children, whose disappearance had scared generation after generation of Australian children, was no more. Penny had said that not all incursions mattered, but I wasn't certain Odysseus would agree.

My phone pinged with another message from Dan. *C are you home? You left your drink bottle at my place.* I felt pinned by my guilt. Would he forgive me and remain my best friend? How could I explain about the Temporal Sinistrum and the last five weeks? For him, it had only been a couple of days. I paced up and down Penny's kitchen before finally texting him: *I'm sorry D, let's talk later. XX C.*

At 10 am, the clocks chimed in Penny's hallway. *Ding-dong!*

Ding-dong! But something was missing. I knew every chime, beat and song of Penny's clocks, but there was no screeching *Cuckoo!* The bird was still imprisoned inside its wooden chalet despite my earlier attempts at repair. I took it off the wall, and with the tip of my pocketknife I realigned a cog on the back, then wound the clock to the correct time. This time no handwritten notes dropped out on the hallway floor as it started ticking again.

Brrr! Brrr!

The front doorbell rang. 'Parcel!' called the postie as I heard his motorbike sputter off. On Penny's front doorstep sat a small package, postmarked Hiroshima, Japan. Wrapped in brown paper and tied with string, the parcel seemed surprisingly old and fragile for something whose postage date was only a week ago.

Carefully, I unwrapped the paper on Penny's kitchen table and found a porcelain cat and a photograph. The cat was white and fat, with one paw by its ear, dressed in a red scarf. I'd seen such cats sitting on the front counter of Currency Creek's only Chinese restaurant, and also at the Asian grocer two blocks over. A Mae-Neki-Neko, according to my internet image search. A Japanese Lucky Cat meant to bring you good fortune and prosperity. I placed him on Penny's kitchen windowsill next to the dish detergent and her old transistor radio, where his hand bobbed up and down in a waving motion. Next was a grainy photograph of a tall domed building in black and white taken at dusk, with each window outlined by the bright lights inside. In a hand I recognised were the words—*Genbaku, 2 pm August 30, 1945*—the same hand and thick-nibbed fountain pen that had left me a note at the old Sinistrum headquarters alongside a photograph of my grandmother, Odysseus, Hinze and its author sitting at a cafe on the Left Bank in Paris.

Hiroshima 1945? I knew from my high-school history class that the atomic bomb had been dropped on the sixth of August 1945. Would this Genbaku building still be standing? Would it even be safe to visit? Two weeks after the bomb went off, the radiation could still be quite high. Odysseus and the Sinistrum were also closely monitoring all incursions. I needed to bide my time, wait until I had done my research, and then make this rendezvous, but first I had to return to the Temporal Sinistrum.

I walked throughout Penny's house one last time, looking at what remained of her things: the armchair in which Telemachus slept, the desk with the roll-down lockable top, the clocks on the wall and the family photographs. I didn't know when I would return. I wanted to ring my parents and say goodbye, but their questions about Dan and university put me off, knowing the lies I'd have to tell. It was easier this way, despite the guilt that felt like a scab whose top was about to fall off. I poured a bowl of cat food and put it outside with some water. I placed a note and a box of cat food in the neighbour's mailbox. I then grabbed Telemachus and dropped him outside. He put his ears back and looked up at me quizzically, his tail twitching with annoyance. 'Sorry, Tee,' I said as he stalked off into the bushes. I then locked Penny's house up, including the safety locks on the windows, and replaced the spare key under the garden gnome. *BEEP! BEEP! BEEP!* Two houses down the street, a large removalist's truck was reversing, beeping loudly and drowning out all other noise.

In the living room, I entered the coordinates for the Sinistrum's new headquarters just as the front door swung open.

'Charlie?' Dan entered the room, holding the spare key, Telemachus at his heels. 'I thought you weren't home.'

The white light growing bright and consuming me.

'I was just going to put—what the—?'

Dan's eyes were wide, his face pale as the light flashed brightly, taking both of us and Telemachus with it.

EPILOGUE

Adelaide, January 2007

Odysseus sat in his car watching a two-bedroom duplex in a housing estate. He could still smell her Chanel No. 5 on his collar from where she'd kissed him. Another ten minutes and he was scheduled to return to the Sinistrum. Days of work lay in front of him at the Dyad. Piles of paperwork that he hated and wished the explosion had destroyed as well. There was a reason why he had never aspired to be anything more than a field adjudicator. Nonetheless, what else could he do? Hinze was dead, there was the Fulcrum still to prevent, and there were very few adjudicators left.

As he watched the duplex, a four-door ute with a tray on the back pulled into the driveway. Out of the back door climbed a small girl, aged nine. She ran to the front door and pressed the buzzer, and Penny answered. Around Penny's feet a tiny, grey-coloured kitten circled, and the child bent down to look closer.

'Grandma, who's this?'

'A gift, a kitten, from an old friend.'

The child picked up the kitten and brought it closer to her chest. The kitten purred as the child patted it.

'What's his name?'

'Telemachus.'

'Cool, Grandma! Can Telemachus sleep on my bed tonight?'

'Yes, Charlie. I can see he already likes you. Now, why don't you come inside? They are some freshly made lamingtons and Anzac biscuits on the kitchen table waiting for you and your mum.'

The child and her mother went inside, followed by Penny, but before she shut the door, she looked across the street at Odysseus in the car and waved.

ACKNOWLEDGEMENTS

I initially wrote this novel as part of my PhD in Creative Writing from The University of Adelaide, with the financial support of an Australian Government Research Training Program (RTP) Scholarship. I would like to express my sincere gratitude to my supervisors: Dr Matthew Hooton, who believed in this project from the very beginning; and Jill Jones for her encouragement over the first two years of my project before retiring. I also wish to acknowledge the editorial assistance of Dr Kerrie Le Lievre of Academic Editing Services, who proofread the creative work prior to its submission for assessment as part of my PhD.

I would like to thank the staff at Varuna, the National Writer's House, for my 2021 Residential Fellowship, and also their willingness to reschedule it to the following year due to COVID-19 state border closures.

I am also grateful for Rochelle Stephens and the team at Wombat Books who helped bring this novel to print. I appreciated their patience and perseverance with the work as I finalised it.

Next, I would like to thank my friend and fellow English

teacher, Louisa Mulligan, who willingly read and provided feedback on an early draft of my novel. I would also like to thank my family, especially my two children, Ryan and Owen, who have tolerated their mother's need to disappear into the study at odd hours with mostly good humour. I will always be thankful for the loving support of my husband, Mark McDonnell, who was one of the novel's first readers.

Last, I wish to acknowledge all the many students I taught as an English teacher over many years, who served as the inspiration for the character of Charlie Lamp, and for whom *The Tempus Imperium* was written.